An Airship Named

Desire

(Take to the Skies, #1)

Katherine McIntyre

Printed in the United States of America

Cover Art by Jillian Renee A

Edited by Summer Ross

First Printing, 2012

Reprint, 2015

ISBN: 1519103670
ISBN-13: 978-1519103673

DEDICATION

To everyone who read and loved Airship when it first came out in 2012 or who shared kind words and support along the way, this is for all of you wonderful people.

Katherine McIntyre

ACKNOWLEDGEMENTS

Huge, huge thank you to Summer Ross for her careful eye in helping me smooth out the edges of this story, as well as Rob Martin, my ever astute first line of defense when it comes to edits. Also many thanks to Jillian Renee who did such a gorgeous job on the cover—she brought Bea and the Desire to life in a beautiful way!

Katherine McIntyre

CHAPTER ONE

At least once on every smuggling job, we reached a point where any sane person would have run screaming. We'd passed that point three days ago when we first snuck aboard this British Merchant ship.

Jensen closed the windowless iron door behind us, and we stepped forward into the mausoleum of a room. I inhaled the lusterless air as the door clicked shut. Steel panels surrounded us, from the walls to the ceiling, and footsteps scraped against the metal floors outside the door as the next guard started his shift.

The hanging light swayed back and forth, swirling the shadows around the corners of the room. I ran a hand over my pistol, Matilda, ready to draw at any second. Most people would have dodged this job from the lack of information alone. Captain always gave us every last detail about our employers down to if the man wore slacks or pantaloons, but with this guy? Nothing. The back and forth clank of the guard's pacing began, echoing like a thousand marching marionettes. I slowly lifted my hand from the gun.

All the bickering, stiff silence, and many hours of waiting— all for this box—Property of the British Merchant Company.

A metal container the size of my jewelry box back home gleamed under the dim light. A clear casing overtop protected it from where it perched on a stand in the center of the room. I wiped my clammy palms on my stained breeches and stepped forward from the door.

"Bea, wait." Jensen grabbed my shoulder.

My hands balled into fists from surprise, and I resisted the urge to deck him. "Boy-o, if you're referring to the thermal alarm around the perimeter, I already noticed." I pulled my leather bag from my shoulder and rummaged around the bottom.

He stepped back and tugged down on the brim of his bowler cap. "Just wanted to make sure. One alarm goes off and we tango with an entire ship of guards and military."

"It wouldn't be fun any other way." I flashed him a quick grin, and my fingers found the corkscrew-sized magnet. "Don't worry. We'll get out of here and celebrate with the Captain's secret stash of absinthe." On the opposite wall, a rectangle protruded several feet down from the ceiling. I dropped my bag on the floor and approached with careful steps while wielding my sharp-tipped magnet. "If I get this, will you take care of the casing?"

"Deal." Jensen exposed teeth with his grin.

Opening the latch exposed the perimeter alarm: a convoluted set of cogs with gears that shone brassy under the off-white medical lighting. Pinching the magnet, I faced the tip towards the alarm. A small bearing ball hid behind the largest cog, waiting for the thermal sensor to trip. If we extracted the ball out without triggering anything we had no problem. Like we'd be so lucky.

I inhaled a deep breath of the stale, sepulchral air and pressed the magnet against the largest cog. A subtle tug from the other end told me the magnet found its mark. A droplet of sweat tickled my cheek as it crawled down the side of my face while a severe case of adrenaline threatened to shake my arms. The lone light in this room exaggerated the shadows, and I struggled to follow the outline of the gears. Jensen's breaths disrupted my focus every time he hissed an exhale. The bearing ball clicked as I brought it to the small entry hole by the top. It teetered there for a moment, and a dry breath caught in my throat.

The ball dropped into my palm, and I exhaled. Around the stand, the slight imprint of the sensor alarm faded.

"This is crap, you know." Jensen pieced his thermal lance together, screwing the top head on.

"What, you don't enjoy the spacious views?" I asked, "Playing a three day long game of hide and go seek?" We'd held our tempers so far, and I wouldn't let the stress best us.

Jensen passed me a glare. "You know—the military on board. The three different sets of alarms just to protect this box. Captain Morris threw us in too deep."

"If you can't handle a job, it's your own inadequacy." I bristled. "Morris is doing what he's always done, and he'd never send us somewhere he wouldn't go himself."

"Fine, I'll deliver my salty words straight to the Captain when we get back." Jensen's smirk wavered, and I could smell the tension rolling off him—granted, the vinegary scent might've just been us. Stress wore at my nerves like the humming of an aether lamp. I glanced toward the doors. Any loud noises and we were screwed.

"Let's get this job over with. I want to smell like posies, not a dung heap," I muttered as we approached the covered box. Whatever blackened sludge crept in the corners of this ship fixed itself on our clothing, and I longed for a clean skirt or anything more feminine than these filthy breeches. The strain of hiding on this vessel affected me too, but after the last botched job, our ship ran on fumes. My rumbling stomach cut through the silence of the room.

Jensen smirked. "Want some of that home cooking from back on the ship? Isabella's jerky with burnt rice?"

"Thanks." I snorted. "The memory of that food just killed any appetite I built up."

He turned on the thermal lance, and the tip gradually burned white-hot. The scent of burnt plastics mixed with Jensen's own musk of rosemary and diesel oil. My fingers tensed. As soon as he finished, I'd have to grab the box. Jensen pushed the lance into the casing like a pastry blender through shortening.

"Ready, Bea?" Jensen grunted. "The alarm sensors should skip for five seconds."

I braced myself, sucking in a deep breath. Jensen grasped both sides of the case with his gloved hands and lifted it from the base, taking his time. We both exhaled when he extricated the casing and placed it onto the aluminum-plated floor. Even though we'd procured stolen goods more times than I changed boots, one fumble and the operation would break down into uncomfortable odds: two to a ship full of armed guards.

With the casing off, Jensen fixed the thermal lance to the base. Once he bored the hole, his eyes flashed in my direction. Using the second we'd have for the alarm to reset, I reached out and yanked the box towards me. A blue circle glowed from the pressure plate until it turned a bright orange from heat. My brows crinkled in confusion. I'd never seen a base alarm react that way.

A light clicked on at the stand and began flashing, followed by the first screech as the alarms sounded, fast.

Jensen's eyes met mine.

"Run." I tucked the box under my sword arm and took off in the direction we entered. Without any further communication, Jensen followed.

I threw myself against the massive iron door, and it slammed into the posted guard with a loud crunch. Jensen seized the opportunity and clocked the man in the temple, knocking him unconscious. Before the body hit the floor, we raced through the first chamber and hurtled through the second.

Behind us, the alarm squawked a constant reminder of how if caught, we'd be screwed six ways to sailing day. When it came to the Brits, they didn't mess around with handling lawbreakers. Official executions took place in a televised arena, and after days of torture, the weakened victims barely struggled. Yet I'd take that fate over a look of disappointment from Captain Morris. We rounded the corner and entered another empty room, but the sound of footsteps clattered behind us. The guards were catching up.

Their guns fired before we took another two steps.

I ducked for cover behind an old rusty frigate crate right as the sharp scent of gunpowder melded with cheap battered metal. I held two fingers to my eyes before gesturing behind me. Jensen nodded and followed my cue by diving from the crate back towards the door.

Bullets darted past him, each one with a death threat, but if we didn't keep moving we'd lose the chance to reach higher ground. My booming heartbeat competed with my shallow breaths. He took the lead, and I tagged close behind while they focused their fire on him. The shots ricocheted around the bleach-white boat hull, and the noise recoiled in my ears. Only after we threw ourselves through the door did I peer from behind the frame.

The room spanned before us past the open doorway. Those wooden crates, not surviving the gunfire, splintered out across the long chestnut floorboards. Hazy smoke from the shots drifted through the air like billows from a grill. Some guards hid behind a cluster of the dented metal crates, and more men peeked past the opposing door. I whipped out my pistol, adjusting my stance, since the stolen bundle weighted down my left side. Once several brazen guards cropped up from their cover, I fumbled for the trigger with sweaty fingers and fired. Of course, a good shot would be too much to ask for.

"Straight ahead, Bea," Jensen stepped behind me and whispered in my ear. His gloved hand brushed by my shoulder.

"Thanks." I batted my eyelashes at him. "I've never shot before in my life, sweet thing." I drank in his laugh like a shot of whisky because craziness helped us survive smuggling missions like this. The external observer would believe I reveled in this insanity— they'd be right.

Another round of gunfire spat past us. My shoulders twitched with the jarring sound, and several stray bullets studded the floor. One veered by my arm. Luckily, I trained under Captain Morris, and the ex-Marine made sure we didn't head into a job unprepared. I swerved in time. The firing squad peeked from the opposite door, and one man darted for the cover of a closer crate. Their alarm system blared on faster and louder than we had anticipated, to the point that the ringing reverberated in each and every room.

I reserved some very choice words for our employer. Stealing from a merchant ship, he said. Difficult but rewarding, he said. Newsflash, bucko, they had stationed more guards around this ship than their stupid Buckingham Palace, and I definitely spotted some military on board.

"Too many guards down here," Jensen said crouching beside me. "We have to reach the top deck or else any chance of escape is shot."

I gritted my teeth and lifted the bundle. "I'm not moving as fast with this thing."

Jensen leaned past me and aimed three shots with his revolver. The near-deafening sound boomed in my ear. "Our only real chance is to book it. They're closing in, but we can pick them off one by one in the hallway."

Five seconds ago, a mere four men had rushed into the room, but now dozens of heads popped up over their crate cover to fire shots. The unabashed clang of the alarm pounded in from rooms away, marching to the same incessant beat as my racing heart. Another round of gunshots burrowed into the whitewashed wall, which reverberated from the force. My grip on my pistol tightened, and sweat pricked my neck. We wouldn't last much longer here.

I peeked out again. At least eight guns had their marks on us, so if we moved past the open door, we'd be clear targets. I scanned behind for anything to use as a shield. The corner we wedged into contained more of that caked sludge, a couple old wrenches, and copper shavings. Lovely.

"Swords out," I whispered back to Jensen. Before the words left my lips, he drew his cutlass. I plunked my pistol into its holster and tried to one-handedly tug out my sword. Since the bundle occupied my sword hand, the sharp edge of the steel sliced into my sleeve. I steadied the blade. "Ready?" A smile broke out on my face, to the teeth.

The mirth in his hazel eyes mirrored my own. He whipped out his pistol with his left hand and fired his round blindly into the encroaching horde. Using the distraction, we lifted our swords in front of us for meager cover over our vitals and darted past the door. Half a second later their rounds emptied into the steel paneling past the doorframe.

"Run," I commanded. We dashed down the hallway.

I shot one-armed better with my pistol, Matilda, so I tucked my cutlass away. We couldn't afford to lose our prize after the sweat, rumbling stomachs, and the wealth of knowledge I never wanted to learn about riot wrestling. The guards' footsteps echoed around the steel-paneled hallways, following our own.

We had several levels to scale before having to think about

the crew waiting for us on the main deck, but at least they wore comfortable black-and-white enemy clothing. When the narrow hallway ended at the staircase, Jensen and I stomped up the shaky metal slats to the second floor. The interspersed clip of hurried footsteps against the splintered wooden flooring hadn't halted, and the sound tangled my nerves to knots. They were coming, and if they caught us, we'd be deader than Jensen's intellect.

Jensen peered down the hall first. "Clear."

We threw ourselves down it, keeping pace with each other. Jensen liked to boast he could take me in a fight, but that was also a challenge he'd avoided. Chivalry, my ass—he knew better. The corridor angled to a sharp end, and I nearly collided with Jensen when he stopped. He peeked into the porthole window embedded in the door. The loud clank of footsteps echoed from both ends. My stomach flip-flopped, and I clutched the locked box closer to my chest.

"How many ahead?" I whispered to Jensen, hoping the noise wouldn't give us away.

"Only a couple," he murmured, "and they haven't spotted us yet." At last we had an advantage. Surprise attacks always helped. Jensen twirled his revolver around his finger.

"Show off," I said. He aimed one of his trunk-like legs and kicked the door open, straining the hinges. The impetus didn't stop him, and Jensen emptied three shots into the men inside upon entering the antechamber. All three dropped. Except, there hadn't been three men. Four more emerged from behind the door, alerted by the sound of gunfire and the thud of bodies hitting the floor.

Apparently, surprise attacks don't always help.

A shudder rolled down my spine as the clatter from the other side of the hall grew louder from the approaching throng of guards. We couldn't fail this job. As the first mate of our ship, I had a reputation to uphold. Bullets pinged off the corner's edge, nearly taking my hand with them. I yanked it back and pulled out my pistol.

Feeding another round into the chamber, I fired from the doorframe. Unlike Jensen, I didn't need a flashy entrance since I was carrying our cargo. One man shouted and fell under my fire. Several short breaths calmed me as I squinted and aimed another shot at the top man peering around the frame. He emitted a garbled sound before slumping over.

Jensen marched to the door before I could blink, and during his parade, he clocked one man with the handle of his revolver while knocking the other one back with a full-throttle punch to the jaw.

"Clear?" I pressed my shoulder against the wall. Jolts of adrenaline pulsed through my arms, which threatened to shake. Jensen nodded and signaled forward.

When racing past the men, I spotted movement. Before the

dying man could fire a shot, I kicked the gun from his hands. One stray bullet and we'd be fish food. After shoving a speedloader in the chamber of my gun, I tucked it back into the holster. We dashed headlong down yet another corridor. The horde of guards advanced behind us, and their footsteps echoed like rain drops hitting a metal hull. My heart hammered in my chest while my breaths arrived in short bursts.

"Two more levels left." Jensen pointed at the stairwell ahead. The tinny flats all but crumpled under our frantic footsteps. This close to the deck, fresh air invaded my senses like the crisp scent of a fall morning, beckoning and caressing me with renewed hope. I pushed through the wind of exhaustion pummeling me, because failure wasn't an option.

"D'you think the communicator will pick up signal from here?" I asked. Our footsteps glanced off the aluminum floors. Yellow stripes followed the walls like guiding lines.

"You could try." Jensen shrugged. I unfastened the copper buckle on my brown leather pack and rummaged for our communicator. My hand landed on the ribbed, black device with its copper antenna and metallic buttons. I struggled one-handedly to turn it on.

"Thank you ever so much for your assistance, Jensen." My sarcasm flowed like the ale I'd drink upon returning home. "I'm glad one of us is capable of multi-tasking." The mesh over the speaker had rusted, and the machine's buttons had been re-glued multiple times, but we couldn't afford to spring for new communicators. The copper antennae vibrated with the low hum from the speakers as I flipped the metal knob on the side to power the communicator on.

"Spade, do you read?" I lifted the speaker to my lips. Crackling sounded from the other end.

"I don't think our connection's stable," Jensen said.

"Well, it has to be, or we're sunk."

He placed his hand up in front of me at the turn and peered past first. The loud beating noise was either my heartbeat or the guards' footsteps, but I was long past being able to distinguish the two. I snuck a peek. A couple men in officer red coats stood attentive by the stairwell, and my blood surged at the sight of them. Maybe a little because I was sick of being on this ship, but maybe a lot because Captain used pictures of the British military as targets when we practiced on board. Old Germany ex-military like him held a grudge.

Some of the redcoats sat on the aluminum steps while the others lined against the undecorated white walls. The boring paint job bleached my eyes from running through hallway after hallway of it.

"What are we going to do?" I hissed.

"We have the upper hand."

I stopped and raised my eyebrow. "Remind me again how the last surprise attack went?" I nudged past him to catch a glance at the officers. The whole lot wore cutlasses strapped to their backs and holstered military guns. As much as I loved my Matilda, mechanized battery pistols like those would outshoot her any day.

"What's in that pack of yours?" Jensen unhooked the strap and rummaged through my bag.

"Nothing we can use, of course." I ran a hand through my damp hair to brush away the tickling strands and crawling droplets of sweat that fought for my annoyance. After blinking the drops away from my eyes, I took a deep breath. Whatever we were going to do, it had to be quick.

Jensen glanced up. "What about the vent up there? It should take us to the top level so we can bypass those guards." Above, a loosely screwed screen covered the vent. Jensen reached up and unhinged the piece with the edge of his sword.

"I'll need a boost." I placed a hand on my hip, daring the man to make a jab at my height since I stood a foot under him.

"Alley-oop." He laced his hands in front of me. The clanking from behind us grew louder as a constant reminder of what little time we had left. I stepped onto his makeshift lift and scrabbled up the side wall.

Grasping onto the vent's edge, I popped our bundle through the opening. Once I pulled myself up and into the tight space, I turned onto my stomach. Jensen waited below for my assist, so I reached down, offering my hands.

At that point, the communicator received our signal. Unfortunately, vents echo. Loudly.

"Beatrice, come in. Do you read me, Beatrice, come in." The sound crackled through the old machine and tripled in sound throughout the corridor. I clenched my jaw, biting down a curse. With a shout, the officer redcoats snapped to attention right as our squadron of chasing guards rounded the corner.

"Jensen, jump." I stretched my hands out and tensed my fingertips. He gripped mine in his while I strained to pull him up. Several shots whizzed past his feet. Lacking in upper arm muscle, I notched the toes of my boots in the crevasse behind me, using the leverage. A shot glanced by, and a howl ripped from his throat.

The officers arrived on the scene. A spurt of vitality flooded through me, and I yanked Jensen up until he gripped the vent and lunged inside. The ropy scar on my left leg throbbed at the thought of his gunshot wound. We forged on through the tunnels above the ceilings even though their shots rattled through the shoddy aluminum.

"This wasn't an ideal plan," I said.

"You think so?" Jensen's voice came from behind. "You're not the one who got shot."

"Buck up, boy-o, we've got more ground to cover." I tried to keep my tone light. "We'll take care of it as soon as we can." I bit my lip to suppress the worry that crawled through my veins. Jensen never got shot. Not in the time I'd known him. Pushing the bundle in front of us, I squeezed through the tight tunnel until the vent stopped at an intersection and peered down both ends.

"Go right," Jensen mumbled behind me. "It'll get us to the top floor."

I shifted into that vent and forced myself through. Good thing claustrophobia never bothered me.

"Beatrice, do you copy?" My communicator sounded again. I cursed myself for not turning the damned thing off. I could barely fit inside the area ahead let alone move around enough to pull it from my bag to respond. That scratchy noise of interference echoed through the vents. Up ahead, the dim square of light at the end beckoned, and the vent widened enough that I shifted my bag around in front of me.

"Hold on. I'll make sure we have an escape route." I yanked open the beaten leather bag and pulled out the blasted communicator, which cast a green glow against the dark tunnel. After pressing down on the metallic button, I spoke.

"This is Beatrice. Cargo acquired. We'll be topside in minutes. Over." I clicked off the knob and popped it back into my pack.

"You make some hefty promises."

"None we aren't going to keep." I grinned. "Either we make it through in minutes, or we're dead anyway."

A numb tingling raced down my spine, and my heart pounded a notch faster. Looping the bundle back under my arm, I crept to the side of the vent. This grate suspended over the ceiling unlike the one we entered through. Jensen crawled over to the opposite side, and we peered through the slatted view. Below us, the halls appeared empty, lined by bleach white walls with evenly paneled mahogany floors. I strained to hear anything besides the engine's whirr echoing through the vents.

"Are they there?" I asked.

Jensen shrugged. "We'll find out." He unscrewed the vent and bent over the side. "Remember, you promised minutes," he said, before jumping.

I grabbed the cargo and hopped after him. Jensen covered my right side while I glanced down the left. Both corridors lay empty with those chestnut floors sloping upward to the main deck where our struggle to the top would reward us with no cover and a whole crew to tangle with. Those odds were something I could get used to. I forced away the fierce smile threatening to take over my face and instead pulled my pistol from its holster. The corridor met the deck on the main level, and the walls stopped up ahead to greet the sunshine spilling in from the entrance. My breaths came out in

17

staccato beats, and sweat slicked my palms. The clamor of footsteps rose behind us again.

We peeked over the sides to view the main deck. Many crew members had charged to the hull upon the alarm, so the deck cleared out more than I expected. Still, pockets of uniforms gathered from both ends of the ship. New wooden planks, cleaner than dry bones, lined the deck. I scanned the area again. Ahead of us lay a clear trail to the edge but no cover.

I stared above at the brazen blue sky. The wind roared with the same intensity as an engine, and the clouds puffed like outpouring steam. Several of the guards holstered guns, but some walked around with mop and bucket in hand. Non-threats made our job that much easier.

"They'll be on us soon." Jensen's voice bristled at the edges.

"I don't see her though." I nodded off to the distance.

"Me neither." He shook his head.

I pressed my body against the wall. Time ticked away faster than an auctioneer's roll. Ideally, we'd have escaped unnoticed out of a side hatch or camouflaged in with the crew. But we bungled that and no longer had those options. I squeezed the handle of my pistol.

"All right." I leaned over to Jensen. "See that clear zone? We're going to sprint to the side."

His eyebrows rose in disbelief. "Are you crazy? With no ship in sight?"

"I said minutes." I pointed to the communicator. "Spade always makes his checkpoints."

Jensen shook his head, but the hint of a grin crept onto his face. "All right, doll, on your orders."

I clenched my teeth. Even though I came up with the plan, I didn't think it stood a chance in hell. Luckily, common sense had never been my strong suit, and my feet moved faster than my brain.

"Go." My calves strained with the jump as I cleared the remaining ledge, and once I hit the planks, we moved. Shouts broke out on deck the moment we emerged, but I ignored them. My limbs burned from all the running, crouching, and crawling while we dashed toward the ship's side. Jensen brandished his sword and slung it around as we ran. I made a mental check to teach him how to use it right. Our movement alerted the clusters of men, and they scattered, all for the two of us. If I wasn't running for my life, I'd have been flattered.

The edge loomed in sight, and I barreled straight into the side, hanging my head over the ledge. Dizzying depths below caused a sickness to spread through my stomach like the flu.

"What now?" Jensen and I stood against the edge, weapons out. The crew closed around us, and we backtracked into the corner. I clutched the package against my chest as Jensen and I bumped against each other. All over a stupid box. A gulp refused to voyage down my dry throat when the readied guns clicked all around the deck.

Propellers whirred overhead.

I glanced up and my face met dangling rope. Spade came through for us. A red striped banner rippled through gusts of wind, and the sight of her polished hull filled my insides with sunshine. Our girl, Desire, loomed overhead in the form of one magnificent airship.

CHAPTER TWO

Circus performers like the Aeronaut Troupe climbed up ropes one-handed, not the first mate of an airship. I steadied myself for the first five handholds, but the higher we scaled the more my hands slipped and legs shook. Especially when the guards below opened fire.

I squeezed my thighs tight around the rope and wedged the lockbox under my arm since I'd move faster with both hands free. Jensen followed close beneath me. Several stray bullets clipped the rope, and it shook, giving me an ample view of the plummeting depths below. My throat tightened as I took in the remote hills and valleys below, but the line held, so I kept climbing towards our ship's boarding entrance far out of reach. An overwhelming blue sky and swollen clouds swirled with the sway of the rope.

In the distance, the squad from the lower levels breached the surface, and their guns glinted under the broad daylight. I glanced up to see how quick the Desire moved when the first shots sailed in our direction. Stopping my climb, I gripped the rope so tightly my knuckles resembled their ship's horrible eggshell-white walls.

The bullets dropped well out of reach, and I heaved a sigh of relief. Spade's timing ticked two notches faster than theirs. As we drifted further out of range, I continued my slow ascent.

If heights bothered me, my term on the Desire would have ended a long time ago. Our ship glided past the merchant ship's deck, and we dangled midair, surrounded by the stark blue. Treetops dotted the ground like miniature soldiers while the hills of the Canadian landscape spread out as clear as a map.

The rope twirled around, but Jensen and I continued our climb since the vessel's gunfire no longer reached us. Sweat trailed down my biceps. The bundle under my arm hampered my movements so much that anyone watching my awkward climb might mistake me for a hunchback. But our rescuer waited for us up above, my girl, the Desire.

A vast white balloon surrounded by an aluminum frame kept her afloat, and the word Desire emblazoned it in bold black letters. The ship hung from the attached cables with propellers whirring loudly from behind. Several short masts and a lookout tower extended up from the deck, but they hovered far beneath the balloon. She had a sleek body of darkened wood and could sail faster than any other ship in the skies. At least, that's what the Captain said. Her real beauty shone on the inside. The aether tanks lined the engine room like pipe organs, and trinkets from our conquests decorated the hallways, unlike the lack of flair in that hulk of a monstrosity we exited.

Their ship's clashing Union Jack flag stuck out like soured

milk against the gaping sky. My fingers trembled from the effort of the climb, but I continued upward. The British government ran the merchant guild boat, so they could afford to spend extra on bells and whistles, but in my opinion, with those boring bleach walls they would've been better off hiring decorators.

A gust of wind twisted the rope and sent me reeling. My senses almost escaped me, but I groped for the lockbox tucked under my arm. With the amount of surrounding security and the price tag for its retrieval, this little bundle must have been special. I mean, we couldn't outwit their alarm system, and between us, Jensen and I had stolen enough cargo to fill a warehouse.

The bundle inched forward from my arm's vice-like grip. I froze. If we lost this, not only did we lose a fortune but we also blew all that money into the operation for no return. And I guess we'd lose some important artifact or whatever it was. While we had this cargo the guards wouldn't blow us up either—at least, I assumed they wouldn't amass all that security just to destroy the item. The muscles in my arm tightened like a wolf trap around the box.

Jensen's head collided with my feet. His shout of annoyance disappeared into the noisy wind kicked up by the propellers.

"Sorry," I called down. "It slipped." I didn't hear any response, so I stayed still. My legs twined around the rope, but I didn't have the tightrope skills necessary to hold on by my thighs alone. Clutching tight to the line, I tried to push the package over to my other side. The swaying didn't help in the slightest.

A gust of wind blew through, and the package jumped from my arms.

I clamped on with my thighs and scrambled for the box. My hands groped puffs of air, and I stretched further into the empty sky around me. The rope bit deep into my thighs as I clapped my hands around our treasure, pulling the package to my chest. Blue and more blue whirled around me, and my legs trembled before I grabbed the cord with my other hand. Taking in a deep, shaky breath, I tucked it under my other, less slippery, arm.

"Bea, what are you doing up there?" Jensen called.

"Thought I'd try my hand at performance. If a trained monkey can do it, so can I," I yelled back. "Next time, why don't we trade? You deserve a chance to keep our merchandise safe."

His loud bark of a laugh carried past the roar of the wind. Jensen might laugh, but I didn't kid. He'd get package duty next time.

The closer we climbed to the top, the more the rope twirled in circles. With nothing to weigh it down, the end rippled in the breeze. My thighs scraped against the strained fibers, and the pain made my stomach flop. If any of those snapped, we'd have a long trip down.

The climb ended when we reached the boarding deck, which opened like a black window of hope from the lower level. Before I even tried to heft myself up, I tossed the cargo on board, hoping the contents weren't fragile as it slid across our smooth floor. I groped for the wooden planks with sweaty palms and used what little strength remained to pull myself onto the deck. Jensen followed behind me, and we slumped against the cool shaded ground of the lower level.

I could have melted onto the floor then and there as our musky smell mingled with the scent of cedar throughout the chamber. The extra oxygen from the vents flooded through me, filling my lungs with air and sparking my sluggish brain to life. I slouched against the wall since my limbs ached something fierce from holding our cargo in awkward positions.

Geoff, our navigator, yanked up the rest of the rope, and his lithe muscles flexed as he pulled the door shut against swelling winds. His dark brown eyes met my own, and the huge smile that surfaced on his face sent a burst of warmth rolling through my chest. Geoff was a welcome sight, the closest thing I had to a best friend.

I sat up, but my creaky limbs burned from exertion, and my legs splayed out in front of me like the loose joints of a clockwork doll. The rope had chafed my leggings, causing the shine of irritated skin from under the holes. Sweat soaked my calves beneath my knee-high boots, so old the leather edges had worn to a dull taupe. After all the grime I'd accumulated, my blonde hair had taken on a brassier sheen, and more than anything, I couldn't wait for a shower. A patchwork coat of dirt covered my skin, and that weird blackened sludge lined the fraying edges of my breeches. I'd look cleaner if I took a dip in the lakes of toxic waste all over Jersey.

"How's your leg?" I gestured to Jensen's thigh. He glanced at it as if realizing for the first time he sported a large open graze. From where I sat the wound didn't appear too deep. It bled, but the blood hadn't spread far. Geoff let out a low whistle.

"You got hurt on this one, big man?" He crouched beside us. Jensen grunted in response.

I scrambled over to where Jensen sat and opened my pack. "Let me get it. I'm sorry we couldn't wrap up your big ol' gash back there."

"Sorry? If we stopped to take care of a measly bullet wound, we'd be dead."

I rolled my eyes. The man pumped out more machismo than a diesel engine. His massive chest heaved in exhaustion and strained the suspenders holding up his stained tweed pants. That glancing shot had split the flesh on the sides and grazed deep enough to cause substantial bleeding. I pulled a bandage and antiseptic out of the bag before opening the vial of liquid. He didn't even grimace when I splashed some onto his wound, just studied me with his soft hazel eyes. Drops of sweat slid down his cheeks and dripped off his square jaw.

"There you go. You'll have to take that leg dancing soon," I said, yanking the bandage tight across his thigh to quell the blood flow.

He tested it by flexing his calf and managed a stiff stretch with the bandage on. "It'll be fine in no time."

"May as well have ox blood running through those veins," I added. "You're as stubborn as one."

"All this over a box," Jensen's voice rumbled through the room like a truck over gravel as he sat back, flashing me a charming grin.

I snorted and threw him a wink. "You've done far more work than this over a box."

"Yeah, except he probably had more of a reward." Geoff scooped up the package from the floor. Besides the large brass keyhole, a geared mechanism off to the side kept it sealed. Not only did you need the right key, but the lock required a numbered combination of turns to open. What could the box contain that warranted such protection?

"So were you waiting up for us Geoff?" I drawled. "Did you have your midnight candles burning at the navigation deck?" Between him and Spade, we had the best team of helmsmen in America, though when Geoff wasn't at the helm he lived in the navigation chambers with his maps, ink, and compasses.

"Three days and we hadn't heard a word since we dropped you off at that port in London. Of course we were concerned." Long strands of dark brown hair shadowed his chestnut eyes and hid the worry. He smirked and leaned over to muss my hair but withdrew fast the moment he touched my sweat-soaked strands.

"Somewhere between stowing away and keeping quiet on board we couldn't manage." I gave an apologetic shrug. "But we made it and with the box in tow." Geoff shifted his stance, but his stiff brown pants barely moved. He towered over me, a foot taller at that, but not in the hulking way Jensen did since Geoff only packed light muscle on those long lanky limbs. Hell, I could best him in a fight. Although, he was still no slouch—Captain Morris didn't recruit slouches.

"While you lounged on your British cruise, we've been hard at work. Not all of us get a break from our duties." His cheeky grin always made him handsome.

"Oh yeah, we sunbathed topside, ate marvelous feasts."

"They put on a firepower show that'd bash the hell out of Texas's Fourth of July Blow-Out," Jensen jumped in.

"Right," I said. "The British Merchant Guild really knows how to give you a memorable send off." Geoff laughed and offered me a hand while Jensen hopped up on his own.

"If you girls are done preening, let's bring this bundle to the Captain." Jensen dusted his pants off. I inhaled, savoring the brined, cedar scent of home. After standing, I adjusted my corset which not only dug into my ribs but also sandwiched my sweat-soaked beige chemise to my chest.

"Actually boys, if you don't mind, I'll take you up on that offer of preening." I pursed my lips. "I'd like to freshen up before we hop to the Captain's room."

"Don't worry sweet thing." Jensen smirked. "Captain Morris doesn't care if you're fresh or not. Most men are more concerned if you have the plumbing."

"I'm sorry, but I take pride in my work. Besides," I said, gesturing down at wrinkles in my shirt and the stains on my breeches. "As much as I love writhing in my own filth, if I don't mop off some of this sweat, we may drive the Captain from his chambers." Jensen threw his hands in the air but didn't argue.

Geoff shook his head, unable to keep the grin off his face. "Bea, you're fine."

"Fine as a laundered skunk. I won't take long, and besides, I need to get rid of all this extra weight I'm carrying on me." My hand remained on my hip, and I dared either of them to argue back.

"All right dear lady—let's get you to that room." Geoff slid next to me and offered his arm. I looped his through mine, and we stepped down the hallway together.

The ship creaked and groaned with the familiar symphony of noises while remnants of the windy day swept through the lower deck with wispy breezes. Not like I'd planned to spend half my day out with them, dangling in the sky like a human anemometer. My palm traveled along the solid metal walls made from sheets plastered over one another and held by welded nuts. Unlike that monotonous merchant ship, our girl Desire belonged to the crew.

I passed a large copper porthole that we'd fastened to the wall one of the first years I arrived on the airship. Further down, an enlarged cameo made a creepy, yet classy portrait. Isabella took a fancy to it during her first reconnaissance trip and mounted it soon after. Geoff had added his own flair with maps tacked onto the walls detailing mysterious air pockets and isolated islands.

The press of his arm against mine provided a solid warmth I'd longed for after our days aboard S.S. British-Craphole. We'd been fast friends when I first joined the crew seven years back, and the longer I'd known him, the more irreplaceable he'd become. During my first month on board, I'd snuck off ship and drank myself belligerent at a cantina even though I landed extra deck work twice that week. Geoff made up a story when the Captain came stomping around looking for me, and I only found out later because Isabella let it slip. He was the sort of stand-up gentleman every gal wishes for, but not everyone deserves. I gave Geoff's arm a quick squeeze when we stopped outside of my room.

Upon entering my chambers and shutting the door behind, I unbuckled that damned corset and shunted it to the floor. Instead of boning like corsets of old, sheet metal made mine stylish, but uncomfortable armor. The goldenrod-and-black patterning across it kept the corset inconspicuous. Another invention I had our resident scientist, Edwin, to thank for—this monstrosity had prevented a couple bullets from piercing flesh in the past.

Next came off my sticky chemise and torn up leggings, which allowed the cool air to caress my bare skin with the promise of dryness at long last. I rummaged through my boudoir and pulled on a black chemise and clean breeches. Plunking my feet back into my boots, I yanked the holster containing my pistol around my waist. As I rolled my shoulders back, my spine cracked with gusto. In fresh clothes, I felt much less like a pickled turnip and more like the first mate of the airship Desire. The door beckoned, but I took a moment to sit back on my bed.

That had been a close one. Too close. My heart still skipped off-beat in my chest, and my shoulders tensed as I readied for the next attack. Most of our jobs required some level of danger, but I hadn't come that close to a bullet in the chest since the rendezvous in Seoul. Whatever the box contained, I didn't think the contents warranted the risk.

Dangling my legs off the side of the bed, I swung them back and forth. My mirror hung on the opposite wall with as large a frame as I could find for it, decorated by wrought iron roses and twisted metal vines. I tugged on strands of my long hair and frowned, since I was unable to finger comb them into any semblance less than mess. No more time to waste while the men waited beyond the door.

"All ready." I offered them a mockingly sweet grin and took the lead. A couple rugs lined the floor to the captain's quarters, remnants from when Isabella decided to gussy up the ship. The maroon rugs blossomed with patterned roses with a golden trim along the perimeter. We paused right before knocking on the door.

"You have the box, right?" I turned to Jensen.

"No, I lost it in the five hours you spent brushing up in your room. I think your vanity devoured it." He cracked a grin, lifting the box to confirm.

My laugh erupted in a sharp bark. "Please. You boys don't see nearly enough tail. It's not my fault I like to look classy." I arched my back, and their eyes followed the motion to my satisfaction.

"All for the Captain, eh?" Geoff gave me the side eye, sneaking the comment in even though he knew better. I slapped the back of his head.

"More of a man than you lot." I stepped past them to Captain Morris' large oak door and stopped. We were bound to pay for our lack of communication during our time aboard the merchant ship but better to face him now than hide about. Sucking in a deep breath, I knocked.

CHAPTER THREE

"Come on in," Captain Morris called with a gruff voice.

He sat behind a long oaken desk, waiting for us with a cigar in hand. Normally, the man bustled around the ship fixing loose knots or practicing his swordsmanship on hapless deckhands, but he must've heard word of our return for him to be sitting around here. Sun streamed through the slatted windows and cast shadows along the sides of the room, enough of a light source that the two aether lamps on the opposite wall had been turned off. Behind his chair, a wooden locker held his private reserves of rum, absinthe, and anything else to take away the edge. A keypad sans-holographic display sat on the corner of his desk, which added one more piece of clutter to the overfull surface. As he rose to greet us, the edges of his khaki trenchcoat swept the ground.

"You retrieved the cargo?" Captain Morris stood as tall as the five-tier bookshelves in his room, and tufts of blackish-silver hair poked out from the aviator cap atop his head. Grays marked his age, but his tanned leathery face gave him a more rugged than wrinkled appearance. The man was a veteran. Morris had fought his whole life and bore the scars to prove it.

"Aye, aye, sir." Jensen stepped forward, presenting him with the box.

"Was the ship well-guarded?" Morris turned the locked side toward him.

"Of course." I swaggered forward, slipping my thumbs through my belt loops. "But you're talking about me and Jensen. Nothing we couldn't handle."

He broke into a smile that tugged against a deep scar on the left side of his mouth. Whenever I faced him, the mark resurrected the memories of the knife he took for me, because this man had done more to protect and raise me in the last seven years than my father had for the first fifteen. Granted, dear old dad's regime rested on pretty shaky standards.

"Good job." He stepped past the desk and enveloped me in a fierce hug. My chest swelled with a pride that burned in the back of my throat. To Jensen, he offered a firm handshake. "This job had a higher price tag than we've seen in years, so it should keep the old girl running for some time. Thank you, both of you."

My mind honed back in on reality. "We're going to want to move fast," I spoke up. "The merchant ship didn't seem too happy about losing their prime piece of cargo. While their crew isn't as capable as ours, that monstrosity's equipped with top notch weaponry. The British Merchant Guild threw more than a couple coppers into construction."

"Where's the rendezvous point?" Geoff asked. "I can begin

plotting the fastest route there." Jensen leaned against the far wall, favoring weight on the leg sans-gunshot wound. Captain Morris struck a match against the desk to light his Camacho cigar. Embers glared at the end, and he took a deep drag. The heady smell of tobacco filled the chamber, and I inhaled a deep lusty breath of it.

"We'll need to get working immediately." He tapped the top of the box. "The contact warned that the merchants might try and track us down. Whatever's in here must be worth more than a bottle of fifty-year old scotch."

"What's our direction, Captain?" Geoff repeated. As he shifted his stance, the toe of his boot tapped a fast beat on the hardwood floor.

"We're going stateside. The contact lies past the Californian divide, south of the Oregon marshes. North of Reno, we'll hit the shores of Nevada, right by the sea at the Sutcliffe port. If you set the coordinates a notch above Reno, we're in business."

"Yes sir." Geoff jogged off to start working his magic. He'd tried to explain his navigation system to me before, but after five seconds of watching variables and scanning for air buoys out the peephole, I gave up. Even the stacks of maps spread over his worktable made no sense to me. His journey book held notations and references to each individual map and the specific demarcations of the land. When it came to navigation, Geoff could plot a route faster than anyone else on board.

"Free to go, sir?" Jensen already stepped halfway through the exit. Morris nodded. He waved on his way out, and the door shut with a click.

Morris stood and faced me with a frown tugging down the wrinkles on his face and his bushy brows drawn tight.

"You report back next time," his voice sharpened. "Three days and we didn't hear a word from either of you. You've been doing this for far too long to ignore your duties, regardless of circumstance—you should have known better."

I bristled in defense and opened my mouth to retort. After all, maintaining radio silence became sort of key when our communicators blared louder than a fire alarm.

His gaze softened. "I was worried, Bea."

Any excuse or retort dried in my throat, and I sighed. "I'll do better next time, I promise."

He nodded, satisfied. I learned after running my mouth for far too many years that explanations and rebuttals were for cowards. Whenever I fought with him and tried to justify my actions, he slapped me with another hefty helping of busywork. I used to go into my bunk to punch holes in the walls and for the longest time thought he hated me. However, after awhile his methods worked: I stopped arguing and started owning up for my mistakes.

"Did you ruffle a few Officer petticoats for me?" A grin snuck onto his face. Captain hearkened from old Germany and had no strong love for the British Merchant Guild. He had served in his country's cavalry before most of Germany disbanded under Britain's regime. Too loyal and stubborn for his own good, Morris took to the skies rather than joining a new army.

"More than a few." I smirked. "Granted, we spent most of our time hiding and then some in the vents. Your contact better pay us proper, because this wasn't the run-of-the-mill retrieval job."

"He will as soon as we deliver the goods." He rapped a fist on top the box. The tap made a hollow noise, but the sound gave no hint of the contents.

"What do you think is in there?" I asked. "Hopefully nothing explosive."

Morris shook his head. "I checked with our employer. Said he needed this box and gave us the retrieval details. I didn't want any harmful substances or bombs aboard our ship, but he promised the cargo was of interest to him, not a dangerous item."

"Besides the price tag though, what made you take him up on the job?" I asked, crossing my arms over my chest. "This mission stuck our necks out further than normal."

"He looked me up because I was an old veteran and asked me to do one last job for the nation we once had. Gods Bea, Germany was my home, my country, and I served her for so many years. A chance to help those who remain?" He pressed his palms flat against his desk and examined them as if he lived through each scar and divot dotting his hands. "Maybe sentimental, but that's why."

"How's Isabella recovering from last time?" I changed the subject, knowing well enough when he was close to losing himself in the memories. Several weeks ago our goods swap failed when a Morlock bastard shot her in the leg because they got a little too greedy. Even though they were our biggest source for jobs, that incident marked the last time we'd do business with the Morlocks. Good riddance.

"She's healing fast, no thanks to those turncoats. Edwin's used a new salve on her that's more effective than any on the market."

I raised my brows. "As long as this isn't some crazy experiment, and he put it through proper testing. We don't want to amputate her leg because he accidentally threw some belladonna in." Edwin's creations landed hit or miss on the board, and one miss a year ago ended with the lot of us heaving overboard for a week. Fortifying meal solutions, my ass.

"How well equipped are we?" I took the leather-bound chair to the right of the desk. Since the rest of the crew had dispersed, he'd be honest with me.

Morris puffed a smoke ring into the air and tapped the side

of his pipe before taking another slow inhale. "I'd be lying to say we don't need this paycheck. After fueling up and restocking our reserves, we didn't have as much to spend on ammunition. That last trade should have tided us through a couple months, but those Morlock bastards screwed that up."

"Do you think they'll give chase too? I mean, we left that squad rotting on the docks." I sat at the edge of the seat with palms printing into the leather in front of me.

"They shot one of ours." The lines deepened around his grey eyes. "I'd waste the whole army for spilling a drop of my crew's blood."

My heart thrummed with pride. All those years ago when I ran away from home, luck had been on my side.

"Some pirates," he scoffed and pressed his cigar into an ashtray to put it out. "Real pirates follow the Code. Those Morlock bastards don't care who they kill and what they destroy. They've torched airships and left them to plummet to the land."

I picked up the cigar before it completely extinguished and took a drag. "Good thing we're not like that, eh?" The taste of tobacco entered my throat, and my nerves slowed to a simmer.

"I suppose I'll go talk with Geoff." Captain Morris roused himself from his chair. "He's probably neck deep in his work right now and could use the help."

"Better you than me." I flicked my wrist to ash the cigar and put the embers out for good. "Our navigational system might as well be ancient Latin. I can't figure out anything from it."

He laughed. "Come now, all this time aboard and you still can't triangulate our location?" We exchanged wry grins, and I followed him out. Morris made the right turn down the hallway toward the navigational chambers while I stopped by my cabin. Opening the locked cherry wood box on my dresser, I rummaged for the long velvet bag and withdrew my brass telescope. We sailed at a fast pace, but my instincts remained on guard for the merchant ship.

I tucked the multi-magnifying scope into the clasped pocket on my holster belt and headed for the upper levels to breathe some fresh air. Wooden steps sloped upward as I ascended and the ceiling stopped upon entering the deck. The old girl's helium balloon loomed overhead, white like the surrounding clouds. Against the side, large black font spelled the word 'Desire.' Anyone from miles away knew who we were, so stealth missions, like the last one, started at the docks.

On deck, the sun pierced the sky and soaked into my skin. Our crew bustled across the faded wooden planks while Spade stood steady at the helm. Because of Spade and Geoff, our ship avoided most turbulent pockets and cut straight through our courses like a turbine bike on the racetrack. Out in the open, nothing muted the sound of our propellers from the ship's rear and the buzz roared in my ears. The mighty chrome blades whirred with the fury of our steam-powered engine.

I walked to the bulwark on the starboard side of the ship, since if the Brits trailed us, they'd be approaching from this side. Despite shoddy navigation skills, I still knew my points on a compass. As I leaned against the wooden ledge and peered over the side, the occasional cloud's condensation kissed my face.

Blue spread all around me, like someone slapped a glob of pastel paint on an open canvas. I stretched the retractile segments of my telescope to full length, the scope spanning from my thumb to my pinkie finger. Peering through the eyepiece, I scanned a horizon amplified by the refracted crystals within the lens. A whole lot of sky came into focus but no flash of their Union Jack flag.

The copper glint of a mail delivery bird zoomed past my view. We hadn't gotten a visit from those miniature mechanized birds since Edwin received his last batch of experimental astragalus. If the Brits pursued us they could always take cover in the clouds, but even still, I should've been able to see the sheen of a balloon or dark splotches of wood. I sighed and leaned against the bulwark. Wind rippled past my face and tossed strands of my hair like pennants until I got fed up and tucked the pieces behind my ear.

"Never pinned you for one of those philosopher types." Jensen sidled next to me. "What are you musing about? The best thing before sliced bread?"

I waved the telescope in my hand. "Come on now, you're thinking too well of me. I figured I'd check for pursuers." I drank in the fresh taste of freedom—the same air I tasted every day since I boarded the ship so many years ago—exhilarating like new rain with drops of adrenaline and a zest of lemon. Jensen hunched over, his massive forearms dominating the ledge. The sunlight gleamed over his tan skin, creating shadows along the angular bridge of his nose, and his thick eyebrows knit together in concentration.

"Do you think they've got our trail?" he asked, his mouth forming a firm line.

"Now, now, don't tell me you're afraid of that little old merchant ship. It's an obnoxious fly but nothing to quake in your boots over," I teased. "We have the goods, and we escaped. Geoff's set our course, and sooner than not, that box isn't our problem anymore. If they pursue, we don't have it." I noticed the quick glance to his leg. Injury wasn't common for him. The man could bench press my weight twice over and outrun most military personnel. He was a top-notch soldier, and even though the bullet only grazed, Jensen wouldn't take that wound lightly.

"Yank the wind out of your sails," he said. "You were right there with me. A whole squad to protect a lock box already under alarm and in a high tech safe? It doesn't add up. If it's that important, they'll pursue us like a stripper crawling after a dollar. We're going to be their primary targets even if we pawn the goods off to someone else. I don't believe they'll want to sit down and sip some afternoon tea after we broke into their ship and stole their merchandise. What did Morris have to say?"

"Same thing he told you. I have no idea what's in that damned box, but it's valuable. Plus, the contents must be personal. The employer asked him to do it for old Germany, and you know how much that means to him."

Jensen didn't respond at first, and his lips formed a firm frown. "This wasn't a good idea doing a job just because the old man's sentimental." He gripped the ledge. "This is messy and our crew's been getting sloppy. We're pissing off way too many higher organizations. If this keeps up, I'll have to find another ship to fly with."

"You'd best stop making excuses and start training harder." I bristled in defense. "You're skilled, Jensen. If the Captain didn't think you could handle the missions, he wouldn't put you on them." Both of us avoided addressing the wound on his leg, but I wouldn't tolerate anyone badmouthing the captain in my presence. His thick jaw tensed, and for a moment I thought he'd argue.

"I think we cut it close out there." Jensen sucked in a deep breath. "It threw me off. I'm used to having more control and definitely more information on the job."

"Had enough of my hare-brained schemes already?" I nudged him in the side. "But we didn't even get to take on a renegade crew armed with an accordion and a soup ladle." Jensen raised an eyebrow, and a smile tugged on the corner of his lips.

I punched his arm. "Look, why don't you get Edwin to check out your leg? I did a quick job on it, but you could use some antiseptic and a cleaner bandage wrap. He'll take care of it for you."

"You're trying to get rid of me, aren't you?" He flashed me a sarcastic grin. "Knowing Edwin, I'll end up worse off. He'll mix antiseptic with the arsenic, and I'll be dead before sunrise."

"Come on now." I adopted a mock serious tone. "He's not that bad. On rare occasion his concoctions end up working." My lips quivered until I broke into a wry grin. "Of course, that could just be a tall tale after one too many drinks. Look, I'll even walk with you."

"Oh?" He leaned in closer to me. "I'm getting the first mate's personal touch, eh?"

I pursed my lips and placed a hand on my hip. "Sweetheart, my personal touch would leave you useless for days." I winked, trailing my fingers down his arm. "I need my soldiers in top condition, not incapacitated because I wanted to have some fun."

"Darling," he said, "you can keep your wrecking-ball style of love to yourself. If I want a riot wrestling match, I'll sign up for the tournament."

"You couldn't handle my heat, Jensen. Tie your apron on and get back in the kitchen." Laughter bubbled in both our grins, and we stepped away from the edge.

"Ready to go?" Jensen extended an arm. I looped mine through, and we walked off toward the infirmary.

A booming crackle in the distance caused me to nearly jump out of my skin in the aftermath of the gunshot-like rumble. The humidity beaded along my neck and chilled there. When I scanned the horizon line, the blue sky darkened, and white clouds grew smoky tails around their edges.

CHAPTER FOUR

I whirled around to the stern side. "Spade!" I called out. My voice carried across the deck. "Storm ahead!"

"Yes, sir!" Spade waved from the helm.

"Just what we need," Jensen said under his breath.

"It's good timing." I grinned, all teeth. "Imagine if rain hit while we escaped. The rope would have been too slippery, and you can just forget holding onto that cargo."

Jensen and I quickened our pace to get below deck. If a storm loomed on the horizon, we'd need the whole crew to help steer the Desire. I should have recognized the signs—the heaving air and the humidity in the wind signaled the imminent storm. But the sooner I stopped by the infirmary, the sooner I'd be back on deck. High up in the air, we bypassed some pockets, but most of the time rain exploded, hard and fast. At least the deck would get a shiny new polish, since as of late the wood had taken some heavy footprints and extra sludge. Deckhands these days didn't clean a ship like I had.

We stalked down the flights of steps to the two connected rooms toward the stem side of the ship that comprised the sick bay. A rectangular plank with "Infirmary" scrawled over it marked the door. I turned the doorknob, and Jensen followed me in.

Edwin's personal labs bisected the main chamber from the back, and the faint smell of bleach lingered throughout the place. Hospital beds, if you could even call them that, covered the front section of the room, some frames with clawed feet, or none, and all sitting at different heights. Multi-colored sheets ranged from olive to neon orange, which provided a splash of color to the menagerie of empty beds spanning the room—apart from the one on the far right.

Isabella perked up when we approached. She'd stayed in the infirmary for the past month after the Morlocks shot her because the wound had dosed her with a hefty amount of poison on top of injuring her leg. While Edwin had found a cure for the poison and administered it in time, the aftereffects slowed her. She'd already wandered around on her own and soon she'd be going on jobs again, but the run-in had swerved too close to casualty. We didn't lose our own. Her taupe ringlets swung around her neck and brushed along her caramel skin when she stood to greet us. Dark eyes glittered against her heart shaped face, offset by full pouty lips.

"The two of you come down to visit little old me?" She coquettishly brushed her fingers over her mouth. Her tart rose perfume lingered in the air around us.

"Always, lady." I grinned and patted Jensen's shoulder. "I brought you a present. He's big, surly, and I can even tie him up with a bow."

"How did I ever get so lucky?" He ran a finger underneath his suspender strap and smirked. "Passed around between two gorgeous women."

"You two best stop that now, or I'll blush," Isabella said with a wan smile. What crap. Nothing ruffled the woman. She stepped past us, and her hips swung side to side like a bellydancer's.

"Now, time to go see Edwin." I clapped a hand against Jensen's back before pushing him forward. He trudged off.

"My leg's been aching," Isabella murmured. She approached the nearest table covered with Edwin's mess of capped bottles and sketched inventions. Testing the bench with her hand, she sat down. "Is there a storm brewin'? It doesn't hurt like this unless there's rain on the horizon."

My lips pressed together in a tight line. "Time to ride out another tempest and pray we're not the bullseye."

She glanced behind me to make sure big and burly had cleared out. "Jensen got injured?" Isabella's brow rose. "Color me wrong, but that man doesn't get injured. In the five years since he's been aboard, he's barely gotten a nick on his shoulder let alone a bullet graze."

"No, he doesn't." I rubbed my temples. "The setup of the mission ended differently than expected."

"A lot of these unexpected scenarios keep cropping up for

48

us." She glanced down. Her bandaged leg poked out from underneath her rust-red ruffled skirt. A strand of golden circles strung down each side of her off-shoulder white blouse, and the hemming scrunched over her ample bosom.

"How's your recovery going?" My voice lowered. She spread her legs wider on the bench and placed her hands on her knees. Though a leather cincher usually encircled her midriff, she hadn't bothered with it while recovering. Not like she needed it. She could loop a belt twice around her waist, and her hips curved like teacup handles.

"Well." Her breath came out in a hiss. "I can walk again. I'm not hobbling around deck any more, and I'm ready to take some damned Morlocks down. Nobody puts me out of commission this long and gets away with it. As far as attempted murder goes, I'm not very forgiving." She glanced to the ground and refused to look up.

Her voice softened. "I'm weaker than I was. The wound's healing due to Edwin's diligence, but I'll get tired if I push myself up above. I guess I came close to falling over the edge." The blackened truth suspended in the air, that we'd almost lost her back there. If we hadn't brought her to Edwin in time, and if he hadn't been as skilled, we'd be one crew member down. A life like ours sizzled with danger, but our crew had been together for so long I couldn't imagine a member missing from our surrogate family.

A boom quaked throughout the cabins, shaking the ship.

My fingers gripped the table so hard I swore I bored holes into the top.

"Not a pretty one at all." Isabella's face paled.

"You sit tight here and worry about getting better. I'll be heading on deck to give that big bad storm what for." I cracked a grin for her.

"Sweet pea, you better tighten your bootstraps." She winked at me. "I see your knees quaking from where you stand."

"Ha," I mouthed. She was half-right, but my job as first mate was to be out there facing the storm no matter what. "Well as long as you're here taking care of Jensen, I guess I can head out."

Isabella licked her lips. "I'll take care of him all right." I shook my head and stalked out of the infirmary. The wolfish grin on her face didn't bode well for Jensen—he wouldn't know what hit him. Not that I blamed her, since a tumble with Jensen had the superficial necessity of a satisfying lay without any emotions shackling me to the mast. I shed that sentimental crap a long time back. Entanglements and feelings interfered with my way of life: trust my instinct and shoot faster than the other guy.

Turning the corner, I quickened my pace as thunder growled again, echoing through the hollow corridor. If a storm loomed, Spade and Geoff would need any help they could get. The sounds of the squall twisted my stomach with the raw anticipation of danger, and I caught a reflection of myself in the porthole mirror

I passed. A wide smile had crawled upon my face while I wasn't paying attention. Apparently my sanity walked a wobbling tightrope if risks excited me this much. Nonetheless, something triggered a skip in my chest with every peal of thunder. Dangerous, yes, but the turmoil of a storm ripped through the entire sector with a clarity I envied.

I walked up the steps and entered the deck where a darkened indigo skyline replaced the pastel hues from earlier. The keen scent of ozone thrummed through the horizon, threading through my veins like tiny pinpricks of adrenaline. Meaty drops cascaded from the sky, and thick as anything, they plopped on board with loud smacks. Upping my pace to a jog, I made a beeline for the helm. The air darkened, and the sky cascaded to the mottled purple of a bruise. The wind batted my hair around, lifting strands clear over my head.

Captain Morris already left his quarters and stood by Spade at the helm while Geoff hid away in the cabin trying to secure our location. Morris waved me over, and I tossed him a quick salute. Rain soaked into my black chemise, and I thanked my lucky cameo I hadn't been wearing a white one, or I would've been leered off deck. Giant droplets splattered against my clothes like cheetah print, trickling down my arms. A storm aboard an airship dealt one hell of a pummeling. Naked under the broad horizon, the sky unleashed its worst violence, and we fought to survive.

Gusts of wind kicked up.

With the first aggressive blast, our ship leaned to the right, and her planks groaned under the pressure. Water cascaded across the balloon overhead, dropping in sheets down onto deck right as I arrived at the helm.

"Where do you need me, Captain?" I shouted. The hum of rain along with the claps of thunder muffled my voice. Morris pointed forward, towards the forecastle. The storm sails hadn't been released yet, and we'd need every ounce of maneuverability to clear the gusts and stay steady.

Wind and rain pounded on my back while I ran. Thunder vibrated through the air again, tense and booming. My boots slipped, but I threw my body back to stay straight since the slick deck made a simple walk dangerous. I kicked up puddles of water as I raced along, pitching myself toward the forward end of the ship. Spade would have plenty of help with Morris by his side, and we needed those sails.

Another thunderclap boomed through the pregnant air, followed by the first flash of lightning. The jagged bolt razed the sky with precision, slicing through the alien horizon and clearing through the torrents of rain. For one instant, the light illuminated the entire deck from stern to stem. It lanced off the curves of the overhead balloon and displayed the exact path I needed.

Streaks of lightning disappeared, and the torrential downpour returned. Water slid down my back, pelted my head, and soaked my pants. The torrents blinded me, and I could barely see three steps ahead, but I stumbled forward, driven by the image seared into my mind.

This time, the airship careened to the left, and my feet slid from under me. As I hit the ground with a thud, my chin slammed against the planks. Though I groped forward for anything with a hold, the downpour slicked the wood across the deck and along the masts. I scrabbled like an overweight fish before pushing myself up again. Lightning illuminated the sky followed by a crack of thunder, which provided enough light to renew my sense of direction. Rain overwhelmed my senses, and even as I choked back draughts of the heady liquid, my heartbeat sped with the thrill. I clenched my jaw, pushing forward. The captain gave me an order, and I didn't disobey.

Those hooked sails lay within reach, so I scrambled for the rope, which slid within my grasp. I needed a fair amount of force to upend the flaps—this was more of a two man job—but we couldn't spare the extra deckhand. Winding the limp cord around my hands, I tugged.

After concentrated effort, the sails rose a little but flopped back down as I lost my footing. This wasn't going to work. My biceps bulged as I tried again, but my feet kept sliding around. I had to edge backwards enough to tie the rope through the brass loop attached to the sides of the ship, however, the tread slipped from under me. Even as my back hit the ground with a thwack, I kept my grip tight.

The force of the fall pushed the sails up, but my body slid as the ship tilted forward. I shut my eyes for a moment to concentrate. Wind, rain, and thunder pounded all around me, pummeling my body.

It had rained the night I left home.

I rolled around the deck and smacked into the edge. The rope tumbled with me, wrapping around my middle. Thunder quaked, and another bolt of lightning flickered through.

During a thunderstorm like this one, I'd stolen my freedom and never glanced back. Years ago, I had crouched on the street side under an old abandoned building. Water cascaded overtop me and soaked my skin as I shivered, alone in the dark. In fact, I'd never been more alone. I abandoned my family, my school, and my friends, leaving my life behind after too many nights of listening to the screams, the crashes, and the thumps from the other room. So many days my mother left the house, a battered hull of a woman. I sat alone under that old building in the middle of a torrential downpour and grinned.

Another loud boom of thunder snapped me to the present. The rope entangled around my waist finally stopped sliding all over the place. I groped for the ledge, and my hand traveled the curve of the brass loop which glinted against the barrage of water from overhead. After fumbling with the cord, I clamped down onto the loop with my other hand.

If I let go, I'd struggle back to the edge all over again. Slithering on its own, the rope kept darting away from the circle's opening. After several failures, it caught, and I jammed the end through. Once I looped it in, I placed my feet against the side timbers and yanked backward. Fully diagonal with the ship, I used the leverage to pull the sails up, straining with the effort.

The time between the thunder and lightning began lengthening right as I tied the rope to the loop and stood back to watch the sails flutter in place. Desire steadied somewhat, and the careening lessened. Rain flew into my mouth causing me to splutter as I rushed toward the stern side.

Spade and Morris manned the helm, directing the ship while deckhands scrambled across the planks. Some tightened ropes and secured cargo, while others clung to anything stable. Near the forecastle, the lay of the ship spread before me with the most stunning darkened wood angles, cleansed by the rain. No time like the present to climb back.

I slipped down the rungs of the forecastle onto the main deck. Water sloshed around me, as if I stood knee deep in the ocean, though up here we were closer to any lightning, and our airship made a clear target. If the Gods played darts with their lightning bolts, we'd be bullseye.

Rain swept past us in buffeting gales. I stumbled over my slick leather boots and hunched to guard my body from the torrents. Maneuvering my way across deck, I coasted back to the captain's side. The flashes of lightning lessened with the following crackles of thunder, and some of the wind even died down. Of course, whenever we pulled the ship into tip-top order for the storm, the wind and rain would dissipate. Storms didn't last long in our sector before they moved on through the sphere. We'd deal with the onslaught and aftermath, but conditions rarely spanned over a long duration.

Raindrops clung to my eyelashes and streamed down my face like tears. A bitter smile twisted my face because I hadn't cried in years—I'd learned at an early age the repercussions of showing weakness. Spade waved, but his other hand gripped the wheel. A fresh breeze cut through the thick tense air of the storm, invading my lungs. By the time I reached the helm, I slumped to the ground where they stood.

"Had enough of the storm, Bea?" Captain Morris leaned down while the edges of his trench dripped onto the floorboards.

"No, sir." I perched with my elbows crutched onto my knees. "I love a wicked storm, gladly take another."

The rain continued, but mere rainfall we could handle. Uncomfortable, yes, but nowhere near as dangerous as those ozone-crunching, climate-changing thunderstorms. I plucked my sodden shirt from my chest, and the material flapped back with a sloppy plunk. My nose wrinkled in distaste. After I'd just put on fresh clothing too. At the helm, Spade's blue eyes focused straight ahead with an intense sort of focus.

"Rough patch, eh?" I called to him, much too lazy to stand.

"Aye." His muscular forearms tensed back and forth with a rhythmic sway of the ship while he guided our path. I rummaged through my pack and pulled out my smaller pouch with the telescope. Peering through the eyepiece, I gazed off in the distance. Rain streaked through my vision, and droplets clung to the lens, but I could still see clear enough. My toes curled within my boots.

A Union Jack flag rippled in the distance.

CHAPTER FIVE

Shit. Shit. Shit.

The red against blue glared on the flag, and the hulking ship penetrated the expanse between us.

"Enemy ship on the horizon!" Jack, the overseer, called out. Blunt interference from the residual rain garbled his voice.

The monolith of a ship must have stayed hidden via cloud cover since the redcoats had enough tech aboard to track us through that storm. At the sight of the behemoth, a shudder rolled through me. I whipped my head towards the steering rig where Spade stood by the helm and Morris at the aether regulators.

"How far away are we from port?" Morris called to me. "Check in with Geoff as fast as you can and return here. We're going to move faster than a hooker on a time crunch and leave this freighter eating our dust."

I stifled my grin. The captain always kept calm, even under this siege which would begin in mere minutes. With a salute, I raced towards the navigation chambers. My feet pounded against the dewy floorboards, and drops of rain pattered across my back.

Gusts of wind whipped past me, and the deck careened

under my shaky view. I threw myself headlong towards the cabin, meters away. Geoff needed to plot our course and quick, because once we had our bearings, we'd have a better chance of outmaneuvering the Brits. Desire was smaller and faster than most ships among the skies, but speed didn't matter if we had no direction. My hands fumbled with the doorknob. Aimlessness created more danger than any landlubber would understand since the skies abounded with storms and atmospheric pockets. After I got a grip, I yanked the door open and hurled myself inside.

Geoff sat at his desk, surrounded by stacks of maps. With his compass in one hand and a marker in the other, he scrutinized the map before him. I leaned against the wall and tried to appear calm—at least as calm as I could manage while puddles formed by my feet.

Even though my entrance had been anything but quiet, Geoff didn't look up. A thick curl of chestnut hair swung over his eyes, and I resisted the urge to walk over and brush it from his face. He blew it away but didn't stop maneuvering the compass. My heart beat faster watching him work, and warmth spread through my extremities despite the rain soaked cold. As much as we teased him, our ship would be a duck sans tail feathers without his navigation.

Besides, Geoff kept me sane. He'd introduced himself with a warm handshake and a gorgeous smile on the first day my life started over. Every time I'd gotten into trouble for running my mouth, he sat with me and helped me calm down so I didn't land even more busywork from the captain. I coughed into my hand to get his attention. At the sound, his head swung up to greet me.

"Bea, please tell me you're here to announce a change into balmy weather and a surprise beacon signaling a treasure trove." He scratched away at the papers in front of him even while sparing me a glance.

I tried running my hands through my hair but gave up when the sodden curls molded together into one cohesive mass. Attractive.

"Of course not. I'm leveling an aether bomb's worth of fun. How do you feel about enemy pursuit? The captain mentioned the words port and fast, so he sent me down to help. You point, I grunt, go push button."

He lifted an eyebrow, and a laugh slipped from his throat. "All right, we're going to chart this course as fast as possible. Grab the Western Coast map for me. You can work through the preliminaries, and I'll finish mapping our current trajectory." As he spoke, the ship trembled.

"Right, West Coast." I stepped past his mess of compasses, chronometers, and rulers towards the hand-painted cabinet of our maps. Of course, the cabinet was covered in more roses, thank you, Isabella. Since our ship traveled all over the globe, we owned a definitive collection. Voluminous, yes. Well organized, no.

I rifled through the folders, but most of the maps blended into the same scribbles on parchment. Pinpricks of nervous sweat tickled my neck and commingled with residual raindrops. At least in here I'd get some solace from the storm, even though my heart raced with the excitement from the torrents on deck. Obviously I had some mental issues if I got off on that sort of mind-numbing danger. My slick fingers printed wetness onto the maps, and I cursed my lack of foresight because I'd ruin our papers within seconds if I wasn't careful. Further in, I rifled past a United States map, so I stopped and lifted it. Bingo, West Coast. Pulling the paper out, I slapped it onto Geoff's desk.

"Here it is."

He placed down his marker and glanced over. "I'm almost done with the first half of our coordinates, so can you start calculating the direction of our entry? We're going to ride an Eastern current there and should be able to use the drift to accelerate our engines."

I blinked several times and pointed to myself. "Push button?"

Geoff let out a sigh and passed me a lopsided grin. "Look Bea, get this to Spade, he'll know what to do. That way we can at least start moving rather than drifting like an open target. I should be able to take care of the second part while we start sailing in the proper direction."

Sometimes I loved that man. He handed me his scribbled over maps, and I folded up the paper, tucking it away into my side bag. Before I left, I bent down and gave Geoff a light peck on the cheek.

"Thanks, chief!" I waved goodbye and ducked out the door before I noticed his blush too much.

I started missing the shelter of the cabin the second the rain spat at my face with ill-tempered slaps. That leviathan of a merchant ship loomed closer, cutting through the space between us, but their cannons glinting in the distance proved more menacing than their proximity. A couple more meters and we'd be within their heavy artillery's range.

"Captain," I called out, scrabbling over the slick deck, "Firing ahead!" My voice scraped against my throat, and my leather bag slapped my hip. I had to get Spade our coordinates. If we didn't move, they'd start using those cannons. But they wouldn't blow us from the sky, would they? If they did, their precious cargo sunk with us.

Along the sides, their crew fired away, and the bullets peaked like fireflies before dropping down towards land. The tiny lights created a spectacular but deadly sight. A couple bullets pinged onto our deck, but most of their men fired for the sake of feeling accomplished. I snorted. Only fools wasted their ammunition. The ship veered closer, coming in parallel to line up their cannon sights for a clear shot. If they took aim, I wanted to be as far away from the side of the ship as possible.

I raced faster under the canopy of our overhead balloon. An aluminum frame and plasma shielding reinforced our balloon, but enough shots would knock us straight out of the sky. And no one survived those crashes.

A crack boomed in the distance.

I scrambled over to the nearest mast, clinging onto it for support. Like a disorienting punch, the cannon hit our ship, and the Desire's body whipped back and forth. My heart soared into my throat, and for several horrifying seconds, my feet floated in the air while I desperately clung to the mast. Several folks who hadn't found a sound structure slid from the force to smack against the sides of the ship. The deafening cannon's roar kept me from hearing the crunch of their bodies. Thanks to Spade and the captain, the ship steadied again.

They needed the maps to catch Geoff's stream. I raced towards the helm where our men stood steady—a feat in this turbulence. Jitters ran up and down my legs, but I pushed myself onward to the navigation bay.

My first thought would have been to fire back on the merchant ship and gun them down, but Morris made a better Captain for a reason. In outmaneuvering them, we'd save our ammunition for when it counted and cut down on the number of casualties. Not for the first time, a fierce pride for my Captain towered in my chest.

"Bea, how far are we?" Morris hollered from his perch. A crew member rushed by me with rope, ready to tie down our reserve masts.

"I've got Geoff's work right here," I said. "He's getting the rest of it ready." I took cover under the slats over the helm.

"A first mate who's rubbish at navigating?" Morris grinned. "One of these days we'll teach you, Bea."

"You promoted me for my ruthless stubbornness and dog-headed determination, not my tech savvy. Plus, I'm a damn good shot." From the merchant ship, a spark exploded in the distance.

"Duck!" Morris roared and we wedged ourselves into the corner of the control bay. Spade clutched the wheel tight, knuckles as chalky as my mother's best china. Even braced for impact, the cannon's hit still disoriented us as white exploded before my eyes, and my ears rang with a tinny whistle. My body began sliding, and I groped the wooden frame next to me. Splinters dug into my shaking fingertips while I choked on my own breaths, sitting for several shaky seconds before my world stopped spinning around me.

"Schiesse, hull's breached," Morris spat. "Quick, pass me our trajectory. We need the fastest route out of here."

I fumbled for the leather purse at my side. Nothing. Panic

seized my veins and coursed through my system. Across the deck, crewmembers raced around, pulling on ropes or tossing buckets of water overboard. Several crouched into whatever corners they found, and some had joined in the gunfire since the behemoth of a merchant ship maintained its parallel position. I inhaled deep, but the breath barely calmed my shattered nerves.

"Bea, where is it?" Morris repeated. Scanning the perimeter wouldn't help because we didn't have that kind of time. The bag must have jostled free after that first cannon shot. With any luck, it'd still be there.

"Be right back, Captain." Ignoring the flare of another cannon startup, I dashed headlong and retraced my tracks. Rain and wind muffled the string of curses from Morris. The world slowed around me, along with the surge of rain, and the crew rushing back and forth. Even the cannon heading straight for us lagged to a crawl. The deck careened a sharp left from the force of the shot.

When my feet gave way, I rebounded and jumped using the impact as leverage towards the mast. Droplets of rain burned in my eyes, so I groped for the wooden structure. The second my numbed fingers touched splinters, I loped my arm around the mast as the ship tilted, ready to carry me past the side.

A maelstrom of darkened blue and charred clouds swirled over the edge. My limbs seized up at the sight as torrents of fear surged through my shaking body. Below, my leather purse slid with the movement. I pinned the bag down with my foot to keep it from slipping out of my reach again before exhaling a sigh of relief.

Our girl, Desire, righted, but the merchant ship readied their rope. They'd try boarding us any minute now and the captain and Spade needed a direction. Hell, we needed Geoff. I surged back onto my feet and with the leather strap wrapped around my hand, rushed for the helm.

Halfway across the deck, a hand clapped against my back. Surprised, I whirled around and almost clocked whoever stood behind me.

Geoff caught my hand.

"Bea, let's get moving. Did you get the coordinates to Spade?" he asked.

I shook my head while waving the leather purse. "Trying to."

We both ran across the wooden panels for the refuge of the helm. Our ship couldn't withstand any more hits, and if we loitered any longer, we'd either have to start returning fire, or they'd board us. Their guards and officers lined the sides and took aim. Now from the ship's closer vantage point, their bullets pinged against our railings. We ducked under the slats, joining with the captain and Spade.

"Sorry sir, here's the coordinates." I fished into the pocket and pulled out the papers.

"I'll take them." Geoff grabbed the paper and stepped up to the wheel. "Spade, stand relieved. I need you on the accelerators. If we're going to make it through, we have to catch the polar jet. Jumping on mid-stream requires precise direction, since we'll have to combat the hellish storms on the outside, so I'll need each of you. Captain Morris, pump our aether to full velocity, we're going to need our maximum amount of pressure for this maneuver." The captain shifted over to the aether manipulator at once. "Bea, you're our bearing taker, the high speeds of the jet stream will muddle our gyrocompass, so I need you to check it against this."

He tossed me one of the regular compasses from his chambers. I bit my lip but didn't argue. Navigation wasn't my best suit, but we couldn't afford errors and didn't have time to grab anyone else. If we didn't leave here fast, not only our cargo but our lives and ship would be forfeit.

I sucked in a deep breath and stepped between Geoff and Spade. Wind whipped through his hair and tossed strands into the air, but Geoff gripped the wheel and stared out at the bruised skies before us.

"We're in your hands now." Morris resumed his post by the aether manipulator. The enemy ship neared so close we could hear its boards creak.

"Bea," Geoff asked, "What's our immediate direction?"

I stared at the black compass and peered close for the exact leaning of the white arrow. "Thirty-three degrees North." I had to shout for him to hear since the winds kicked up louder.

"Aiming sharp West," Geoff called, "Veering left now. Captain, maintain pressure. Spade, on the count of three, push the accelerators." He gripped the wheel, stationing his feet flat against the ground. "Three, two, one...Go!"

Geoff threw his body to the left and whipped the wheel along with him. Our ship groaned with the sudden effort, but Spade picked up the excess impetus by firing the accelerators. I peered at the compass.

"We're still not full West." The white arrow danced out of reach, "We're fifteen degrees off."

"Couldn't be easy, right? Those degrees will cost us the jet stream," he growled and let go of the wheel. It whirled back into place, and the ship righted. Already, Desire pulled away from the merchant ship, but we weren't clear of its firing range yet. Normally we'd zoom past the monolith, but those hits, they slowed us down. If we missed that jet stream, we'd be sunk in no time.

"All right, again," Geoff called, "on my cue...Go!" He used less force this time and careened her left. Desire lurched under us, her timbers creaking with renewed effort. Spade pressed forward, and the captain lessened his pressure since we didn't want to overshoot this. Rain drifted in from beyond the slatted overhangs, while around deck, crew members struggled to keep our masts following proper direction. The merchant ship had stopped firing their cannons, but behind us they picked up the speed of pursuit.

I glanced at the compass. The needle landed on West and didn't stray, minus the occasional interference.

"We hit West!" I called out. "West ahead!" Nervous energy prickled up my arms and across my back. I didn't like how fast they gained on us. Even if we did find this jet stream, if they found it too we'd have accomplished nothing.

"All right, crew." Morris took over. "Thrust ahead, we're going to dodge this ship!"

"Aye, aye, Captain!" Geoff saluted, and Spade revved the acceleration. Our ship darted forward into the gray skies. With a course, Desire moved fast. We had to be nearing the streams, since gusts of winds whipped around the ship, as fierce as that storm.

"Hey Geoff," I said. "You had to go and pick the most dangerous route, didn't you?"

He gave me a wide grin.

"If it wasn't dangerous, it wouldn't be any fun," Morris called over. "Now quit your schoolgirl gossiping and man this station, First Mate." Captain Morris pointed to the aether manipulators. "I'm going to prepare the crew. We'll need all the deckhands at full capacity to fight into this jet stream."

"So this is how the merchant ship won't follow us," I

mumbled. "They aren't insane enough to join the party." The wind carried Morris' laugh out onto the deck.

Our ship trembled under the voracity of the wind, but Spade and Geoff maintained our position. Captain Morris raced out onto the deck and gathered the crew who snapped to attention at the sound of his bark. Between our crewmates raising the masts and the fast push ahead, our ship zoomed forward into the frenzy of a gale. The tubes of green aether pulsed up and down with the strain of the force. I flipped the switches to my right when the bubbles peaked near the top to stabilize our pressure. The last thing we needed was an engine malfunction.

Behind us, the merchant ship lagged and didn't keep the same pace they had. Before us, the wind roared like a living beast.

"Ready?" Geoff's warm gaze met mine.

I matched his grin. "Always."

I flicked three of the switches on the console, and Spade fired one last request to our accelerators. We pulsed ahead with the wind, soaring straight into the polar jet stream.

CHAPTER SIX

I slumped against the beams behind me, using them for support. Seconds after we entered the jet stream, the roaring gale petered to a minimum, and our ship sailed along the current smoother than a journey through clear sky. With the mellow change of weather, rain no longer assaulted our steps. Personally, I just appreciated the return of feeling to my fingertips.

The waning light of early evening tinted the sky a much more comforting shade of gray than the nonsense from mid-afternoon. A backwards glance towards the stern end of the ship rewarded me with a clear view. We lost the British Merchant ship.

"Not so shabby of an escape route, eh?" Geoff tossed me one of his lopsided grins. Several crooked teeth poked out, and his eyes gleamed from the excitement.

"This is that balmy weather you mentioned," I purred. "I have to say, I'm a fan."

Captain Morris lumbered towards us. "Geoff, slick navigating there. You pulled us out of a tighter pinch than we've seen in a fortnight, and I'm grateful. We'll have to break out the absinthe tonight and celebrate before we hit the docks."

"Should be reaching the docks by tomorrow, sir," Geoff said. "Besides giving us a smooth, sweet ride, this current's faster than anything." Captain Morris nodded and walked across the deck. Our crew faced him.

"Tonight, crew, relax," he called out, "we'll be riding fair weather courtesy of the polar jet stream!" A round of cheers filtered through the air. I couldn't keep the smile from my face and pumped my fist during the next round. Spade laughed. A gentle zephyr swept through the deck and spread hope with a renewed fervor around the ship.

I hopped up and leaned over the aether manipulator. Flipping several switches stabilized the tubes in flux to put the machine on standby.

"I'm going down to the infirmary. I'll let them know we stopped rolling around like a power turbine."

"You going to make sure princess Jensen's hanging tight with his scratch?" Geoff asked.

"Now, now." I placed a hand on his back. "Jealousy colors you black, Geoff. If you wanted to be a pretty princess too, I would've bought you a crown. I'll be back soon." I flashed the boys a grin and dashed across the deck.

Warmth and damp humidity from the passed storm glued my leather boots against my legs, and my matted waves shifted across my back in a large clumpy mass. Under the changed light, the mahogany panels of the deck sparkled from the brand new storm wash, better than any crew could accomplish.

I stomped down the steps to enter the cabin's canopy. Blood still hummed through my veins like a chant after the day's excitement, and my damp boots squelched along the cabin flooring. Dim light filtered in amidst the electric candles decorating the halls, but the shadows deepened with the onset of night, chilling my skin. I paused before passing my room. After three costume changes in one day, I should've stolen away with those vaudeville girls, but I claimed this one as necessary.

The door creaked when I pushed it open, and I crept inside the darkened room. After grabbing the lamp on my dresser, I flicked the electric candle on as false light flickered from its brassy cage. The smell of lemons and salt water permeated my room, even though we were well above the ocean. My chemise and pants clung to me like a second uncomfortable skin, so tight they outlined the deep ropy scars over my left thigh. At least I'd escaped alive. I couldn't say the same for the smuggler who gave me that scar.

My clothes landed with a squish onto the floor. With one foot, I nudged the sodden mess towards the bed before rummaging through the clothing in my trunk. We'd be celebrating tonight.

I pulled on a black ruched skirt, pinned up twice in the front. A little ruffled, yes, but I had to remind the crew of my feminine side once in awhile. My leather boots needed to air dry, so I left them under the narrow window. Instead, I yanked out trendy taupe slippers from Thailand. I strapped on a forest green bodice with considerably less boning and tied back my sodden locks with a piece of twine. The simple change of clothes transformed me into a new person again.

After exiting my chambers, I made a short detour along the way. Seth always stayed close by the engine room to keep an eye on the important machinery and fixed it when parts loosened, so she ran at optimum efficiency. But we were celebrating tonight, and he could afford to cut loose. I made the first right into the descending stairwell, following the turns I knew by heart. When I first arrived on the ship, I helped Seth out most days because ship mechanics made more sense than navigation. Give me a wrench and diagnostics issue over the crazy jiggery pokery Geoff did any day.

The second floor hallway stretched out like a boardwalk since it spanned the entire length of the ship. When I reached the end of the corridor, I made another right down the next stairwell. Midway down the set of steps, the air grew hotter, and steam drifted from the door of the engine room in hot humid tufts. I snorted before rounding the corner. What was I thinking? Seth wouldn't want to join in our merriment. The sober ex-marine avoided most of our shenanigans.

"Seth." I peered in past the doorframe. My voice echoed around the wide room, bouncing off the boiler tank.

His stout figure almost vanished under the dominance of the giant aether towers, huge pipes that lined the sides of the room like organ tubes. Bubbles slid up and down in unison with the flow of the large engine pumping out billows of steam. Airships swarmed the sky mere decades after they began harvesting aether, and these batteries converted to the steam that fueled the Desire. The mist outlined him from where he stood by the engine, but once he walked over, his flushed face contrasted the murky room.

"Beatrice, how have you been?"

His expression rarely faltered from serious, but when the crew got silly he'd bestow us with one of his small smirks. Seth stood a foot shorter than me, but his extra muscle gave him a burly profile. Oil stains covered his dark blue jumper and patches of sweat drenched his wife-beater. Tools lined his pockets, which he could've kept in the toolboxes lining the room, but Seth preferred to be prepared. Steam made his ruddy skin glisten with droplets of fresh moisture.

"Peachy." My arms swung along my sides. "Just an average day robbing British merchants, running through a storm, and dodging fire from an enemy ship."

"Dodging, you say?" He lifted an eyebrow. "From the damage to the hull and how much the ricochet offset her pressure sensitizers, I'd say you did a pretty poor job at dodging."

"So we may have a received a couple of nicks along the way, but that's why you're here!" I slung an arm around his shoulders.

"You're telling me we're heading to a port soon, right? That enemy ship knocked more than a couple screws loose. The hull breach caused enough of an issue that once we dock I'll need a crew to repair the siding and take care of the bent metal of the exhaust case unless we want to be inhaling toxic fumes."

"No worries, we'll be sailing into port within the day." I played with one of the leather straps along my bodice. "We're following the polar jet stream right now, so at least the smooth current will take some of the stress from her. We're celebrating the escape tonight if you'd like to join us, Seth." I pursed my lips.

He gave me a look, because both of us knew his reply. "I have a handle of rum down here, I'll take a swig."

"You'd take a swig regardless." I slapped him on the back and headed towards the door. "Don't come crying to me when you're lonely down here."

"How could I get lonely?" He patted the giant boiler of an engine with a gloved hand. "She's always talking, never shuts up." The side of his mouth quirked into a half smile. Seth saw a couple wars years back, so he didn't associate drinking with merriment—for him the swill took the edge off bitter memories. He and the captain fought in the Great European War together, but Captain took his mind off his past by barking orders instead of drinking in the engine room. Even still, a smile from Seth warranted the trip down to ask. I waggled my fingers before jogging up the steps. The voices grew louder the closer I approached the infirmary, so I threw the door open.

"What, a party and I wasn't invited?" I called in. Isabella, Jensen, and Edwin huddled around a table in the back, but Isabella turned her head at the sound of my voice. I sauntered over to the table. A pile of cards and some loose coin lay scattered across it. "Playing Faro, eh? You lot missed a bunch of fun. Our friends visited, you know, the ones Jensen and I made on our trip."

"I heard them." Jensen pressed his palms against the table. "They were begging me to come out and play. Loudly."

"Neither of you should leave the infirmary until you're well. Running amok atop deck will land you back in here and worse off than before," Edwin piped up in his reedy tone. He presented himself as authoritative without even trying. Pointed eyebrows and dark eyes transformed his long face and beak of a nose into a disapproving look. Bony elbows protruded from his oversized ash suit jacket, and the long pants hovered above the ankles of his lanky legs. If he popped on a pair of glasses and a lab coat, the man would be the perfect illustration of a mad scientist.

"Doc, it's only a graze. I'll be walking smooth on this leg in a couple of days, so no need to chain me here much longer."

"Jensen, you're being too cruel," Isabella chided. "Edwin's been a lovely companion down here. Besides, if we have one more player, we'll have enough to play cribbage next." Isabella pushed on the knob above her tea press and the filter squashed the fragile leaves to the bottom. Several of the dark black flecks escaped and floated to the top while she poured herself another cup.

"Why thank you." Edwin waved a hand toward her. "It's been a pleasure having you ill. You've provided a welcome distraction from my studies."

"I'm sure Isabella's loved being out of commission." I enjoyed her sour frown and slapped her on the back. She met my gaze with a weary one of her own. "Now Edwin, what has she been keeping you from? More of those potions you made at your shop back in China?"

"Don't tell me it's another meal supplement." Jensen groaned. I swung a nearby chair over and took a seat around the table.

"Look," Edwin said. "Had my one calculation not been off, we would have dined on those supplements for months."

Isabella smirked. "Instead we puked for weeks."

"I don't know why I try with any of you ruffians. No appreciation for the finer aspects of experimentation and the sciences." He sniffed.

"We appreciate you, Edwin," I said. "Our digestive systems just don't remember you fondly."

"This is why we need a cook," Jensen interrupted. "A whole crew and nobody can make a decent meal. Hell, you and Isabella can't even make sandwiches. What kind of women are you anyway?"

"Obviously subpar. I mean, what am I doing here?" Sarcasm flowed from my mouth in tomes. "I should be landed and popping out babies, not getting stabbed and shot at thousands of feet above ground."

"Is that what your people do?" Isabella lifted one elegant brow. "Mine have always roamed, for centuries. The sky's our next frontier for travel."

"You mean your gypsy clans?" Jensen placed one of his beefy arms onto the table. "I thought you people always stayed in groups."

"Usually." Isabella drank a quick sip of tea and avoided Jensen's comment. "My people have remained throughout time, past industry, and weathered every war. We've never been captured or enslaved. We know no nation, no leader, only governed by an open sky like an eagle at flight." Her mixed accent of British and French threaded her words with a musical resonance.

"Here, you want to know more about my people?" She wandered over toward her bags and rummaged through the nearest one. From it she pulled a larger pack of cards sealed in an engraved bronze box under a twisting latch.

"Not your mumbo-jumbo witchcraft again." Jensen rolled his eyes and stretched his arms over his head, uninterested in the whole idea before we'd begun.

She pursed her lips while arching an eyebrow. "It's called

tarot, my dear. It's a shame not everyone shares your boorish inflections."

"I'm from America, haven't you ever paid attention to stereotypes?"

"So am I, don't go looping me in with you, boy-o." I rested my hand on my hip and gave him the side eye.

Isabella snorted. "Well, I'll read your fortunes. A tarot reading from a gypsy woman is the best telling of the art."

"Count me out." Edwin shook his head. "I'm not a fan of the arcane or predictions that can't be quantified. They don't follow any projectors, and the hypothetical objectives cast such a wide net they'll always find some form of emotional manipulation to fit the scheme."

"It's called mysticism, sweetie." Isabella placed a hand on her hip. "And we've been practicing it for years. You can't put the power behind tarot into a classification box."

"How to you explain the conclusions you come to then?" His eyes glinted in excitement for the onset of a debate. "For if you're referencing any level of belief, that's a subjective experience manifested by the brain as a coping mechanism."

"People aren't robots." Isabella shot him a dirty look. "We feel, we make our own choices, and those choices make us unpredictable." Her words clipped with frustration, but from the smile on Edwin's face, his argument had just begun. "Haven't you done anything rash, something that couldn't be explained away?"

"I've made rash decisions, yes." He clasped his hands overtop the table. "But nothing that couldn't be explained by simple psychology, pseudoscience though it may be."

Isabella passed him a flat-lidded stare. "You know, a simple 'no' would have worked."

Edwin's mouth twitched until he released his grin. "But it wouldn't have been nearly as much fun."

"I'll do a reading for Jensen and Bea." Isabella waved her hands in the air. Edwin stood up from the table and walked over to his lab.

"Oh, Edwin," I called out, "We're celebrating on deck tonight. Are you going to join?"

He stopped and rubbed his chin. "I suppose I can pull away from the lab for the chance to further degrade my liver. Might the captain be breaking out the ale?"

"Maybe." I winked. "You'll have to head up there to find out."

"Do you have to do my prediction?" Jensen complained, nudging his boot against the floor.

"I, for one, am looking forward to it," I interjected. Isabella flipped open the latch and pulled out her deck. Her cards fascinated me. Unlike the regular playing cards we used for games, she owned a holographic tarot deck, so whenever she turned a card over, the structure flickered with a blue hologram overtop.

"I'll read your past, present, and future. It'll be quick and painless."

Jensen placed his hands behind his head. Isabella's chest rose with her deep breath as she shuffled her cards, and after quiet contemplation, she pulled three from the deck. A slight exhale passed her lips before she placed each one in a row. Ornate purple diamonds covered the back of the cards, which were interspersed by indigo runes of varying gypsy descent—though Isabella knew every one by heart. She closed her eyes and focused. From where we sat she appeared to spread her energy out over the cards, and after a slight inhale, she turned over the first one.

"Five of cups for the past," she said. The holograph flickered on, and five transparent blue cups towered over the card. "You had a deep sorrow in your past, something that's stayed with you your entire life." Jensen's jaw tightened, and even I noticed the tension that descended upon the room. Time to clear the air.

"Hear that?" I spoke up. "Even the cards are telling you to stop crying over that poor bet you made last time we played Faro." Jensen narrowed his eyes, and I laughed. Isabella scrutinized the card before resting her gaze on him.

"Did something happen to your mother?" She asked, as her dark eyes filled with curiosity.

His frown deepened, and though he didn't say a word, the slight flare of his nostrils told plenty. Before she could continue down that line of questioning, he cut her off. "So what's my present?"

"Come on, I have daddy issues. It's okay if you have mommy ones," I joked, trying to lighten the mood. My back pressed against the wall, and I folded my arms across my chest while I watched the master do her work.

She took in another deep breath before turning the next card over. A frown turned her lips, and her forehead creased.

"Your present is the Tower." The card lit up, and a tiny holographic tower teetered over the piece. "A reversed tower makes things ...interesting. A strong change or upheaval in your life."

"I'm about ready to heave up the rest of my lunch with this crap. Why are you holding onto this junk anyway? Didn't your gypsy people reject you?" He leaned back in his seat and crossed his arms over his chest. The first card must have triggered something unwanted for Jensen because he wouldn't throw Isabella's past in her face like that.

"Classy." She glared at him. "My ex-fiancée may have gotten me banished, but I still appreciate my roots and heritage. It wasn't the elders' faults he manipulated better than I could."

"Well this tower card must mean I won a fortune. I'll take my retirement on a tropical island." Jensen pushed his chair in. "I'm going for a walk. You can keep your future, doll—I'll make my own." He stalked out of the room, but not before Isabella shot him a miniscule glare.

"I think the first one bunched his panties," I said. "Although he's never said much to me about his past." Isabella met my gaze and nodded. She peeked at the last one in his spread.

"Ace of wands last. Card of breakthroughs and new beginnings." She placed his cards back into the deck. "Maybe he will leave us for that tropical island. He can take that attitude with him."

"Something must've hit him the wrong way. He wouldn't have brought up—you know."

Isabella scooped her cards and dropped them back into their holder. "I'd be lying if I said I wasn't a touch bitter about my cheating whore of an ex-fiance. Jensen knows better. I'd say for sure my cards were on their mark." Her dark eyes glittered with unspent anger, and her lips pressed together in a firm line. I didn't need to ask her how she'd still be so sour about the banishment from her clan after all these years. I understood holding onto baggage.

"Maybe you can read my cards some other time." I tapped a finger on the sealed deck. "When everyone's not on edge. Here's a change," I said. "Let's get you out of this infirmary and out onto the deck. The captain is breaking open some of our stores to celebrate the cargo pickup and evasion of the merchant ship. I'm talking the ale, the grog, maybe even some absinthe."

"Well darling, all you needed to mention were the spirits." Isabella brushed down her red skirt and stood from her seat. "I'll drink to celebrate anything." Her hips shifted back and forth as she exited the infirmary. "Try and keep up, I'll see you above deck."

I lifted my arms over my head for a stretch and then pushed myself away from the table. My fingers tapped a percussive beat against the door frame before I gave the infirmary one last glance and exited the room. A pint of ale would take the edge off all this tension bubbling on board.

As I jogged up the steps, the floorboards creaked underneath me. Once I emerged topside, I noticed the sky had changed, and night coated the horizon with her velvet touch while a full moon glistened overhead. Millions of stars twinkled across the sky, interrupted by purplish-blue tufts of clouds. Nights upon an airship were like nothing else.

Our men huddled around the stern side of the ship, which meant the Captain must have brought out the casks of ale and grog. The wind carried the crew's laughter out past the deck, towards the stars. I plucked my empty flask from the loophole on my belt and dodged crewmates to get to the casks where Isabella stood by the ale, drinking the fresh poured brew from a mug.

"A little overeager, are we?" I said, dipping my flask into the ale. The muddled golden liquid filled it, and I pulled a full flask out.

"The captain's been stingy with the ale since our last job fouled. We've been drinking grog for the past couple of weeks. It wears down on a girl. This however—" She held her mug aloft. "This is liquid bread. It throws some color on your cheeks and provides proper nourishment."

"More nourishing than the food we concoct," I said, "Jensen's right. We need a cook for the ship—I'm tired of gruel." I gazed towards the helm where Geoff and Spade steered the ship at the navigation deck. After tucking my flask back into my belt, I filled two mugs. "If you'll excuse me, I'm going to take these over to our helmsmen." I winked at Isabella, dismissing myself.

Her laugh rang into the air, and she swaggered off to terrorize a throng of men by the main hatch. I carried the mugs across the deck, one in each hand. At least this trip over to navigation didn't involve dodging cannon fire or a stormy gale.

"You're being sweet?" Geoff called out when I approached. "I didn't know the world was ending. Let me light a cigar."

"Sweet?" I sidled next to them underneath the canopy. "I don't know what you're talking about, these are for me." Spade snorted, and I passed him a mug. I lifted the other one to my lips before glancing to Geoff.

"What about me?" Geoff pointed to his chest. I peered at the mug and back at him before pursing my lips.

"Well, I guess you deserve it." I passed him the ale. "I mean you did navigate us out of a storm from under enemy fire."

"Damn straight I did." Geoff took a hefty draft of ale. I leaned back against the wooden pillar and lifted my flask to my lips. The sweet taste of beer coated my tongue and tingled down my throat.

"How confident were you we'd make it?" I asked.

Geoff ran fingers through his thick brown hair with his free hand. "With your help navigating? I thought we'd die." His eyes locked with mine, and his darkened gaze told me we had played our cards pretty close. Ever since last month, we'd done nothing but play it close. "We've had pursuit from stealing cargo before, but that wasn't an average rogue ship. That was a state of the art, well-equipped merchant ship with military personnel on board. Did the captain know what the job threw us into? What's in that box?"

"I haven't the slightest," I said with a shrug. "But we need that payoff, more than the captain's let on since we're taking these risky missions."

"First pissing off the Morlocks and now the Brits. I hope he has a plan up his sleeve. We'll need to stay under the radar as much as possible." Geoff took another swig of ale.

"I know." I heaved a sigh and lifted one leg over the other.

"But the captain's never steered us wrong before, and I doubt he'd start now. He wouldn't risk our lives without a reason." Geoff nodded. The breeze whipped several loose strands from my messy bun and tossed them over my forehead.

"Any opinions over there, silent one?" I glanced back to Spade, who sat perched by the thrusters, watching the two of us.

His shoulders twitched with surprise, but he shook his head. "I have no qualms. I just steer the ship." A smile tugged on my mouth. Good old Spade. He rarely strung a full sentence together, but his silent presence offered a much needed sturdiness to our crew.

"Boy-o, that's good to hear."

Geoff caught Spade's eyes and looped his free arm through mine. "Care to join me for a stroll?"

"What's wrong, Geoff?" I raised an eyebrow. I didn't like that look he gave Spade. Those two gossiped worse than the deckhands.

"Nothing, nothing. It's a balmy night for a walk." He smirked.

"Right, 'cause I haven't done enough walking, leaping, and running today to last me a year."

"Stop complaining and come with me." Geoff tugged me away by the hand while Spade took over at the helm. My heart thumped offbeat in my chest, and a nervous sweat pricked the nape of my neck. That unspoken tension rose between us the second we walked off. He'd tried to talk feelings before, but I always dodged around him because in our line of work they interfered with getting the job done. Don't get me wrong, sometimes I wanted to throw him down and run my hands all over his lithe body, but that couldn't happen between us. It wasn't simple like a tumble with Jensen. Where Geoff was concerned, attachments came into play, and I didn't mess around with those.

We walked past several crew members who watched Isabella dance with the natural grace of a gypsy. Based on the way her hips sashayed, I couldn't blame their open leers. A lot of the crew's fantasies centered around that woman.

Geoff's warmth mingled with my own. He always smelled like ink from his stained hands and cinnamon from the sticks he chewed when he pored over maps. Firelight from lanterns flickered across the deck and cast winsome glows with checkered shadows onto the floor. We passed Jack, our scout, and Captain Morris kicking back mug after mug of ale. Jensen lumbered by and nodded as greeting.

"So, tell me what's wrong." I spoke while we walked. "I caught that look between you and Spade."

"Just wanted to talk. I don't like blasting my personal affairs to everyone," Geoff said. We reached the edge of the ship, and he let go of my arm. "I know we joked about the last job and all, but I

89

was worried sick about you. I have full faith in your skills, you know that, but these stakes don't make me comfortable. After we messed with the Morlocks and Isabella got hurt, it drilled the message home."

Geoff wrapped his arms around me and pulled me into a tight embrace. "Gods Bea, contact us next time. With our jobs getting risky like this...I can't imagine losing you..." he trailed off. His body against mine sent shivers tingling up my spine, and his warmth made my insides melt. Emotions I didn't want to deal with surfaced, so I stepped away.

"I'll be more cautious next time. I know you're watching out for me."

He caught my eyes with his intense dark gaze, and for a moment I aged backwards to a time before I put my guards up. My defenses dissolved. I wanted to fall into his arms and surrender to the mind-searing passion that wrung my stomach and twisted my heart. Couldn't let that happen though.

I leaned over the side and placed my arms along the ledge, changing the subject. "We'll have some smooth sailing soon anyway after this next payoff."

He sighed but leaned over next to me. I lifted my flask again for another sip to wash away residual feelings. This distance—this was comfortable. Safe. Any time we strayed past those borders, my mind ran screaming in panic.

Geoff bumped my side with his hip. "You got to spend a vacation with Jensen, so I'm sure that made the trip worth it."

"The intellectual experience of a lifetime." I rolled my eyes. "If I heard one more story about how he used to practice riot wrestling with his brothers back in Texas, I'd have practiced some on him." Geoff's laugh cheered me and wiped away the last bit of awkwardness between us. Footsteps creaked from behind, and I turned my head as Captain Morris approached.

"What are you two lovebirds doing over here?" his voice boomed. I fought the blush that surged and won.

"You call this romancing?" I showed some teeth and squeezed Geoff's shoulder. "I'd take a bodice ripping any day."

Captain placed his large callused hands on both our backs. "Mind if I cut in?" he asked. Geoff opened his mouth to protest, but after glancing between the two of us, he shrugged and tossed a hand up as he walked off. Captain Morris took his perch over the ledge.

"It couldn't hurt to give the boy a break now and again. It's been obvious since I took both of you young'uns on board that there's something between you."

"Not so, sir." I pressed my lips together. "They switched me out with a robot and I'm incapable of processing these feelings you refer to."

"Schiesse," he cursed, and a steady grin took his face. He reached into his leather pack, pulling out a half empty bottle of the translucent green liquid.

"For me? You're too kind." I placed a hand over my chest with mock surprise. Morris pulled out the cork and took a swig before he passed me the open bottle. Fumes of anise and trouble wafted my way before I followed suit. The absinthe seared my tongue and erased my concerns, replacing them with fuzzy-headed abandon. He turned around, leaning his back against the side to face his crew.

"Update me, Bea. You hear more than I do. What has the crew's been up to?"

A sigh escaped my lips as I tossed around what to say. The crew had been murmuring, but Captain didn't need to know every last detail of their whines and complaints.

Morris shook his head. "That bad, huh?"

"The past month unsettled folks. People are growing concerned because we're taking larger risks. Nearly losing Isabella and the Morlock betrayal sparked a huge panic and now we're pissing off the Brits. A lot of the crewmates wonder if we're going too far."

"Are you concerned?" he asked.

"No." My reply was firmer than I let on. "You wouldn't

needlessly throw us in danger. This last one was personal for you, I get that, and I suspect the upped stakes have to do with our lack of funds. You don't run an airship on dreams."

Pride shone in his eyes, and his wrinkles creased with his smile. "You're unshakable, Bea, that's why you're my first mate. We need this payoff. I didn't like associating with the Morlocks, but since our contacts with them closed off, our supply of jobs dried up which leaves us more of these difficult ones. Losing the Morlock jobs has put more financial strain on our pockets than a missed payday." The light of the full moon glistened over his scarred face. His expression sobered, and he stared out far into the distance. Lifting the bottle of absinthe to his lips, he took another draft.

"It bothers you, doesn't it," I murmured. He raised his eyebrows. "That they'd believe you'd put them in unnecessary danger." For a moment he didn't respond, and we swapped the bottle while basking in the silence.

"We protect our own, Bea. Always have." His voice grew thick, "I would never put a crew member in danger we could avoid and send them to do something I wouldn't myself."

"I know, Captain. You don't need to prove that to me."

"Hah." He gazed at the sky. "Wasn't it just a couple years back you were a speck of a thing we found shuddering in an alleyway? Now look at you."

"Your age is addling your scope of time." I crossed my arms

over my chest. "I joined with this crew seven years ago."

"So it was. Although, you're still a slip of a thing." He grinned.

"Desire's been my home for some time. I'd know no other." My face darkened with the remembrance of the house I spent my childhood in. I never considered that a home. Gesturing for the bottle, I took another shot of absinthe. The harsh liquid cleansed away the soiled memories.

"She's a sturdy old girl, isn't she? In all my time I've had her, she's always come through for me, truer than any woman I've dallied with. When I saw her years ago in that junkyard, I knew, even back then. Seth helped me. We cobbled together a crew and rebuilt her with scrap parts from the yard. Something told me she'd be worth every penny."

Both of us lapsed into silence, lulled by the thrum of the wind through her lower sails as moonlight glided over the balloon, glinting along the metal frame. The Desire cut through the sky resiliently, reflective of her Captain. She knew no fear and accepted any challenge.

Pride thrummed through my veins like a victory chant. The crew had started singing an old shanty, and their rough melody drifted over towards us, pouring renewed strength into my bones. Joy filled my heart overfull, and in that moment I was light as a feather, unburdened and free.

Across the deck Jensen had his arm around Edwin, convincing our resident scientist to imbibe the grog. The scientist spluttered, but under Jensen's hand began to guzzle down the contents. Off to the bulwark side, Isabella flirted with a hapless crewmate, pulling off her hair twirl and lowered lashes bit, while Jack stepped in to harass the newest deckhand. By the helm, several men joined Spade and Geoff, and they huddled under the cover of the navigation chamber. The circle of deckhands who began their shanty trickled off until only one voice drifted by in the errant breeze. Through it all, the lanterns shifted like fairy lights on a summer night, and stars twinkled overhead.

"Captain. She's absolutely beautiful," I breathed. We lapsed into silence again and gazed at the horizon, full and free as the deck we stood upon.

CHAPTER SEVEN

My wake up the next morning sucker punched me in the stomach. The bright sunlight caused my head to throb, and I may as well have downed a keg of cotton balls. Upon second check I lay under open sky, not in my bedchambers. The roar of a steady breeze filtered through my ears, and the wind carried along the sharp vinegar scent of morning. I blinked, running a hand through my messy hair.

I sat up and groaned as pain lanced up my back. Apparently, I'd spent the night on the deck, tucked in a corner behind some barrels. A couple of guys laid propped upright by crates, and I sighed with relief that I hadn't been the only one. What a night. The last thing I remembered was joining the crew in a rendition of "Take to the Sky," but the rest of the time blurred after I drank absinthe with the Captain.

The smell of ale lingered on my breath, clinging to my coated tongue. I tossed an arm overhead and regretted it as my muscles protested with fiery strain. Slower this time, I stretched both arms forward, ignoring my creaking joints, and with a roll I heaved my aching body up off the floor.

Everyone around me slumped over in slumber, which meant

no one caught my walk of shame. My pace quickened the more my legs adjusted to movement, and within minutes I stood under the shade-darkened canopy of the cabin. My blurry vision dissipated, but my migraine turned up a notch, so I lumbered to the infirmary. One of Edwin's weird cocktails would do the trick.

A smile plastered my face at the memories of last night. After a tense couple of days from the job, we knew how to wind down, but times like that had to be treasured because peace and quiet could depart in the blink of an eye. I stalked down the corridor and flung open the infirmary door. Jensen and Isabella lay curled up together on one of the beds—apparently someone got some last night. Edwin sat around the same table we crowded yesterday, but this time, he pressed an ice-pack against his forehead.

"You too, Edwin?" I mumbled.

He nodded and pointed to his lab. "They're back in there."

Following the direction, I nudged open the crooked door. Beakers and tubes lay askew on his workbench, and the unorganized shelves contained different types of stopped pale powders and corked fluids. A clear ball crackled with electric currents by the edge of his desk while the smell of burnt rubber clouded the room.

I stepped past his mess to pull one of his labeled vials from the shelf. The whole crew knew where to find Edwin's hangover remedies. I unplugged the vial, pinched my nose, and downed the serum. That liquid burned my tongue, and I spluttered even as I forced it down. The sour taste of bark and dirt clung to the back of my throat, and when I swallowed, the acrid taste still lingered. With a shrug, I tucked back the empty bottle onto the shelf, since Edwin would use it again at some point. Although slow-acting, a tingle around the fringes of my headache signaled the serum's effects. I left the lab and waved at Edwin as I passed.

Feeling more human than before, I stalked back up the steps and returned to deck. Sunlight pulsed across my throbbing temples, but I shrugged off the pain. The air around me thickened with humidity as we descended towards land. I didn't even need to survey the skyline after so many years on board and just gauged the shift by the drift of Desire. Geoff manned the wheel over at navigation, and upon catching sight of me, he raised an eyebrow.

"Did you sleep well? You looked pretty comfortable wedged between barrels." His grin widened as he teased me. "I'm glad the first mate holds her liquor well." Damn him. I hadn't escaped unnoticed.

"I slept wonderfully." I forced my lips into a smile and delivered a sweet tone. Dropping the banter, I cocked my head starboard side. "We're near port, aren't we? I can taste the ocean air."

"We exited the jet stream early this morning since Spade took care of her through the night. We're close to the ports, but the captain hasn't made contact yet. He's aiming for tomorrow morning since he wants to examine our meeting spot. We'll want every advantage after last time."

"Smart," I said. "Someone really wants whatever's inside that box, but we don't want any double-crosses or extra risks." I clapped a hand against Geoff's back. "I'll go recommend myself for the scouting job. Catch you in the quick wind." I jogged across the deck and peeked over the side.

The port city of Sutcliffe lay next to Pyramid Lake, less flashy than Reno. We couldn't afford flashy, not with the British Empire on our tails. The ports hit the cerulean Pacific like a stone wall, and the vast sea twinkled brighter than a jewelry vendor's stand under the sun-soaked sky. Sutcliffe's fierce rectangular buildings juxtaposed the tide while large pillars marked the landing strips, which were equipped with tiered notches. They suspended her when we powered down the engine and deflated the balloon inside its metal frame. Below us, seagulls circled the sky, hunting for scraps.

I stepped away from the ledge and returned to the cabins. Once below deck, I strode towards the captain's room and knocked on his door.

"Come in," he called. Seth stood beside him at his desk as they pored over a map.

"Captain, I heard word of a reconnaissance. I'd like to

recommend myself."

He nodded without raising his head. "Bea, you already knew you were going. I'm sending Jensen with you."

"Way to take the fun out of my preplanned argument." I stepped beside Seth. "So, what are you searching for?"

"Plotting out where to get parts," Seth said. "The job took us for a tumble and the Desire's running sluggishly."

"And we're pinpointing the goods drop." Morris spread his palms wide over the desk. "I alerted our employer with the update. We're to meet him at one of the warehouses in the freighter district at five in the morning tomorrow. I'm not risking another crew member, so I'm making the drop myself." He glanced at me. "Meanwhile, scout and stay quiet. Keep out of trouble." He shot me a look.

"Why Captain, that's easy as baking a cake."

"Considering you're the worst baker I've met, color me concerned."

"Fine, fine. I promise I won't cause too much trouble." I gave him the toothiest grin I could swing. "We're close to the dock, so if you give me a location, we'll be off soon."

"Sure thing." Morris grabbed a scrap of paper and drew up a makeshift map. He folded the square and passed it over to me. "Here's the area I want you and Jensen to check out. Make sure he's up and ready."

"Aye, aye, sir." I saluted and took my exit. If I was rousing Jensen, I knew exactly where he'd be. I clattered down the steps to the infirmary, and upon flinging open the door, the same sight as before greeted me.

"Feeling better?" Edwin asked. I paused and took inventory. His remedy must have kicked in while running around, since my head stopped throbbing.

"Yeah, your mojo did the trick."

He leaned back into his mug of coffee, and the fragrant smell drifted towards me. Edwin drank that stuff like an opium addict, using his metal percolator over a hotplate. I enjoyed the occasional cup, but this man consumed enough coffee per day to fill a bathtub.

I approached Jensen and Isabella's sleeping forms. Their eyes were closed in the peace of dreams, and their chests swelled with the soft breathing of deep sleep. A wolfish grin spread over my face. Exactly why I'd relish waking them.

"What kind of slouches sleep through mid-morning!" My voice boomed around the cabin causing Edwin to wince.

Jensen shot out of bed, and Isabella whipped her head up at the sound. I snickered. Both narrowed their eyes with irritation the second they spotted me. Jensen's bare broad chest heaved up and down with surprise while the blanket slumped by Isabella's feet as she shifted out of bed. She only wore a chemise made of flimsy fabric that did a poor job of covering up anything. Out of the corner of my eye, Edwin spluttered on his coffee.

"That's a lot of thunder for a slip of a thing." Jensen rubbed his head and gave Isabella an eye scan. A leer broke out on his face. "Some night last night, eh?" Jealousy trickled through me. Not over Jensen—I stifled a snort—never over him, but a fair amount of time had passed since my last tango in the bed sheets.

"Well rise and shine," I drawled. "We're docking soon, and you won the lottery to join me on a scouting mission. We're giving the drop site a once-over, making sure no ticking bombs or trap doors hide out of sight."

"Let me go get changed." Jensen grunted. I stopped to admire his muscular back as he exited, and Isabella's eyes followed the same route. The boy had a spectacular body, even if he was ignorant as get-all.

"I suppose I should be doing the same." Isabella glanced over her slender bare legs, and her lips curled into a smile. Edwin's coffee splashed onto the table as he almost dropped the cup back onto the saucer. "Have fun, love."

"Oh, I will." I caressed Edwin's shoulders and stifled a laugh when the poor man nearly jumped from his seat. "You better keep Edwin here busy."

"Yes, ma'am. I already have some lovely sorts of entertainment in mind." She gave him a coy wink.

Edwin's cheeks flushed a furious red, and I bit my tongue to keep from laughing. Isabella waggled her fingers towards me while I exited the infirmary.

Before marching back up to the deck, I swung by my room. Ditching the skirt, I pulled on pants, which were much more practical for roaming the city. The torrential downpour from the day prior had soaked my usual leather bag, so I pulled out a different one from my trunk. After shoving a couple rounds inside the bag, I tucked my pistol into the holster along my belt. Although we planned on keeping out of trouble, I always arrived prepared.

Looping the leather by the hoops, I pushed my coin purse onto my belt to rest against my hip. My jewelry box sat unattended on the dresser, so I flipped the top open and pulled out one of my lucky blue cameos. I fastened it around my neck for good luck—we could use it. Checking my appearance in front of the mirror, I pushed my bosom up from inside my bodice and gave my cleavage a chance to breathe. Distraction meant less suspicion.

After closing my door, I made my way back onto the deck. We decelerated and descended to the port. Lucky for us and unlucky for the Brits, only major docks took foreign ships around here. They'd have to go one down to Reno, and by the time they tracked us, we'd have already made the switch with our merchandise and flown away. Skyscrapers rose into the surrounding view, and seagulls zoomed past our ship. Desire creaked and groaned under the slowed velocity as the dock markers flashed into sight.

Geoff and Spade guided the old girl in past the bay with careful precision as they loosened air from the balloon, and we skimmed over the Pacific like a worn pebble. Geoff steered her straight ahead through the first set of markers, slowing her pace to a crawl. The metal balloon frame caught first along the ramparts, and the suspension cables tensed under strain while the body drifted further forward until it stopped, pinioned by the overhead balloon.

An official ran across the wooden walkway to approach our ship. I jogged to the edge and unraveled our rope ladder over the side. Captain Morris emerged above deck, roused by the grinding halt of the ship.

"Time to give more of our hard swindled cash to those bureaucrats." The captain climbed over the side and descended the rope ladder, and when he jumped onto the boardwalk from the last slat, the planks shook. The uniformed man's foot tapped anxiously against the ground before he thrust a pen and clipboard towards Captain Morris.

Jensen advanced from below deck with a fresh pair of breeches, a collared tan shirt, and his revolver strapped to his side.

"Ready?" I asked and lifted the map Morris drew. Jensen

grunted a yes.

While the captain dealt with the docking officer and paid our fees, we climbed down the ladder and hit the deck with a thump. I saluted the captain when we passed him and opened the map. Based on the drawing, the freighter district didn't stretch far past the regular docking bay, so we strolled along the boardwalk in that direction. Officials in navy jumpsuits clutched their clipboards, rushing off in the direction of the airship lineup. A traveler strode by with a suitcase packed fuller than his overbearing stomach and skated an inch from bumping into us.

"So we're finally rid of this cursed cargo?" Jensen adjusted his bowler cap to cover his buzz cut.

"Tomorrow morning at five. Captain himself is going to do the trade."

Rising from the sea-soaked wooden planks, the salty smell of brine tickled my nose. The ocean glimmered under a full sun, and waves surged with cloud-like crests of foam. Beaches spread out in the distance, marking the land with their amber shores, but ahead, the shipping districts rose above the ramparts and their markers.

White square buildings wedged between rectangular gray, but all wore a uniform coating of streaked black smudges, sunken doorframes, and paint weathered by time to a ruddy rust color. The occasional tan tenement rose over the whole mess like a sentinel guarding his castle. Refuse and rotten clams mingled with the ocean breeze, and shouts from dockworkers echoed through the air as they unloaded freight from laden ships.

I pointed down the pathway at the intersection. "Looks like the warehouse district lies to the left." The landscape changed into strips of flat boxy warehouses with aluminum siding and accordion doors. Yellow arrows lined the walkway, providing direction meant for the workers, but we followed them anyway.

"Nice and open. Why do you think they chose somewhere like this? Witnesses galore," Jensen said with a frown.

"Well if they're hoping for a quick exchange, the random worker won't make a huge difference. Besides, the captain marked a specific warehouse. We'll be trading inside there." I poked the circled box on his drawn map. "This one, number fourteen." I squinted. "Can you make out any numbers from here?"

"Barring hawk-like vision, no," Jensen said, pulling out a pair of binoculars, "But I have these." He scanned the area as we approached the freighter district. "The ones nearest us are in the twenties. Fourteen must be further in." While we strolled along, Jensen and I surveyed the perimeter. Like I said, Captain hired no slouches. At the end of each line of warehouses, a ladder led to the connected roofs, and that, I didn't like. Unless you stood by the loading dock, the rooftops weren't in line of sight.

"Smart spot for a sharpshooter." I tossed my head in that

direction. "As long as we place one of ours out here, we'll have the rooftop in range. As for the warehouses, most look like one entrance, one exit deals." I spotted a scraggly stenciled number fourteen on one of the doors down the lane. Jensen and I strode past the dock workers to approach the building.

"Home sweet shithole." I turned the knob, and we entered the darkened warehouse. Jensen quick drew first while I fumbled around my leather bag, and he flicked on his aetherlight, part of a multi-tool he kept on his person at all times. The aetherlight's dim orb of greenish light brought dozens of boxes into visibility. I brushed a hand over the nearest crate, which was marked by numbers and odd letters giving no inclination as to the contents.

"What do you think, doll?" Jensen jerked a thumb at the box. "Any chance they're filled with tobacco and aged scotch?"

"As long as they aren't filled with flammables or explosives, we're safe. We don't want anything dangerous." Under the ray of his aetherlight, a crowbar glinted in the corner of the room. I picked it up and wedged the end into the top of the nearest crate. "Jensen, come shine that thing over here." He stalked over, and the light shook with his steps. He held the aetherlight over the open box. Rows of bright pink parasols stacked inside.

"This is where you left your stash!" I offered a cheeky grin. "We could have used these during that storm."

"Those cads stole my pretty pink parasols." Jensen smirked.

He shone the light over the ceiling, but atypical to other warehouse cells, the flat aluminum provided no entrance to the roof.

"Well, we're counting on a clear meet and greet. The only sore spot is the rooftop, but we'll work around it." I scanned the room one last time. "The outside crates too—we need to keep an eye out for any hidden snipers and maybe station one of our own."

"Aye, aye madam. Are we finished?" Jensen stood by the door.

"Should be," I said with a shrug. "All we can do is hope for a smooth trade at this point. Got to get rid of that damned box."

"You're telling me." Jensen pressed his palm against his forehead. "Can we swing by a bar on the way back?"

"Why? It's not even lunchtime."

"Hair of the dog." He grunted.

"Let's get going, I could go for a mug of ale." Before I followed Jensen out the door, I placed a hand against the frame. An inexplicable shudder traveled down my spine. Without Jensen's light, gray misshapen shadows contorted throughout the chamber. Not lingering any longer, I turned and exited the building.

A crowded town street lay past the right turn at the crossroads. Laundry lines hung across tenement balconies, and canopied tents littered the worn dirt streets. Jensen batted a large loaf of fresh bread out of his way after one of the peddlers kept trying to shove it in his face and shout about his loaves to anyone in the vicinity. A nearby stand with cameos of all different sizes and colors caught my eye, but I stayed on task. Within seconds a neon 'Bar' sign with an arrow pointed down came into view.

"Why not try the obvious?" I pointed, and we descended the stairs into the basement of the building. The doors swung back and forth, and fluorescent lights cast a bluish hue over the room, making the ceramic black tiles of the long bar counter gleam. Liquor filled the shelving behind it from the rounded bottles of aged brandy to the long, thin vodka cordials they produced nowadays. In my younger years I'd made the mistake of trying the peanut brittle variant—it looked similar to the candy coming back up.

I swaggered in, and Jensen followed close behind. A few older men loitered around the pint-sized room, most with a five day old scruff and wearing stained trousers. I snagged a seat at one of the torn red leather barstools.

"Barkeep," I called over to the man slouched behind the counter. "A mug of ale for me and-" I turned to Jensen. "What do you want?"

"Just a shot of whisky. It'll clear this straight away."

"You heard the man." I shrugged. The barkeep's sunken brown eyes bored into me, but he flipped the tap handle. With his free hand, he poured the whisky into a shot glass. I rummaged into my bag and pulled out the satchel of coins to slap one onto the table in exchange for my ale. Jensen picked up the shot glass and held the whisky towards me in acknowledgement before tipping it back. Lifting the mug to my lips, I sipped a deep draft right as the door opened behind us with a smack.

"Owen, get the hell out." The barkeep didn't hesitate, spreading both palms over the countertop. I peered behind me. A hulk of a man stood by the swinging doors with a red kerchief around his neck, and a beard rivaling the mythic pirates of old. His arm looped around the waist of a younger woman who couldn't have been more than sixteen or seventeen.

"You'll just bring us trouble. Out," the barkeep commanded. Owen growled like a deranged mutt but listened. He exited, dragging the silent girl behind him, her lip trembling all the while. A glimpse had been all I needed to realize their relationship. The baggy man's shirt she wore slipped off her shoulder, same with the straps of her oversized overalls. Mottled purple bruises covered her arms, and the dark spots glared against her pale skin.

Slavers.

Anger boiled within me, sparked by the life I left behind. I would not stand by and tolerate the sight of an abused woman. Never again. I chugged my beer and slammed the mug onto the countertop.

"Jensen," I barked, "We're going."

"Didn't the captain want us to stay out of trouble?" He placed a palm onto the counter. "It's just a girl, and she's none of our business. Leave it alone, Bea." Wrong words. I gripped his collar and shoved my face inches from his.

"We saw it. That makes it our damn business. Get your weapons ready. We're going to go stir up some trouble." I pulled Matilda from my holster and checked the safety. We stalked out of the bar without a backwards glance.

CHAPTER EIGHT

I gripped my pistol so tightly my knuckles whitened and pressed my tongue against the back of my teeth. Owen stood down the street with the girl he held captive next to a fruit stand teeming with ripe oranges and apples. The shop's yellow-and-green striped canopy marked it out from the rest on the street. With all the innocents wandering through the crowded marketplace, I couldn't get a clear shot at Owen, or people would get hurt. Before all this rage sent me rushing in with my pistol waving, I forced several deep breaths back and placed a hand on Jensen's chest.

"You wait as my backup. Let's see if I can't manage a diversion." I unlaced the top loopholes from my bodice, and my cleavage spilled out. Blowing Jensen a kiss, I sashayed over to handle the slaver.

Owen's eyes probed me the moment I stepped into his sights, though I refused to meet his stare and arched my back a little more. Men always fell for a touch of aloof and some feminine sex appeal. My boots scraped against the worn dirt path as I swerved past a group of larger women carrying thatched baskets. Owen's dark eyes followed me, and saliva pooled at the corner of his mouth. I winked.

"Hi, sweet thing," I managed my smokiest tone, holding

back a shudder at this greasy mammoth of a man. Within close proximity he smelled riper than the garbage lining the street sides. His gut swung over his ratty leather belt, and his eyes hadn't moved from my chest. "I couldn't help but hear you were searching for a place." I glanced down both sides of the street before continuing. "Why not swing by mine?"

His bushy eyebrows rose, but the leer stayed on his face. I pushed my chest forward and extracted the pistol from my holster. Distracted, he didn't notice the movement until I jammed Matilda's muzzle straight into his side.

The click of my pistol menaced, but I maintained my sweet smile.

"This can be real simple, lad. Hand her over and walk away. Any trouble and I won't hesitate to shoot." The poor girl's eyes widened as her jaw dropped. I dug the pistol in further, glancing to my side. No odd looks flashed our way, and no authorities patrolled the streets. To anyone watching, we had a civil, rather close conversation. "So what will it be?" A harsh metallic edge ringed my dulcet tone.

"This girl?" Owen's voice bellowed. "What's she to you?" He jabbed her side, and she flinched.

"Consider me an interested party." I gritted my teeth. Owen opened his mouth as if he'd argue, but shut it.

"Fine, fine." He waved his hands. "Take her and go, she's not worth any trouble."

"Good choice." With my free hand, I gestured towards the girl. "Please, follow me." The girl took two steps forward but paused and viewed me with terrified eyes. "It's okay, I don't mean you harm."

"Well I do," A foreign male's voice came from behind as the click of a cocked gun sounded at the back of my head. Frosty metal bit past my thick tresses, and I froze. The gruff voice continued, "Why don't you remove the pistol from my boy here and place it on the ground. We'll proceed from there." The young girl took a step backwards.

"And why should I do that? You'll just add me to your slave cartel. Besides, I guarantee I'll pull the trigger faster on Owen." I stalled, scanning around the marketplace in front of me. "If that didn't compute, my answer's no." Without a clear view behind me, any premeditated moves became impossible.

"I'll chance that bluff." The man growled, digging the muzzle in deeper. Bravado or no, there was nothing as jarring as the shiver of icy steel against skin. A sweat broke out on the nape of my neck and matted down loose strands of hair. I scanned the crowd past Owen. People began staring. Nobody neared us—they weren't stupid—but the man behind me didn't mess around. If he had the audacity to pull a gun in public view, he'd follow through. I gulped, and my tongue scraped against my pinched dry throat.

Around the edge of the crowd, a head adorned by a bowler cap stuck out over the others. Jensen kept close behind like I'd asked. Our eyes met, and he jerked his head down. If we didn't get out of direct eye soon, we'd garner official attention, and the captain would be angrier than a prodded lion. Sometimes a situation gave you a cornucopia of options, but sometimes the ballsy move was the only route to go.

I ducked.

Spinning around, I kicked out behind me. My boot hit solid leg, and his knee gave way. Matilda moved off Owen, and I dropped right as Jensen lined a shot, taking fire over the crowd. The bullets pummeled the man with the raised gun, and he hit the ground like jettisoned cargo as the sharp stench of gunpowder filled the air. The sound reverberated in my ear. His blood pooled on the worn dirt street, mingling with dusty pebbles.

Unfortunately Owen pulled his gun in the meantime and hid behind the girl. Several shouts ripped through the air on the sound of bullets, and a crowd gathered in the distance. Jensen muscled past the growing throng of people, but Owen's finger jumped the trigger. I dove towards him and knocked the line of fire askew with a tackle. The bullet flew astray, ripping into the crowd. A scream flared through the air, and a young man's knees buckled when the shot burrowed into his leg. Blood spurted from the wound as passersby swelled around him.

"Thick painted bastard," I swore. I tried to bat the gun from

Owen's hands, but a horn pierced through the air, startling both of us. He took the distraction and scrambled up.

Owen yanked the girl by her shirt collar and dragged her away, still using her as a shield. Renewed anger seared through me at the sight of him batting her around, since I'd seen the same plenty of times before through younger eyes while I had watched from my cracked door. I whipped Matilda in his direction, but the girl stood in the way of any clear shot. I darted after him, and Jensen followed close behind.

Several people stepped forward as if they'd follow us, but the fluxing crowd closed around the injured man and dragged in the stragglers. Owen shoved past a vendor stand and knocked over the pearls and pendants lining the counter. We wove around the merchant while he bent over to pick up his wares. The girl's collar bit into her neck, and she wheezed while they ran. Her face turned two shades bluer, offset by the dangling strands of her black hair. Anger tore at me like a rabid dog unable to let go that he dared to treat her that way.

"You're a pro at staying out of trouble, darling," Jensen murmured.

I clenched my jaw. "We're getting the girl away from him."

"What about those authorities?" He jerked a thumb back at the suited officials filtering into the square.

"We'll need to pick up our pace."

Owen dodged behind another bright canopy but managed to vanish into the crowd. I squinted, cocking my head to the left. His overgrown shoulders protruded from behind several caravan tents stationed where the street emptied into a clearing.

I slapped Jensen's shoulder. "Besides, what better way to deal with your hangover than to run it off?"

Jensen grunted and reloaded his gun. The sun struck the canopy, exposing Owen's large shadow, so I sidled towards the clearing. We crouched behind the several low-lying bushes fringing the edges.

"Looks like he's hiding there. Coward," Jensen said.

"Slavers always are," I agreed and stopped in my tracks. Slaver rings weren't run by one singular person, and the man who dodged in to help Owen had proved that. But how had he arrived so quickly? I placed a hand out to keep Jensen from moving forward. A man with a thick coarse beard peered out from one of the tents on the far left. Owen's hands flew with signals, and the man ducked back inside. Of course. He'd go straight to his own caravan. We'd have to move fast if we wanted the girl, so Jensen and I crept around the other side with our guns cocked and ready.

The bright mid-day sun exposed their silhouettes on the canvassing. Owen's hulking form squatted on the right, and the petite girl cowered beside him to the left.

"You tackle the big guy, I'll grab the girl," I mouthed. He

nodded, and we jumped into action.

Jensen swung around the tent to confront Owen, and I looped around the opposite side. The girl crouched with her back against the canvas while she trembled. Her eyes widened as Jensen appeared. Owen turned at the sudden sound and raised his pistol, but Jensen didn't hesitate. He smashed the butt of his revolver against Owen's head, and a crunch echoed as the metal connected with his skull. Before I grabbed her wrist, I stared her straight in the eyes and nodded in the direction of the town, hoping she understood we were trying to rescue her. She followed without a fight.

Owen collapsed from the blow, but now we had a whole new problem. Jensen crouched beside us. The bearded man emerged from one of the other hovels and brought several burly friends. I guess we'd invited one too many to our tea party.

Our silhouettes from the sun's glare against the fabric made us easy targets. I scanned behind for any sort of cover, but aside from the bulky set-ups in front of us, no good rocks or crates cropped up along the empty campground. Several yards to the right, a leftover wooden merchant stand stood without canopy. I jabbed my finger in that direction, and Jensen followed my gaze.

A shot ripped through the canvas, and the bullet whizzed by my knee as I slammed to the ground. Anger still simmered through me, boiling too strong to allow fear. We couldn't just stand there. The gap between the tent and the stand spanned several meters but under the glorious impossibility of open fire. Granted, our sad strip barely counted as cover. Jensen shoved us to the side right as another shot ripped through. That made my mind up.

I grabbed the girl's hand, and we broke into a sprint towards cover. The loud booms of their sawed off shotguns blistered my hearing. I cocked Matilda and fired bullets into the fray, hoping they'd find their way into those blackened bits slavers called hearts. A couple screams burst from their end because even blinded, I was still a better shot than most.

A bullet tunneled into the dirt next to us. I rebounded using the soles of my feet and pushed us the extra distance toward the stand. Jensen dodged under the cover, and I followed, dragging the girl with me. This flimsy wood wouldn't hold under the gunfire they emptied on us.

A shot burst through the front panel of the stand, and I motioned for the girl to get behind us. Silent, she followed our direction, even though she trembled with every step. I didn't want to know what those bastards had done to her. Poking overtop the stand for a moment, I emptied my rounds into three different targets. Matilda gave off a hollow click, and shots stopped firing.

I ducked back down with a curse and pulled open the leather pouch by my side. No more ammo. Jensen peered over the stand but dove back when another round of gunfire bit into our shoddy cover, sending splinters flying and chips scraping past my arms. An alarm sounded from behind, and the officials ran towards the clearing.

"We need to get out, now," I spat.

"Really? We shouldn't have gotten 'in' from the start. You and your sentimental crap tossed us into this." His eyes darted over to the girl. I clenched my jaw, and my free hand tensed into a fist. Matilda dangled in my other. Jensen might have logic on his side but that didn't make him any less of an ass.

"Well, we're in it now. How are we going to dodge the authorities?" A bullet whistled by overhead, so we ducked again as shots rang through the air and bounced around us. I glanced behind. Three uniformed men jogged down the trail towards the clearing.

They didn't care about our Robin Hood heroics to save a girl from slavers. We killed several men at this point, and they'd throw all of us, slavers included, into a holding cell. That cooked up a big batch of dead man's stew. We were no use to the captain there, and we still had to report back about the warehouses, and all the while those officials barreled into a hot zone. My mind ticked like the hand of a pocket watch as they approached. Who would draw more attention, men firing at them or three lone escapees?

I placed an arm over Jensen's broad back and drew him in close. "All right. Here's the plan. Once the authorities cross into the clearing, we're going to run. Do not fire at them or at the caravan. Don't even brandish your gun." My heart pounded inside my chest.

We'd have to get our timing on this perfect. If we used the authority arrival to our advantage, the slavers might focus on the new intruder entering the scene. I pinched Jensen's cheek. "Don't you love this gorgeous bed of roses I planted for us?"

"Wouldn't know what to do without your bed planting." He winked. I counted the seconds, and the men drew closer. Their strong and uniform strides carried them swiftly across the distance. The group of five or six men carried military grade shotguns. I honed in on each step, shutting out the noise from the bullets littering the ground around us.

The authorities entered into the clearing.

"Now!" I shouted, and we ran. A pregnant pause held like a tensile bubble through the air while we sprinted back towards the path. The authorities whirled toward us with guns drawn and ready to open fire.

I'd tucked Matilda away, and Jensen plunked his pistols back into the holsters, but I prayed they didn't perceive our headlong run as a threat. I bit my lip. If the slavers didn't start firing again soon, we ran straight into the embrace of a holding cell. My skin crawled with anticipation, but my legs kept running. The official nearest to us placed a finger on his trigger, and my self-preservation begged me to stop. I didn't.

Before the official took a shot, bullets splintered the air from the slavers huddled around the caravan tents. The threat of gunfire commanded immediate attention from the authorities. In turn, the slavers turned their focus onto the officials.

A sudden weight tugged my wrist, and my body jerked backwards. My legs carried me several steps further before the weight whipped me around. The girl collapsed onto the ground. Blood trickled from above her ankle, and a busted round lay next to her on the dirt. Panicked, she let go of my hand. Jensen stopped up ahead but didn't come over to help.

Several feet past the authorities, we stood under open firing range. We had to move. I grabbed her wrists and pulled her over my back since she weighed little more than a midsized dog. Shifting my mass, I planted my feet against the ground to lift us up. Her ankle needed a compress, but we didn't have time to make one. The bullet had ripped in past skin, yet her foot didn't dangle the way a snapped tendon would. My pace dragged with the weight of another person, so I clenched my jaw and summoned any remaining strength to carry us past the ring of officials.

Once I caught up with Jensen, we both continued racing down the pathway away from the clearing. Gunfire seared the air behind us, but our fast pace carried us out of range. The girl's breaths puffed against my ear in short bursts, and strands of her dark hair brushed by my neck. Her muscles tensed when I stumbled or bounded over stray rocks, and wetness splashed onto my calf. Her blood trickled out fast. Bullet wounds were nothing to mess around with, and we needed to dress her ankle soon.

After the first shot, people clustered around the streets in throngs. More and more came to watch the officials battle the slavers below. I pushed my way past a huddle of women who gossiped in loud voices about what could have started this all. Several children armed with sticks hovered along the sides of the street, eager for their chance to rush into a fight. In the distance a cry sounded out from the caravans and continued gunfire.

We passed a merchant who packed away his assortment of used cutlery and tin mugs as he called in an early day. The streets swelled with an increasing number of people drawn by shouts and children's cries. Passersby jostled into stands, knocking over apples or ripe bunches of spinach from displays, so most of the merchants followed suit with closing up shop.

Jensen took the lead and muscled through the crowd since I struggled to maneuver with the girl on my back. The sight of her bloody ankle sent a round of sharp whispers from the few who noticed it but not many did amidst the chaos. Her fingers dug into my shoulder and relaxed. The girl's body sagged, and she began careening backwards.

"Jensen!" My voice came out a sharp bark when I tried to get his attention. "She passed out."

He hefted her onto his shoulder as if she weighed no more than a sack of rice, and her feet dangled against his back. Relieved of my burden, I moved faster. Jensen kept up regardless since he had the strength of a steam-powered engine.

We hurtled through the street until we reached the turn for the docking bay. The girl bounced around against Jensen's chest, and strands of her hair waved with his steps. My breaths shortened, and our fast pace twisted my chest. I chanced a glance behind. We exited a street now swarming with people. Merchants hustled out of the way tugging half-rolled canopies and overflowing boxes of merchandise with them while their boxy stands stood unmanned. Shouts and gunshots cut through the murmur of voices since the little town wasn't prepared for this much action.

Smoke filtered into the air, and a squadron of officials arrived as backup. They cut in through the teeming crowd and shouted for people to move out of their way. Several children dove out, but the parents got shoved back. One of the officials fired his pistol straight skyward, eliciting screams from the crowds around them.

"I think we did a grand thing back there," I panted beside Jensen. "Took out some bad guys, livened up the place. Thank the Gods they didn't get our names 'cause they won't forget this little soiree for awhile." Jensen grunted in reply.

We followed the boardwalk until the town lay out of sight and airships loomed ahead. Desire's sleek form stuck out as stylish amidst the bloated monstrosities. The rope ladder still dangled over the side from earlier since docking bays were well regulated and safe enough. Besides, anyone attempting to board would be spotted from far away, like us.

Jensen gripped the slats first and started his one-armed climb. The girl's body bobbed around as he maneuvered up the ladder, and I followed suit, ascending with the ease of a fatigued marathoner. Jensen swung his legs over the ledge and landed on deck. I did the same moments later. With little care or precision, he dumped the girl's body on the deck and stalked away. I scrambled over to her while tugging open my leather pouch. My bandages were tucked inside, so I focused on straightening her body out.

Blood from her calf soaked into her torn shoes. The flesh had been sliced open above the tendon but not severed. I sent a blessing to the Gods, doused the wound with disinfectant, and fastened bandage around her ankle. Edwin could fix the rest later. Footsteps clattered across deck, followed by a shadow looming over me. Captain Morris stood before me with his arms crossed over his chest and one eyebrow arched high on his forehead.

"So," his deep voice sounded, "I take it you stayed out of trouble."

CHAPTER NINE

"Unavoidable, sir." I saluted.

Morris crouched beside me. "That's not what Jensen tells me. All this over a random girl?"

"Unavoidable," I repeated and lifted her bruised arms. "She can't be older than seventeen."

Amidst the chaos I never caught a decent view of the girl. Under the direct sun, her skin paled to light goldenrod, accented by long thick black hair that trailed past her waist. Bruises lined her arms like a camo covering, and the right side of her lower lip swelled. Rips and streaks of dirt covered the lengths of her dirty brown overalls, and she wore a loose shirt that turned off-white from dust and grass stains. The poor thing still trembled even while fainted. When I met the Captain's gaze, he dropped his argument. I didn't need to explain my motivations to him. He remembered how he found me all those years ago.

"Here." The captain slid his arms under her neck and behind her knees. "Why don't we take her to Edwin? He'll patch her up, and we can discuss the meeting place there." He rose with the girl in his arms and trudged over towards the hatch. I placed a hand on his shoulder, leaning in.

"Thank you," I whispered, and a wave of relief cascaded over me. My Captain always understood. His smile crinkled the scars lining his face.

"Bea, you've always been headstrong, but I can't fault someone whose heart's in the right place. I've seen too many horrors in this world to ignore more."

"Me too." A dark memory surged, and I suppressed a shudder.

"So damn young," he continued as we walked into the shade under the deck. "Do you know who she is? Why they did this to her?"

"Slavers." The word suspended in the air like a blackened storm cloud. The captain grunted, and we entered the infirmary. Isabella must have wandered away hours ago, but Edwin still sat at his table. He stood from his seat when we walked in and furrowed his brows.

"Who?" he asked.

"Someone who needs your care." Morris placed the girl on an empty bed. Her head rolled to the side, and her arms dangled over the edge. Edwin glanced to her swathed ankle before scurrying into his lab. Already blood seeped through my impromptu bandage job.

Jensen stepped into view, gripping the top of the doorframe. "Captain, are we discussing the exchange site?"

Morris nodded and took a seat at the nearest table. I grabbed a chair to join him. Jensen entered with his arms swinging side to side, but rather than taking a seat, he leaned against the wall. Edwin emerged from his lab carrying a giant bottle of antiseptic, bandages, and his container of smelling salts. He pulled up a stool by her ankle and started his work.

"So tell me your thoughts. Does the arrangement seem clean? Anything out of place?" Captain Morris asked. Edwin's percolator simmered with freshly brewed coffee, casting the scent of roasted beans to cut through the room's ammonia coating.

"It appears pretty stable." I rested my elbows on the table. "We're going to do the trade in a private warehouse."

"What about the inside? Any cargo?" he asked.

"Only Jensen's pretty pink parasols." I smirked. "Nothing flammable, no explosives, and no weapons."

"One door for the exit and entrance. Besides the aluminum folding screen, it's the only way out," Jensen added. "We'll have to put someone up on the roof to cover the blind spot."

A splutter interrupted us as Edwin lifted the container of smelling salts to her nose. The young girl's eyes blinked open, and she pushed herself upright on the bed. I strode over to crouch

128

beside her.

"I'm the First Mate, Beatrice—what's your name?" I asked. The chair behind me creaked, and Captain Morris joined me. Jensen's footsteps echoed down the hall. I made a mental reminder to give him hell later for being such an ass.

"Adelle," her quiet voice crept above a quavering whisper like a child's.

"Where are you from?" I asked gently, "What were you doing with that man?"

"Took me." Her gaze dodged towards me, but then she fixed her eyes on the wall. I didn't press her for more because sometimes more hurt too much to voice.

"Well you're aboard the airship Desire now. That man won't hurt you again."

Captain Morris bent over next to us and placed a hand on her shoulder. "Do you have a place to go?" his voice was gruff and menacing, but I knew what came next. She shook her head 'no' and bit her lip. "How are you with cleaning up? Can you follow orders well?" Her eyes still didn't register what he offered, so Morris continued, "What I'm saying is if you don't mind some hard work, we can give you a place here on board."

Her eyes widened with surprise, and she sat up a little straighter as she clutched the sheets tight. "I-I'll do whatever work you need me to." Adelle's voice shook, and the tears slipped down her cheeks. Captain pulled out his pocket watch and glanced at the time. I fiddled with the blue cameo around my neck since neither of us knew how to handle her crying.

"None of those tears." Captain Morris tugged at his aviator cap. "You'll need to be tough on this ship." She nodded and sucked in a deep breath. He gave her a nod before stalking off. I handed her a handkerchief and waited for her emotional display to be over.

"So what do you know about cooking?" I joked to break the tension. She wiped her tears away with the edges of the oversized shirt she wore and choked back her remaining sniffles.

"Some. I've been told I can cook. Point me to a kitchen, and I'll make a meal." Her dark brown eyes shone, but they were tinged with the wary caution of a cynic. For one so young, her gaze aged her years. Edwin rose from attending to her ankle.

"Well, you won't be doing anything until that wound heals up. If you aggravate it you could cause some permanent damage. It might affect the way you walk and cause a slight postural imbalance."

"And he claims another victim." I cracked a grin. "Edwin you're turning this infirmary into a speakeasy."

"You always bring me the clientele." He packed away his smelling salts and antiseptic, carrying them over to his room while whistling a bright little tune along the way. Such an odd man.

I turned toward Adelle. "Will you be okay in here for now?"

She nodded and glanced down at her lap. Her words came out in such a hushed whisper I almost didn't hear them, but a faint 'thank you' broke through the silence of the room. A smile tugged the corners of my lips, and I strode out. Captain Morris stood waiting by the door.

"Not much for tears, are you sir?" We walked along the corridor towards his room, and I ran my fingers along the wood grained walls. Up ahead, the porthole glinted under the electric candlelight, the one Jensen, the captain, and I found three years ago.

"Never did deal with them well. Not hers or yours." He passed me a knowing glance. His trench made a rustling sound against the hardwood as we strode along, the noise interspersed by the clomp of our boots.

"I never cried." I placed my hands on my hips, unable to stave away the wry twist of nostalgia. "You must be mistaking me with some other young girl."

"And you must have a selective memory." He laughed. We stood before his door, and he turned the knob. "Seeing that girl must've hit you where it hurts." Walking over to his desk, he took a seat in his massive leather chair.

I pulled up another one and joined him. "It's the one thing I still can't abide. I'll never let myself be put in that position again, but when someone else is, I flip the furnace."

"Wounds like that don't fade, ever. You carry them with you for the rest of your life, but the best you can do is fight against those evils. I understand why you did it." Morris's voice emanated warmth from that bottomless well of his because he had plenty to spare.

I took a deep breath before I continued. "Thank you for giving her a place on ship."

"We could use the extra hands. I won't turn down people in a rough place." He couldn't help the hint of a smile that breached his grizzled features. The old man had given a home to this ragtag group of vagabonds in the first place.

"I know you won't."

"Plus," he said as he leaned back into his seat, "I thought I heard mention of cooking? I can't tell you how amazing it would be if we had an actual cook aboard the ship, one that didn't make boiled potatoes and overcooked meat. Edwin's tastes like rubber, and whenever we try rotations our meals alternate between burned lumps or gruel." I nodded in agreement.

He reached into his drawer and placed the box onto the table. It sat and mocked us for all our trouble on this job. The brass keyhole and geared mechanism shone under the lamplight, and faint, near indistinguishable engravings imprinted on the metal lining the sides. I peered closer before picking up the box.

"Did you notice these before?" I squinted, but the faint etchings weren't any clearer.

Captain Morris shrugged. "Not my issue. Come tomorrow morning that thing is another man's burden. I don't like that we've been forced to take jobs this risky, and I also don't like the amount of attention that box has garnered. British military? I know how brutal and persistent they can be. The sooner we give that cargo away, the better." His face darkened at the statement, and his scars deepened under the shadows. Memories from the war evoked a distance in his eyes.

"That had to be rough, I mean, since most of Europe lost to the red coats."

He tapped his fingers against the desktop. "You must have been only a couple years old back in the thirties. The land by the Rhine in old Germany? Breathtaking. But what's left barely counts as a country because the Brits stole more than their share." The tapping stopped, and he stared at the wall in the grips of a faraway time and place.

I rubbed at one of the etchings, trying to make it out. "Hard to believe this payoff will keep us free and clear for the next couple months. It's been small job after small job for the past year or two."

He passed me a faint smile, knowing full well I switched the conversation for his sake. "We need the money too. We'll barely have enough to fill up, repair, and leave port without it. Hopes and dreams don't cover costs for the Desire. Running an airship turns into some serious work when you're not a private entrepreneur."

"None of us mind the jobs." I shrugged. "If we sat aboard day in and out many of us would turn into harpies. Adventure is a feast for the soul."

"I think you're confusing adventure with absolute utter danger." He pulled out a cigar and lit it. "Only those with a special kind of crazy enjoy the jobs we go on." I nudged the box with my finger, feeling the coolness of the metal edges and gears.

"You know the main reason I'm first mate is because no one else skated the edge enough. Plus, I scare you." I passed him a grin.

"You might be the craziest on board, second to Edwin, but you're the first mate because of the stunt you pulled today." His gray eyes met mine. "I protect this crew like family, because they are. My first mate needs a heart in the right direction, and not everyone has that. You have the gumption to act on those crazy impulses, but you watch out for the weak and the abused. We may skate the law, but I don't run a crew of brigands and floozies. We're here to defend each other, and you understand that better than most."

I lost my words, and a content embarrassment stained my cheeks. "Still clinging to that military mantra, aren't you?" I teased.

He shrugged. "We may have lost, but I took 'no man left behind' to heart. Back then, we didn't play around with people's lives. When you've seen battle, seen real war, you realize how much life is wasted. I never took anyone for granted again. You could be talking to them in the barracks one day, and the next they'd be lying dead in a ditch."

"Why Captain, are you being sentimental? Am I on the right ship?" I punched him in the arm but met his eyes with a serious gaze. Even though we played light, I understood how deeply the war had impacted him. Trauma lingered and shaped survivors like us rather than vanishing. I stood from my seat. "Well Captain, I'll bid you farewell. It's been a long day, and we'll have an early rise to make the exchange tomorrow morning." As he picked up the box, the dim light gleamed across the corners.

"Who said you're coming?"

"I'd like to see you try and stop me." I placed a hand on my hip. "Tomorrow morning, I'll trade out Matilda for a sniper rifle and take the high ground. Someone needs to watch your back."

"Good. We wouldn't want you running your mouth and ruining our trade." The deep scar on his mouth crinkled with his smirk.

"Why dear sir, I can't believe you'd think such things of me." I placed a hand over my mouth, feigning mock horror. "I'll have you know, I've been called the epitome of a lady."

"Get out of here, scamp. Leave this old man in peace." He shooed me away. I smiled and waltzed out of the room.

Although below deck had no windows, after spending so much time aboard the ship I knew the sun had set. I could just tell. The lamplight flickered through the empty corridor like a lone landing strip. Shadows stained Desire's wooden hull a cherry red, hollowing out the hall like a rind. My stomach flopped with anticipation for the trade tomorrow because of how much hinged on this exchange: our food, our fuel, and our lives. After our run of foul luck, we needed a win.

The whispered complaints aboard ship proved enough because even the most loyal people like Geoff started questioning the captain's motives. None of them realized the pinch we were in though, because it was a Captain's job to not let them know.

I rounded the corner and entered my room, grateful to sleep in my own bed tonight rather than passed out on deck. The tiny flame of my lamp quavered behind the frosted glass and cast an orange tint around my room. I placed Matilda over the stained wooden rose embellishing the counter on my mahogany dresser. Once I removed my boots, I sat them in the corner by my sword. My sweat soaked feet basked in the cool ocean breeze sweeping through the cabins. After donning a loose chemise and less restrictive pants, I hopped into my bed.

For several moments, I lay still. My muscles began relaxing, and my head simmered to a slow boil at long last. The ceiling above me, straight wooden lines, drifted in slow dizzying circles. I pulled my blanket to my chin, sinking into the comfort of an old weathered mattress that knew me by name. Concerns over tomorrow skittered through my mind, and I turned to my side.

Jobs usually played a backburner role on my nerves because we'd always rush in, do our work and laugh about escaping death once more. Several deep breaths barely helped, but I forced them anyway. I closed my eyes, trying to focus on the sound of the ocean tides roaring from our berth. The cyclical motion of the water's crash and roll seeped into my veins, and my heartbeat slowed to a normal pattern. I shut my eyes until the blackness overtook me.

***

Sleep had only stolen me for a moment when I sat up with a start in a darkened cabin. My lamp quavered in the corner of the room. Dread settled into my bones, and my heart twisted in pain. Something was drastically wrong.

CHAPTER TEN

My heartbeat pummeled my chest, but I couldn't explain the spiked adrenaline. Peering around the corners of the room, I caught shadows loitering around the edges and crawling into every crack in the wall. My eyes adjusted to the murky blackness. The objects in my room from an open trunk to the vanity by my bedside appeared undisturbed.

The several deep breaths I took barely helped, and numbness raced up and down my extremities. Even after shutting my eyes and counting to ten, I still couldn't shake the instinct that something was wrong. That feeling soured my stomach, drenching my body with sweat. The gentle back and forth thrum of the tides filtered through the silence, but even the ocean's quiet murmurs didn't stifle my unease.

I blinked several times until the fuzziness left my eyes. My heart still sped, but at least the numbness shifted into my fingers and toes. I picked up my arms and shook them out, trying to rid myself of the pins and needles. Despite the important day tomorrow and the rest I needed, after this wake up, I wouldn't fall back asleep. I pressed my bare feet against the cold wooden floor and wandered out past my door into the hallway.

Dim lamplights trickled down the corridor and cast a greenish orange hue from their surrounding glass capsules. Goosebumps crawled up my arms. The cool minty breeze swept into the cabins and seared doubt into my mind whether any of this was real. I pinched my cheek just in case, but sure enough, it hurt.

The ethereal mist of early morning filtered through the cabins, clinging to my bare skin like a second sweat. Apparently I woke up several hours off from dawn. My soft footsteps padded over the wooden planked floor of the ship, each one slow and irresolute. The sleeves of my chemise tickled my swinging arms. Even out of my room with some fresh ocean air, I couldn't shake the wrongness burrowed deep into my marrow, spreading fear like I hadn't known in years. I suppressed a shudder.

A cautious warning wrenched my gut like the press of a gaze with someone watching. Nervousness wouldn't consume me from a simple exchange like the one in a couple of hours. I'd been on so many jobs that a drop off caused less stress than changing my socks. Nor was I still afraid of the dark. My father helped rid me of that fear when I turned six—physical pain was an easy motivator, and he knew the right techniques.

Rustling came from the captain's chamber several doors down. Relief passed through my chest. Although I had been there before I retired for the night, I always welcomed our talks.

If the captain already woke up, I could plan out the drop off with him and shake this weird feeling. He must be restless over the exchange too. Maybe I had a simple panic attack and let the dark mutate my reaction into something worse. I strode down the hall until I stopped and paused at his door. Morris might want time alone to reflect and figure out a plan for the morning—tough, because he was in for a surprise visitor.

I opened the door.

No.

No, no *no*.

My brain stopped functioning. It refused to process the scene in front of me. This had to be a nightmare, some twisted mess of a nightmare. Moments later I'd snap out or wake up in my bed, and this would turn into something we'd laugh about later when swapping stories in the mess hall. If this was real, some part of my brain tucked this away as a memory that would stick with me for the rest of my life.

His long oaken desk stretched across the middle of the room like always. The maps lay across the tabletop from earlier, remnants of our discussion that morning over location. Even the short dark chair I pulled up mere hours ago remained the exact way I left it.

Morris must have switched his two aether lamps on before he retired to bed because a greenish glow coated the room. The illuminated green liquid set apart the brass fixtures and amplified their golden tones. Even the keypad on his desk lay in the same spot as before, still turned off since he rarely used it—the old man ignored that type of technology. But the captain's chambers looked wrong.

The contents of his desk drawers scattered across the floors, and the drawers themselves hung open, some teetering off the edges. Permits, old jobs, and the multitude of scrap heap papers littered his desk while several had fallen onto the hardwood. Old maps with gilt edging and faded colors shone under the dim lamplight. Even the captain's toy water ship collection, little Spanish ones and Italian rigs with miniature sails, lay capsized along the ground.

His wooden locker had been busted open, and the chest lay exposed though untouched. He kept liquor in there, visible on first glance. The door against the back wall leading to his bedchambers hung ajar.

The acrid scent of rusted tin hit me before I caught the spatters of red painting the desk and his items with freckled dots. Tiny flecks, almost unnoticeable, led to the trickle, which led to the pool of blood. My gaze stopped, and my brain screamed white noise.

My mind didn't whimper, and it didn't yell; instead it shrieked with the same caterwaul of blind rage as an animal taking its prey. So strong, the feeling blinded me, but I forced through my body's shutdown to follow the trail.

The blood pooled around the stiff body of Captain Robert Morris. My Captain.

He lay still on the ground with his tanned features paled and painted with the sickening green sheen from the lamps. The brackish blood took on a blackened hue under that light, coating the floor surrounding him. His arms sprawled by his sides, and his head had rolled to the right with a clear view of his face. Permanently dulled eyes stared at me with a shocked expression, and his mouth hung ajar.

Those eyes, hours earlier had conveyed a world's worth of love and pride, but now glazed over, they witnessed nothing. His scars darkened under the shadows cast across his face, which burrowed deep into the pockmarked crevasses. Strands of his blackish silver hair matted to his forehead, but most formed disheveled tufts. The aviator cap he always wore lay inches from his head on the ground.

Jensen stood mere feet away from the Captain, gun still pointed.

CHAPTER ELEVEN

I lifted my head to meet Jensen's gaze. The couple of seconds between us stretched out like the sprawling pace of hours. His broad shoulders rose up and down with exerted breaths, and his wide chest swelled. The man standing before me wore the same clothes, the same bowler cap as yesterday, and even hunched over with the same terrible posture as always. But his gaze changed my whole view.

Dark, bleak and grim, this person before me transformed into a different creature from the man I called Jensen. His hand quivered on the trigger of his gun, and his other arm clamped around the box. The Jensen on our crew would never steal our cargo. He'd never...the captain. My numb brain refused to wrap around the word.

We stood in perfect stillness, the traitor and I. In the bleak distance the sound of mocking tides swelled with that cyclical steady thrum. This whole thing had to be a nightmare—even the syrupy air I breathed tasted unreal. This scene unmade my reality, stripped down what I believed true, and rewired my psyche.

The misty air choked my throat as my muscles strained with

the labor of each breath. Every molecule of my being protested the view before me, and my mind didn't dare to interject. Jensen pointed the revolver he brought on every job, the one I trusted in his hands all these years. However, Morris hadn't had the same chance, with no gun in hand or anywhere around him. Jensen had given him no quarter.

Something snapped within me—something dark, dangerous, and loathsome. It twisted my stomach, and bile rose in my throat. Morris still wore his bedclothes, a striped flannel shirt, and loose black pants. He probably stumbled from his bed when he heard the noise but hadn't grabbed the gun on his desk. The man never even suspected or imagined Jensen would do such a thing. Not after having him aboard these past five years, sharing meals, jobs, and risking their lives together.

Anger seared my chest and scorched my senses. I'd been called hotheaded many a time, but rarely had such clear righteous rage governed my brain. It bubbled up and spilled over with hot, boiling fury.

I reached for my gun, breaking the stupor between us. My hands clenched on nothing since I left Matilda by my bedside dresser, and Jensen swung his revolver around to aim for my forehead.

Some self-preservation mechanism must have kicked in because my mind exited the stage awhile back. Before Jensen took a shot, I slammed the door and ran. Bullets meant for me pinged against the wooden barrier as I raced for my room. The image of Matilda's place on my dresser roused my mind from sluggish torpor, but if any other thoughts intruded past that, I'd crumble. I threw myself into my chambers, shutting the door behind.

Once inside, my mind blanked for a moment until it burned. I stood and groped at the air before me, but nothing registered, and no train of thought followed. Jensen's heavy footfalls pounded through the hallway, triggering my body into motion. I picked up Matilda with shaking fingers and fed her rounds. His footsteps passed my room. The bastard was going to run.

Thankfully, pursuit, gunfights, and chases were second nature for me. Had I been some deckhand or serving wench, I'd have crumpled into a dark corner of the barracks, seized up, and rocked back and forth driven mad by the events of the night. However, as the first mate, I didn't have that option. My body took autopilot and left my numbed mind behind. With Matilda in hand, I charged out of my room in desperate abandon. The slam of my door rang in my ears. My numbed feet barely registered the steps below me, but I hurtled up regardless.

As the deck emerged into view, I processed several scenes at once. Jensen ran headlong like a tiger lumbering at full speed for the ladder by the edge of the ship. Several deckhands strolled around up top, but every last person froze with surprise when he emerged. Except Geoff, who had stepped out from the navigation chambers, roused by the noise.

Unable to see Jensen clearly, he held his gun up but squinted at the backside of the figure. Jensen turned around with his revolver raised and took advantage of the confusion torn across Geoff's face. I stood an equal distance from both of them. If I chased after Jensen, I could stop him, take our cargo back, and avenge Captain Morris, but Geoff would be at risk. If I helped Geoff, Jensen would get away.

It wasn't even a damned choice.

I raced towards Geoff and tackled him down as Jensen shot. The bullet zoomed overhead, but Jensen didn't bother firing another. Instead, he jumped over the ledge, using a cord to rappel down the side at a blinding pace, our cargo in hand. I pushed myself off Geoff and ran over to the side of the ship, Matilda out and ready. Jensen loped across the boardwalk until his massive figure blended into the shadows. I fired several shots, but they uselessly studded the wooden panels below. I didn't care. Shots rang from Matilda, bullet after bullet until the chamber clicked, empty and done.

I sank to my knees, collapsing onto the deck. Geoff jogged up from behind me.

"Was that Jensen? Did he shoot at me?" Confusion painted his voice sharp. I opened my mouth, but no words came out, only hollow breaths. Geoff knelt before me on one knee and tried to stare me in the eyes. My head hung low, and my chin brushed against my neck while Matilda dangled in my loose grasp. I tried again to open my mouth and say something, but I couldn't speak. Geoff's warm hand circled my chin as he lifted my face to greet his.

"Bea," his voice steadied to a slow, clear and commanding pitch. "What happened?"

I swallowed the lump in my throat, pushed back my panic, forcing it into a partition of my mind. It was all I could do to keep from screaming.

"Jensen. He betrayed us." My voice was foreign to my own ears, vacant and resigned. "Took our cargo for tomorrow morning— the box. And the captain." My mind paused, stuck on repeat, on the vision from the room of Jensen standing over Captain Morris. It wouldn't push through, the word wouldn't budge. I couldn't let it. Geoff's gentle brown eyes widened in shock. Between his gaze and the heat from his hand, my mind started functioning again, one tentative step at a time. It chugged along, slow and sluggish, but there. I squinted, hard.

"Grab the crew—everyone you can rouse on deck. We're only going through this once." A pause stretched between us, and for a moment, I lost myself in his eyes. He knew. Reflected in them was desperation, the horror of what he feared, but also the futile grasping onto hope, onto anything but the truth. He hadn't witnessed that nightmare of a scene.

Geoff broke our gaze and dashed off in the direction of the cabins. While he ran, he signaled a couple of the deckhands over to my direction. Using the ledge, I pulled myself up, even though my legs shook too much to stand on my own. I leaned against the edge of the ship, drawing on her for support. Our girl held me up right now, and deep down, I knew she'd be the only thing to pull me through this. The deckhands approached, but I didn't say a word and just gestured for them to sit. We waited in silence.

The sky overhead remained dark from the passage of night, but an ozone smell surrounded us, hinting of dawn's arrival. Clouds smothered the starry horizon, and the first tinges of reddish orange seeped through the sky.

Geoff reappeared from the cabins with Isabella and Edwin in tow. They circled around me while Spade, Jack, and several other men rushed onto the deck. Even Adelle limped her way over to our growing circle. Finally, Seth emerged from below deck with the grimmest expression I'd ever seen on his face. He'd known Morris the longest and must have prepared for this day, though no one could truly prepare for loss.

Even though the crew still woke up, wide-eyed shock painted many a face in the crowd, while others glanced around, as if waiting for the captain to appear. Their motions sent a lance of pain through my chest. I drew in a deep breath of the laden dawn air and forced myself to stand straight. Planting my bare feet flat onto the deck, I tapped into my girl's strength before I spoke.

"Crew of the Desire," my voice rang out strong and loud, but cold like the distant surrounding sea. "Captain Robert Morris is dead." Several gasps filtered around the crowd, and a shaky sob came from Isabella. "Jensen killed him over the cargo we were meant to deliver at dawn." My voice stopped working for a moment, and Geoff's eyes met mine. Between that and the solid grounding of the Desire's planks under my feet, I mustered the strength to continue. I honed in on those totems because watching any of the crew's reactions pained me more than hearing their cries.

"We're at an impasse. Our ship's running low on fuel, food, and excess supplies. We relied on this job to replenish our stocks, since the captain knew we'd be in dire straits if we didn't. The traitor, who we trusted, stole that cargo. Who Captain Morris trusted." Anger rose within me again, as constant as the dawn's light.

"Our Captain is dead, but we aren't. If we don't intercept Jensen, we'll lose cargo that we can't surrender. There will be time to mourn him later, but that time is not now. Captain wouldn't want the Desire berthed, and he wouldn't want his murderer to run free. If we stand any chance at catching Jensen, we have to assemble a team to meet at the spot before dawn and wait for the parties to show up. I understand if you can't gather the strength to join me, but I'm heading out now to stop that bastard. Step forward if you're willing to help—I'll need any I can get if I'm to claim revenge for the captain."

The second my voice stopped, silence breached the air like an intruder lurking through a home. Not a person stirred.

My heart sank. Going this alone would be a suicide run, but I'd take that over letting the captain's murderer and traitor of our crew run free. I took a deep breath, edging towards the rope ladder. Geoff stepped forward.

"I'll follow you in. Just tell me where you need me." His face darkened with shadows, and his eyes gleamed somber but determined. Several deckhands stood with him. Isabella moved forward, Seth, even Edwin. Before I counted to five, the entire crew shifted toward me, including little Adelle. Pride ached in my chest and mingled with the intense hole that Jensen left by stealing our Captain away. The conflicting feelings battled, but I pushed them aside and took command.

"Geoff, Isabella, I'll need the two of you. Any more than a couple may draw too much attention."

"Let me arm myself." Isabella nodded and walked off. Geoff followed suit. Seth placed his arms over his chest.

"I'm coming." His voice held a tension as if daring me to argue—I wouldn't. Morris was his dearest and longest friend. "Captain, direct me wherever you see fit, I'll go arm up." I blinked several times, not realizing he referred to me. The words sounded wrong from his lips, unsanctified, but as the first mate, I took up that duty now. The chill of such a serious responsibility settled into my limbs. Seth met my eyes because he'd chosen his phrasing carefully. Those words, that affirmation from the oldest crew member here, quelled any potential challenges to my captainship.

Geoff emerged from the navigation chambers with his pistol tucked into his holster. The wind chilled my chapped bare feet, which reminded me that I'd do no good unprepared—I had to get ready.

"I'll be right back, the rest of you remaining on board, stay vigilant. If you see Jensen, show him no quarter. He's an enemy now." Several crew members nodded.

Upon descending below deck, the corridor smelled like a rusted medallion even though the blood only covered the captain's quarters. That aluminum stench refused to leave me alone, haunting me like the crawling chill of a cemetery. I entered my room, yanking on the nearest pair of boots. My chemise could stay on, but I strapped the steel plated bodice overtop for added protection. Grabbing my leather bag, I threw in a couple more rounds before I looped it onto my belt. When I glimpsed my reflection in the mirror, I froze, and a tingling roar rose in the back of my mind.

Shutting out my last ounce of panic and pain, I willed myself onward. If I stopped now, I'd fall apart, and I couldn't. The crew needed someone to stay strong, and like it or not, Seth nominated me. Hell, the captain nominated me by placing me as first mate. The Captain. My mind buzzed again, but I stomped my foot, hard. The pain shot up my leg, distracting me enough to keep my thoughts at bay. I reloaded Matilda, and the chamber clicked when I closed it, all while I ignored the mirror. Later, I'd have time to face reality.

I emerged from below. The circle of crew members had scattered, but they still wandered across the deck. A toxic air of hopelessness lingered throughout the bay. Isabella, Geoff, and Seth stood by the ladder, armed and ready. How Seth managed to grab his weapons before me remained a mystery, but that man packed an enigma-filled punch. I approached them.

Isabella appeared the worst. Tears stained her tanned cheeks, and the whites of her eyes reddened under the emotional onslaught. My jaw quavered at the sight, but I clenched it firm. Under no circumstances could I falter. A blue kerchief pulled back her light brown hair, and a foul frown turned her lips. Throwing knives rested in the straps on her back, and holstered pistols weighted both hips. I didn't bother asking if she was up to the task because the question dried on my lips. Even though the poison still weakened her, she'd blame me forever if I excluded her from this.

Seth wouldn't forgive me either if he got left behind. With his rifle strapped to the back of his jumpsuit and the revolver at his side, he'd already prepared. Despite the shock, Seth's face hadn't changed expression—after all, Morris wasn't the first friend the grizzled war vet had to bury. Geoff favored a single pistol but kept rounds of ammo on a belt around his waist. Seth and Geoff hadn't shed a tear, but a cold fury akin to my own burned behind their eyes.

"I scouted out the spot yesterday," I spoke before my

sluggish mind caught up. "Unfortunately, so did Jensen, so here's what you need to know. We'll split up by the warehouse. I'll need you, Seth, to take the rooftops. You're an excellent sniper shot, and that's what we need there." Seth grunted, but his arms remained folded over his chest, and he didn't protest.

"Isabella, you'll take the docking bay and find cover by the crates. That way if anyone's stationed on the roof you can aid Seth. It also gives you a clear shot at anyone entering or exiting the buildings." She nodded, and I turned to Geoff. "You'll follow me into the building. I scouted it out, so I remember the crate positioning and the layout."

"How do we know Jensen will show?" Isabella asked.

"He has to if he wants the payoff, because the exchange requires him to be there with the cargo. We have that in our favor. If anything goes foul though and they planned a double cross, take the employer's men out. We just want Jensen and the box, those are the priorities." My chest burned. "And when we find Jensen—I'll kill him myself." Three grim expressions stared back at me. "Ready crew? We protect ours, so I don't want any heroics. We're all coming back," I said. Isabella bit her lip hard, and Seth's eyes widened.

My own stomach flopped, realizing whose words I repeated, whose mantra had become such an integral part of my own, and whose boots would never pound these planks again. I clenched and unclenched my hand to keep myself together.

"Let's move out." My words rolled out smoother than a steam engine. I placed my hands on the rungs of the ladder, and we descended.

CHAPTER TWELVE

We treaded over the familiar boardwalk I'd crossed yesterday with Jensen. An aching bitterness simmered through my body, and I grasped onto that because anger dried the sodden rag's worth of tears I bottled away. Anger kept me from breaking down. Early dawn's dew-laden fog had dissipated, but the thinned air didn't change the sober atmosphere. No one spoke, but I didn't think any of us could. The events of the night robbed us of words.

A bloody sunrise broke over the sky and pressured the ocean with its carmine hues while wisps of daylight glided over the boardwalk as we headed to the warehouse district. The bursting melon of a sun littered pink and crimson pulp across the horizon this dawn. I gulped hard and tried to not remember the similarly crimson puddle on the floor of the captain's chambers. My chest tightened. We had a traitor to kill.

I glanced over my crewmates and paused on Geoff. His brows furrowed, and his glazed brown eyes gazed off into the distance. A long undershirt trailed over his black slacks, and a wrinkled, askew button-down trumped the mismatched ensemble. He handled the tragedy the exact same way as me, the way we learned from Morris. No tears. I choked back the lump in my throat and ran an idle hand over Matilda, finding comfort in the cold steel.

Those warehouses rose into view like boxy leviathans in the distance with sharp corners that jutted out, merging into long rivers of aluminum and concrete. The sunrise coated them a burnished copper and glittered over the sullied tin roofs. I hadn't scanned the docks as much yesterday while I had focused on the drop site. After all, they weren't designed for subterfuge since businesses liked to keep them clear and organized.

The empty wharf resounded with the menacing quiet, and the silence lingered in the back of my mind. Dock workers normally unloaded warehouse shipments at the early hours of dawn, but the bay lay deserted. Placing a hand out, I stopped our party.

"Slight change of plans. Seth, you'll still go up top. Isabella, we're joining you behind the crates until the coast is clear rather than walking straight into the entrance. The silence here doesn't sit right with me. Besides, we don't want Jensen to escape with the box."

The closer we advanced, my fingers tingled as I readied to seize my gun at a moment's notice. In the past, I shut out the little voice in my head during my jobs since dwelling on what-ifs wasted time. Yes, impulsive moves tossed me into trouble, but they also kept me alive. Now I led a crew. My new position as captain weighed on me like the title to a broken-down fixer upper. We walked past the first rows of warehouses, and I recognized the scrawled number fourteen a ways in from ones lining the pathway.

"That ladder's the route up." I nudged Seth and pointed to

the metal slats leading up the side of the building. "We'll swing over to the opposite side and watch your back." Seth detached from our group, and with his rifle strapped to the back of his jumpsuit, he scaled the rungs. My stomach flopped, and I gestured to Isabella and Geoff. Quick and silent, we padded over to the crates littering the docks. We crept around the side of them and crouched down behind several stacked in clusters that made for the perfect hiding spot.

Unfortunately, our employer thought so too. And these men didn't hesitate.

A weapon glinted under the early light as the nearest one brought his pistol up. I yanked Geoff and Isabella with me. The bullet already left his gun and cracked as it hit a distant target. He loaded another one, but I pulled Matilda from my holster and tossed my uncertainty off the wharf. Several shots buried into his chest.

The man hit the ground, but the mercenary behind him already started lining up targets. Luckily, Isabella didn't hesitate either and looped around to the other side. Two throwing knives glinted behind his knees as he collapsed to the ground.

"Double cross, is it?" Anger, my familiar friend, surged again. The man scrambled for his gun, but I bent down and scooped the piece up before he grabbed it.

Geoff pointed his pistol at the man's skull. "What do we do

with him?"

A sigh escaped my mouth. I couldn't kill a man in cold blood like that, not while he was unable to shoot me back. Headstrong, impatient, and foolhardy I might be, but straight murderer I wasn't. I didn't kill unarmed men.

"Bind him and gag him. He won't be going anywhere." I pulled out some rope from my bag, and in a couple efficient strokes, Isabella had him tied up. Standing behind the lowest crate, I peered over the top. From our vantage point, Seth's sturdy figure cut a deep shadow against the blooming horizon. But so did the other sniper's. I sank my teeth into my lip to stop from calling out a warning since the noise would alert anyone down here of our position. As if the gunshots hadn't. Aw, hell.

I whipped Matilda up and fired three blasts towards the sniper. All fell miserably short, but Seth's head jerked, and he pulled out his sidepiece. Smart. He bulldozed in and emptied his clip into the man's head. Snipers were lethal but only from a distance. With his short range, Seth took the advantage, and before the other sniper could swing his rifle over, the man dropped. Seth claimed his spot and the sniper's rifle. He signaled to us below.

A sigh of relief slipped past my lips. I barely needed to worry. Seth might be our mechanic, but old Germany built their soldiers tough, and he'd seen some wars.

I narrowed my eyes. "If Jensen came through this way, he'd

have to take out or deal with these men."

Isabella's eyes widened. "Do you think he's working with the employer?" she asked.

I shook my head. "If he was, he wouldn't meet them here, nor would they station men at an unnecessary rendezvous. I must have missed a way in."

"Didn't you scout it yesterday?" Isabella asked while she stared at the throwing knives she'd pulled out. The fresh blood on the tips held her gaze.

"I did." My hands clenched into fists. "With Jensen. He held the light and controlled our sights. He might have withheld a spot from our vision on purpose. I—" my voice cracked, but I continued, "I trusted him to find what I didn't."

"Well, time's dropping like coppers in the ocean." Geoff checked his pistol. "Why don't you and I get out of here, sweetheart, since we have a party to attend." His voice came out hoarse and thick, but his banter meant the world to me right now. My heart bounced from its vise for a brief second. I met his eyes gratefully, and he offered an arm.

Isabella cracked a watery smile. "Bye, darling." The words shook from her throat, but the effort gave me strength. Geoff and I, arms linked, strode to the site where the traitor waited in the only way we knew how: with style.

Warehouse number fourteen surged into view bringing with it a murmur of paranoia as urgent as a rising mob. I didn't like going through the front door, but we didn't have much of a choice. The exchange kept us in the game. Jensen wouldn't shoot the second we entered, since the employer would be arriving right around this time. At least, I banked on that because otherwise this plan threw caution over the ship's ledge. I gave Geoff a tight smile as we stood before the door. Stepping forward, I turned the knob, and we entered.

Same as before, darkness smothered the entire warehouse with its insidious, crawling touch. The shadows shifted around the room like spots on my vision. My muscles tensed. With Jensen possibly lurking around, Geoff and I stood out like two red bulls eye on a cloudless day.

Resurrecting my mental map of the place from yesterday, the pile of crates containing the parasols were to the right. I prayed Jensen hadn't thought of the same hiding spot. Geoff brushed by my side, almost causing me to jump in fright. My fingers scraped over the wooden grain of a crate, so I tugged Geoff's sleeve to drag him down with me.

We breathed in the gloom, and around us the deceptive silhouettes of darkened figures lurked along the walls. After several minutes, my eyes adjusted to the dank warehouse with the shadows morphing into identifiable shapes. The place smelled like balsa wood and welded steel. I focused on the silence and listened as our shallow breaths commingled with the gentle rhythm of our heartbeats. Geoff's warm body pressed against me, and my own responded with a shiver of comfort.

I closed my eyes and honed my focus past us, trying to grasp onto any other sounds. The overburdening silence jarred my attention like static. Either Jensen's skills masked his sound or he never entered the building.

"Don't move." Jensen's gruff voice sliced through the quiet. My eyes widened, and I tried to locate the direction—along the backside of the building. I must have missed a back entrance or side crawlspace, but Jensen hadn't. Geoff's arms tensed against me.

My eyes honed in on the dark shapes, and I peered over the ledge of the crate. Jensen crouched behind boxes at the other side of the warehouse. Only a slice of his shoulders stuck out—not enough to get a clear shot on. His training taught him to choose a good vantage point, and the paranoid nature of our field kept us one step ahead. I cursed every last day I sparred with that man.

Silence resumed again, but at least now we'd know if he shifted from his spot. We were stuck. If we made the first move, he could escape through wherever he entered, but if he moved, we were on the defensive, and I performed better rushing in, guns blazing. My nerves ticked with an impatient irritation. Fury demanded I rush over, sword aloft, and run him through, but luckily for me I only sometimes listened to my anger. Geoff's hand pressed against my leg. In the darkness he couldn't see me, but I smiled, grateful for his presence.

"Walk out now," Jensen's gruff voice sounded again. "You're going to turn around and exit the warehouse. Do that and I'll spare your lives."

"Just like you did with the captain, right?" my voice slid out seething and dangerous. I reined back my temper before I stomped my foot in anger. "You know the word of a traitor means nothing. You'll stab us in the back like you did with him."

He didn't respond.

We sat crouched behind our respective places, neither willing to make the first move and expose ourselves. Quiet in the darkness, those memories—those horrible memories of our new reality—fought to breach the walls I'd hefted up. Without the gunfire, action or something to throw myself into, despair numbed my veins like a hefty dose of novocaine. My hands shook—I was dying to make the first move. Geoff's touch on my leg remained the one source of stability reining me in from rushing over to Jensen and doling out all this pent up pain with my bare hands. But even his presence only helped to a point, and the images, those terrible images, encroached with the stillness.

Gunfire barked outside, and Jensen's shoulders jerked. Coming around the back he hadn't seen the men waiting, so he didn't know the ex-employer already double crossed us. Ironic that the traitor didn't know we were betrayed. But all I wanted was the box my Captain died over and the bastard who killed him. Damn the rest.

The door burst open, and our plans sailed to hell.

Geoff and I skittered off to the sides of the crates since the open door compromised our position. Jensen sprung into action and shifted against the wall seconds after we moved. The light from the open door silhouetted the intruders and granted us a clear view.

Three men loomed at the entrance. Thick muscles built off hard work lent them the appearance of dock workers along with their dirt streaked rags they called clothing. The elastic on one man's suspenders wore thin and threatened to snap. They must've handpicked the finest fashion from the grave. The man in the front possessed a beard the size of his face that almost covered the gun he pointed at us, but behind him, the two had their weapons out, ready to shoot. One glimpse at them confirmed the hunch I had. Our venerable employer sent these men in his place.

"Hand over the box, and this doesn't have to get ugly," the bearded man bellowed. I bit out a hiss. This whole situation had turned deadly and emotional, and I didn't like emotional. Feelings made me stupid. But nothing happened like we planned, absolutely nothing, so I threw my sense out the nonexistent window.

"He says exit and he'll spare our lives." I stood and jabbed a finger at Jensen, tossing my safety to the breeze. "You say this doesn't have to get ugly." My voice darkened, deepened, and a fury burst from it like no one in the room had ever seen. "What none of you seem to understand is that I don't believe a *damn* word from traitors," the scream ripped from my throat, and my eyes flashed. "This got ugly when that damned bastard killed my Captain."

The room stared at me in stunned silence. And then the bullets flew.

I tuck-and-rolled down by Geoff and the crates, but a stray grazed my arm sending a tendril of shearing pain through me. Didn't care. Didn't matter. I rolled away, gunning for Jensen. Occupied by the men at the door and with cargo to defend, he one-handedly shot back at them. I dove towards him.

Unfortunately none of the geniuses in the room thought before they started shooting the place up. We stood inside a metal box with no windows and one escape route. Bullets pinged around the room and ricocheted from ceiling to wall and back. From behind me, Geoff's pistol roared into action, but being one of the few with common sense, he aimed for the door.

My hands latched onto Jensen's broad back, and I swung with Matilda. One powerful jerk from his right shoulder pushed me off before I could whip him in the head. A bullet whizzed by me, seeking a way out of the room. I ducked behind Jensen while he aimed for the guy pointing a gun at his face. Attacked from both sides, he couldn't place full focus on me, and I used the distraction to my advantage. I lobbed a kick behind his knee. It connected, but he didn't go down like I hoped and instead swung towards me.

With the box tucked under his left arm, he aimed a shaky shot with his right.

That motion put the box into full display, and once the men caught sight, they turned their attention to him. I had the feeling they weren't getting paid until the box landed into their coward employer's hands, so they'd hone in on Jensen. But I wouldn't let one of them steal my revenge from me. Geoff used their changed focus to his advantage and pistol-whipped the nearest man in the head.

The man dropped to the floor, and one of the ricocheted bullets buried into his chest. Jensen's foolish shot added another bouncing ping around the room, and we stood in a hotbox of bullets. If we didn't get out, we'd end up dead. Jensen and those turncoats could end up full of holes for all I cared, but I wanted Geoff out alive.

Jensen always put his own preservation over anyone and anything else. I'd gone along on so many jobs with him that I didn't even need to process what he'd do next—I went by instinct. He leapt over the crates, rushing past the hired men towards the main entrance, and a second behind him, I jumped into the broad daylight. Geoff and the two remaining men followed, but I had the lead. Jensen ran several paces ahead of me, and even with extra adrenaline, I couldn't catch up.

Isabella and Seth stepped in front of him.

Judging by several corpses littering the field, the three attacking us had been the only to escape their wrath. Jensen dove to the side and changed direction, but I expected that. I already circled around to tackle his leg. My body thudded against the ground, and loose dirt flew up in choking billows. Wind flew from my lungs, but my hands latched onto his thick leg as I dragged him with me. The dive sent the box flying from his arms, leaving that accursed cargo lying right in front of Isabella. She scooped it up and aimed her gun at Jensen.

The other two men burst between us, scrambling for Isabella since they were here for the goods, nothing else. Seth lifted his shotgun and used their focus to his advantage. He rarely shot, but when he did, he hit every target on the nose.

Jensen wrested away from my grasp and surged forward. I scrambled up, but he already had a lead on me, and Geoff stood on the other side, too far to catch up. Jensen burst ahead, in good enough condition to outrace anyone from our crew. The two men dropped with a thud under Seth and Geoff's shots. By the time they turned around, Jensen had vanished into the distance.

Smoke wafted in the air, residual from the gunfire into a gray morning, and the rusted scent of blood rose from the splatters across the deck. Lone seagulls whirled over the wharf as if to greet the oncoming tides while the four of us stood on a deserted warehouse dock littered by bodies and burdened with some costly box we never wanted.

CHAPTER THIRTEEN

I barely recalled our walk back while we stumbled through the sluggish haze of dawn. No one said a word. Jensen had escaped, our employer turned on us, and we were stuck with a box that we didn't want but the rest of the world did. None of that mattered compared to the real problem. Captain Morris was dead.

We remained wordless when we boarded the ship, and since each of us was grimmer than before, most of the crew scattered. Hiram approached me holding a bunch of stuff wrapped in a blanket. He stood in weighted silence though his eyes kept darting away from me.

"What do you need?"

"Sorry to bother, Captain," he stuttered. "But we have Jensen's—I mean the traitor's belongings from the barracks. What do you want me to do with them?"

"Throw them overboard," I muttered, slamming my back against the shipside. Thinking of Jensen made the ache in my chest twist bitterly.

"A-Are you sure?" Hiram asked as he walked towards the ledge. I sighed and pulled myself up from the ground.

"Give his things to me."

Hiram dropped the bundle into my arms. While the load was surprisingly light, sharp corners jabbed into my arms from whatever the blanket held. I strode off to my room, not bothering to give him a goodbye.

Once I shut the door, I dropped the bundle onto the floor, and several books tumbled out with untouched covers and fresh pages. A stack of "Busty Wench" magazines slapped on the floor followed by the clatter of riot wrestling figurines. He hadn't brought much with him, but he never had a lot of belongings on the ship anyway. The important ones, he took: his arsenal of weaponry and his gear to cut through alarms like the thermal lance, which he'd had since day one aboard the ship. Seeing his belongings scattered on the floor only reminded me of my Captain. Unarmed. Blood seeping in a pool around the traitor's feet.

Hatred as bold as a brand burned into me again. I yanked one of his magazines from the floor and hurled it against my wall as hard as possible. It clattered to the floor, making my mirror tremble, so I ground my heel into the cover. When the cover didn't break, I kicked the book across the room. All I could see was Morris lying on the floor and Jensen standing over him. I picked up another magazine, ripping it in half. He killed him. My Captain.

The pages crumbled to shreds underneath my anxious fingers, and I ripped and ripped until the pieces flew like muted confetti at my feet. I seized one of the riot wrestling figurines with their stupid painted faces and their ridiculous costumes and just squeezed it in my hand. All that time we spent aboard the ship. Nothing.

I hurled the figure against the wall with the rest of his things. My body gave up supporting me, and I just stared at the ground on all fours. The floorboards swirled around, and water threatened to creep into my eyes, but I blinked them shut before that happened.

As I tried to sit up, I careened backwards. My back slammed against the hardwood floors, and a piece of paper fluttered from one of the opened books. It landed right next to my head. I slowly extricated myself from the floor and picked up the leaf of paper.

'39° 31′ 38″ N, 119° 49′ 19″ W

SSN-571'

My fingers closed over it, ready to crumble the paper like everything else, but I stopped myself. Those looked like coordinates for a map. Folding the note, I tucked it into my pocket and surveyed Jensen's belongings scattered across my floor. The shredded magazine bits snuck into the cracks of the floorboards and splattered across the planks like drops of blood. I shuddered. The mess in the captain's room waited for me as if begging to shred apart whatever coherency I still clung to.

Sighing, I stalked out of my room and to the galley for a bucket. Filling it with water, I gripped a mop and several rags before making my way down the corridor to the captain's quarters. My stomach dropped, and my mind retreated to a faraway place. None of the crew would see this scene because no one should've had to experience that horror.

My hand paused on the door because hours ago, I had stumbled onto my worst nightmare. I closed my eyes and took a deep breath. The responsibility passed to me, not my crew—I hesitated for a moment—I said my crew. Loathing coated my entire being to think I'd be so presumptuous. The bodice compressed more than usual, and my breaths left me in short erratic spurts. Grabbing the knob, I opened the door, toting in the cleaning equipment.

My Captain lay in the same place as he did before, sunken into the pool of his own blood. The coppery stench turned my stomach, but I ignored the queasiness. This was my job. No one else's. His face had paled further, and a filmy gaze stared back at me, so I shut his open eyes and closed his shocked mouth. An acidic bubble of grief lodged in my throat, pushing up bile, and I sucked in three shaky breaths before continuing. I pulled his aviator cap from the floor, red dripping from the earflaps. The same red that formed into the puddles.

The mop wouldn't suffice, but it paved the way. Captain always kept a clean ship. He said keeping her tidy showed our pride in her, and the Desire deserved the best. I dipped the mop into the bucket, sloshing the water onto the ground. Before I cleaned any more, I picked up the captain and tugged him away from the mess. The coldness emanating from his body sent a racking, silent sob through my own. I clenched the mop handle. Control. For awhile I just pushed around red liquid.

After some time and the towels I brought, the mop cleaned the floor. I gathered his belongings and placed them back into the desk drawers. They shouldn't lay scattered around like discarded trash. The door to his bedchambers still hung open, so I walked inside and pulled out a spare blanket, resting it over the stiff form of my Captain. Although the large pool of blood cleared up, a mark on the floor remained, staining a shade darker than the wood.

I picked up the mop, bucket, and the bloody towels. My mind rejected most thoughts, so bleached from the tragedy this morning. Walking out onto the deck, I flung the sullied water over the side, ignoring the deckhands around me. Memories kept trying to breach the surface, but I shoved them away. They'd only bring me pain.

Ocean air invaded my dulled senses, which had been raped by the stench and sight of blood. The breeze turned my stomach with the realization of what I'd smelled that entire time. My Captain's blood. I scrabbled to the edge to heave my guts out.

I didn't stop until my stomach emptied its meager contents and then I turned and slumped against the side of the ship. Several deckhands averted their gaze from me since they didn't want to get caught staring. Not like I cared. My limbs draped at my sides, and I glared at the mottled gray sky. The dimmed sun hurt my sore eyes even though I hadn't shed a tear. That's not what a first mate did. We couldn't appear weak before the crew, me and my Captain. I glanced at my rumpled chemise, the edges draping over my dirt-streaked pants. So much for looking classy.

Geoff crouched in front of me. His body cast a relieving shadow over my weary eyes, but I turned my head away from him. Sympathy wouldn't aid me right now. Dulcet words, pretty little memories, they meant shit when the captain was dead. He didn't move away.

Seagulls zoomed overhead, flapping their greedy wings and cawing out to the breeze. They circled around the beached ship, interrupting our silent pause. Neither of us said a word, but I was painfully aware of his presence.

"You need a drink." Geoff didn't ask, he commanded. "And I have some whisky in the navigation chambers. Come with me."

I exhaled a grateful sigh that Geoff knew the exact words to say because most statements would brush me the wrong way. Anger bubbled underneath my surface and waited to rip someone's head off. Besides, a drink would do me an open sky of good. He offered a hand up, and I let him pull me forward. For such a lithe man, he had a powerful grasp and yanked my weight around effortlessly. Numb tingling ran up my legs as I stumbled along towards the chambers. When we reached the door, Geoff tossed it open, and I followed him in.

Sunlight cascaded through the circular windows, but I strode towards the shade. I didn't feel comfortable sitting under broad daylight with the sun's warmth taunting me from afar. Right now I wanted a dark corner, an endless supply of mead, and one of Edwin's weird concoctions. If he could whip up a memory erasure potion, he'd be a god. The stacks of maps didn't litter the room like they had the other day since Geoff had put them all back into the cabinets and individual folders they belonged in. He'd even tucked away all the chronometers and compasses into the many drawers lining the stained maple dresser along the side.

I sat on the ground, not bothering to pull out a chair, and pressed my back against the wall. The leather soles of my boots tapped against the wooden floor at a slow and steady pace, and strands of my unkempt hair brushed against my shoulders. The pit in my stomach still hadn't left, our unsaid words making it harder and harder to keep the pain at bay. He'd have questions, hell the whole crew had questions, but I didn't have any answers. Geoff pulled out a miniature cherry wood trunk with an ornate brass lock.

"Don't trust anyone, do you?" I swung my foot back and forth before me.

"With liquor around here? You don't think I'm that big a fool, do you?" Our banter continued like it always did, but a somber undercurrent dwelled below. Geoff and I ran on autopilot because we had to, since both of us worked on this ship long enough to know our roles. Breaking down helped no one. My arm ached enough to draw my attention. The spot on my wrinkled chemise was torn and soaked with blood from where a bullet had grazed earlier. Genius I was, I left the wound unattended.

"Damn," I swore. My head tingled, but my mind had numbed after the scene from this morning. Flecks of blood stained my white chemise. After cleaning the...mess from the chambers, I hadn't registered my own open wound causing the residual stench.

Geoff glanced over. "You never took care of that? Are you asking for an infection?" his voice came out sharp.

"Ideally, yes," I said. "But for the time being, pass me your cheap liquor." He pulled open the drawer from the cabinet where he kept his maps and passed me a glass bottle filled with rum. A thin layer of liquid coated the bottom. I took it from his hands and sat it down beside me. My chemise was ruined. The blood would stain that white fabric forever, so I ripped my other sleeve to shreds.

"You know, Edwin does have bandage downstairs." He pulled out the chair and took a seat. "I'm sure he'd be glad to fix you up. He also has antiseptic that doesn't burn like hundred-proof liquor."

"Maybe I'm a masochist." I passed him a half smile through gritted teeth. "Besides, I managed to make it in here, but my legs aren't going to carry me much further today."

He nodded and crouched beside me. "Let me help at least.

You can't tie a tight tourniquet at that angle on your arm."

I shrugged and right after wished I hadn't. The pain had been blissfully numb until my acknowledgement, and now the ache roared into the forefront of my perception. I pulled up my bloody, tattered sleeve, rolling the rag around my shoulder.

Geoff positioned my arm out straight despite the protests of my muscles. He pulled the cork out with his teeth and spat it on the floor. Rum hit the open wound, causing my body to tense with the sudden burning onslaught. Bullets had grazed me before though and would again, so I gritted my teeth and kept my mouth shut. Geoff wrapped the strips of cloth tight around the wound to stop stray drips of blood from trickling down my arm. I relaxed against the wall when he tied the knot to close the bandage off and let my arm drop back to my side.

"Good, now that you're all wrapped up, I'll bring out the real stuff." He opened his dark wooden chest and pulled out the whisky. Long and thin with a twisted neck, the glass bottle's curves suggested a class higher than the cheap booze we normally drank. This one was seven-eighths full. He pulled the cork nice and slow, and I shifted my hips against the floor. Geoff handed me the open bottle first. "Here. You need this."

I anticipated the burn before the whisky ever reached my lips. The golden liquid swished around the bottle and coated my tongue. It seared my throat, sending warmth running through my extremities the way aged, smooth whisky did. I choked the splutter but wriggled under its numbing prowess. With my clean arm, I wiped my mouth off and passed the bottle back to Geoff.

"To Captain Morris," I mumbled. The words barely passed my lips before Geoff shoved the bottle back in my face for another draught.

"To him," his voice rose a shade louder than a whisper but echoed with bitterness. "Where are we going to find him?" Geoff glanced into the bottle before taking another long sip.

"We'll find a lead from someone. The traitor abandoned his crew and doesn't have a ship, so he's stuck down here."

"Good." Geoff took another swig before handing the bottle off again. "What'll we do about..." He didn't finish his statement. His mouth opened, but the words wouldn't come out.

"Tomorrow." I shook my head and took a deep swig. The whisky burned and numbed but in the right way to stave off that horrible scene. I blinked, realizing we had already demolished half the bottle. Half a bottle and I hadn't drank nearly enough. "Any plans can wait until tomorrow." He sank back into his chair, as much of a broken pocket watch as me.

I studied his figure before me.

Long strands of brown hair dangled over his sunken eyes which burned with a dull, helpless anger from the onset of this massive blow. The corners of his wide mouth turned down. Several buttons of his bedraggled black shirt had opened and exposed his lithe chest. The man stood too tall to be burly like Seth but contained a deceptive amount of muscle to his lanky frame.

My eyes trailed down the length of his body, and my cheeks began burning. Must have been the whisky catching up to me. I averted my gaze when I realize I sat there gaping at him. That motion rushed my head with the dizzy swirl of alcohol, and I basked in the sweet bliss the feeling brought me.

The wet stench of blood stunk from my clothing, particularly my damp and devastated chemise. Pressing my back further against the wall, I popped the first buttons of my bodice. Geoff snuck a glance, not very subtly either. His cheeks had reddened, and the whisky bottle he held only contained a mere quarter of liquid left inside. Slowly and deliberately, I arched my back, fumbling with another few buttons lining my bodice. The black piece slipped off my shoulders, and my shirt slumped onto the floor. My dark brown bra crept into vision from the rips and holes in the deteriorated chemise.

Before I could go any further, Geoff passed me the bottle of whisky. I gripped the neck with one hand, lifted a finger, and winked before I took a deep draft. Whisky flowed through my veins this time, and I no longer spluttered with my sips. My chest burned but with a different sort of tension, and I squeezed my legs together. I offered him the bottle back, but his eyes hadn't left me. Under his attention, I writhed with restrained lust.

My chemise became a burden, and my chest heaved with excitement and the quixotic allure of whisky. The broad daylight cast several husky strains over my skin, and I loosened the strings keeping my chemise up. Slowly, I peeled the ragged fabric off my body.

With a light thump, my shirt fell to the floor, and Geoff placed the bottle on the desk. I rolled my shoulders further back and thrust my chest forward, the exposed, damp skin prickling under the open air. Geoff tried to glance back at the desk as if unawares, but the reoccurring looks my way didn't help him in the slightest.

My cheeks burned, and my body tingled. Finally, my brain stopped whirring and gave up to the sweet abandon of smooth, smooth whisky. Something so pure and animalistic required no thinking. Feeling stirred within me, pushing my body forward without permission from my mind. I had Geoff's full attention.

His dark brown eyes studied me with a hunger I longed for, so I lifted myself from the floor, closing the space between us. The couple steps stretched out like an endless stairwell, but I stopped an inch from him. So close, his furnace of a body heated me further and threw more fuel to the blaze already burning within.

I pressed myself against him and met his lips with a fierce, passionate kiss.

CHAPTER FOURTEEN

He kissed back, and the adrenaline thrilled my veins. I tasted the sweet cinnamon on his lips from those sticks he chewed, and it tingled against my own. Seven years worth of pent up passion flooded through me. For all the times we'd visited each other's rooms late at night, sat together under the open stars on deck, and passed a quick peck on the cheeks or caress to the back, we'd never kissed. I'd been sorely missing out. My lips sought his again, and I ran my fingers down the side of his neck.

Geoff stepped back from the kiss, away from me. I frowned. My entire body ached with eagerness, and I stumbled towards him. He placed both hands on my shoulders, staring into my eyes.

"I want this. Gods, you know I do, but not this way—not now. You're spurred by grief, and I won't be some fling for you." His words hit me with a sharp rebuff the same time the alcohol rose to my head, and I stepped back as if struck.

My breaths came out slow and husky. Vague guilt bubbled in the back of my mind, but I was so drunk my feet wobbled beneath me, and those feelings took a backseat to my confusion. A blush burned my cheeks, and I staggered. Luckily, Geoff caught me. He placed a blanket around my shoulders and walked me over to his bedroom. The ceiling spun above me, and several times I tripped over my own feet.

The door opened with a creak, and I stepped inside, guided by his arm around my shoulder. Dull rays of light spilled into the blackened room from the entrance where in the corner, Geoff's bed lay covered with rumpled sheets and bloated pillows. I stubbed my foot on something hard and glanced down. A model of a copper robot stared back at me with a glare from its porthole eyes and a helm's wheel gracing its tiny stomach. I took a seat on his bed as my head whirled with the spins. My body protested the change from lusty onslaught to nothing, but my respect for Geoff trumped any more drunken impulses.

He pressed his hands against my shoulders, and I collapsed onto the bed. After he pulled the blanket over my body, he brushed wisps of hair from my face, the motion sending electric shivers across my skin. I yanked the blankets tighter. The bed dipped beside me, and Geoff sat. He tilted my chin up with his finger, placing a soft kiss on my forehead. I writhed in the bliss from his touch, and my eyes fluttered with weariness. His presence emanated safety, and the whisky tinged my nerves with mindless abandon. Warmth flooded through my body, carrying me off to slumber.

***

I awoke to a darkened room, and my head pounded with an earthquake-sized hangover. Once I tossed the blankets off me, I glanced down at my chest, only covered by my bra. My foot stung, and I glared at the little robot statue planted on his floor. Piles of Geoff's pants, tailcoats, and fitted shirts rose to meet the top of his bed. Seven different clocks sprawled overtop his dresser, from old brassy ones to the neon blue glare of a holographic display. Whatever organization he used in the navigation bay obviously didn't apply to his own chambers.

Geoff sat slumped in a nearby chair, strands of his long brown hair dangling over his face. His arms crossed over his chest, and his shoulders jutted upwards in a way that couldn't be comfortable. For a brief moment I couldn't remember why I lay in Geoff's bed without a shirt, and I sat, rubbing the crust away from my eyes. My back seared with the strain of a long rest as I pushed myself over to the edge of the bed.

The sobering memories of what I'd witnessed upon my last wake up flooded through me in such a strong torrent my body convulsed. Embarrassment and guilt wore me like a new peacoat after what a sweetheart Geoff had been last night. He stopped me from doing something stupid and took care of me even though he had his own hurt to deal with. Just another reason why I should've listened to Morris's advice about Geoff and I while I'd been a carefree first mate. But I couldn't now. I had a crew to oversee, a traitor to kill, and a dangerous box we didn't want.

I approached the door but paused, watching Geoff's chest swelling under the lull of sleep from where he hunched over. My hand gripped his chin and I gently lifted his face an inch away from mine. Tension bubbled between us, heating my skin, but I shook my head. We shouldn't go down that path. I couldn't. I let his chin drop and rifled a hand through his ragged hair before exiting the room.

Early light streamed into the navigation chambers. I'd slept from yesterday afternoon through the night thanks to a whisky inspired slumber. My tattered chemise and bodice marred the otherwise clean planked floor, so I looped my arms through the bodice and buttoned up the front. The torn chemise lay crinkled on the floor, but I picked it up anyway. Jittery anxiety crawled through my veins like coffee on an empty stomach. Today I had to do some housekeeping.

Dew-chilled air settled over me when I exited the navigation chambers. A couple crew members stole glances but still none spoke. I strode down the steps into the cabins. Edwin's hangover cure couldn't help this whisky laden brew of grief and besides; the pain helped me focus better. The more my head roared, the less I dwelled on memories.

The stale light of electric candles cast sullen shadows along my parchment stained walls. I closed shut the jewelry box I'd left open on my dresser and avoided my reflection, even though the mirror's glint taunted me with glimpses. My trunk hung half-open from yesterday with stray sleeves drooping out from the top like octopus tentacles. A breeze wafted through my doorframe carrying with it the salty tang of salt water air.

The bloodstained bodice and pants clung to my body like a filthy memory. I ripped the clothes off, rummaging through the trunk for my olive breeches and dark brown leather tunic. They'd do. I pulled on the fresh clothes and tied back my long tangled curls. A slap to the face sent tingling through my numb, clouded mind.

With a sigh, I stepped in front of the mirror. Grief sucked away any vivacity from my sullen blue eyes.

"Dammit," I cursed at myself. The woman in the mirror had bags under her eyes and a sour frown, accompanied by slumped shoulders as her knees bent from unsteadiness. Her Captain passed away, and she couldn't fit into the aviator cap. But I was all they had. If we didn't move fast we'd be helpless as a bloated tick riding a puddle. I glanced back in the mirror. Although buried deep, a spark of determination returned to my eyes, and I lifted my chin. Time to face the crew.

The tough soles of my boots thudded against the steps leading to the deck, and I took a deep breath before emerging topside. No one stood by the navigation bay since we were docked, but Jack spotted me from his lookout roost and gave me a salute.

I called to him, "Come on down."

The broad-shouldered man jumped down from his perch and approached me. "What did you want?" He avoided my gaze.

"Gather the crew. We have some business to take care of."

He nodded and without a reply, ran off. I stalked over to the helm. The elevated location gave me enough of a height and space to view the crew. Taking a seat on the step, I waited. Soon everyone filtered across the deck, and my heart skipped a beat when Geoff stumbled from the navigation chamber clutching his head. Before long, the crew stood before me passing quips and whispers until their voices hummed like a freighter's steady thrum. I clutched my forehead with a silent apology to my pulsing mind at what came next.

"Listen up, crew," I shouted in a bellow that rivaled the captain's. My headache hated me, but the crew silenced, and I had their rapt attention. Quiet somber faces stared back at me.

"I tried on the maid outfit and it didn't fit. I'm not that talented at this housekeeping business." A few smiles broke through the crowd, and I straightened my back. "Look, I may not be who you want as Captain, but I'm what you have. So take your complaints and throw them overboard. I've as much use for them as empty whisky bottles." I caught Geoff's eyes but kept going.

"We're not in a perfect spot. We were counting on that job to keep the Desire running, but we saw how that ended. We hold the cargo still, so the British merchants will be after us. Our ex-employer double crossed us, so he'll send men too. If we stay here, we're asking to get boarded. But the most important issue is Jensen. Traitors don't roam free, not after taking our cargo," loathing crept into my voice, "and especially not after murdering our Captain."

"He doesn't have a ship, but the man's resourceful. We have to stop him before he runs out of our sights. But that surfaces another problem. Jensen was our recon man and now first mate duties are open. Let's be honest, if I don't have a counterbalance to my insane plans, we'll plummet nose first into the sea." I quieted to test the crowd and see what whispers arose. None did.

"Geoff." I gestured him forward. "You'll be taking over my old duties as first mate." I cracked a half smile and fought to keep my composure. "Captain Morris always said I should've known my navigation better for my position. Plus, you keep a level head. We need that." His mouth dropped open but no words came out. Somehow, he hadn't expected this.

"Spade." I pointed in his direction. "You'll take over Geoff's duties as navigator. We'll work on finding a helmsman to replace. Any of you deckhands, if you've had an inclination, talk to me later. As for Jensen's replacement, we need someone who's already adept and trained with so many enemies after us." Spade and Geoff stood beside me, but neither said a word. Despite their new positions, any celebrations fell by the wayside in lieu of action against our immediate threats.

"To you all, take what time you need between now and sundown. If you're hoping to stretch your legs, do so. Watch your back, and be careful. We don't know where Jensen ran nor do we know if the ex-employer has us identified. Regardless, be here tonight at sunset. We'll see the captain off then." As soon as I finished speaking, the crew dispersed. I waved Isabella over and placed my hands on Geoff and Spade's shoulders, so they'd stay too.

"You three are coming with me," my voice lowered to a less head-splitting pitch. The four of us walked into the navigation chambers where just the night before I drank with Geoff. We entered the room, and I claimed the seat. If being Captain meant anything, I won dibs on chairs. Spade's expression hadn't changed throughout my speech, and weariness sunk his blue eyes while frown lines tugged on his black whiskered chin. Isabella wore a mask of indifference to hide her anguish. The occasional tremble of her lip gave her true feelings away, but otherwise she held herself together. Geoff opened the cabinets and pulled out maps of Sutcliffe and Reno.

I lifted an eyebrow. "Less than five minutes on the job and already you're reading my mind, boy-o. I couldn't have made a better choice. Everyone gather round and we'll talk."

"You don't waste any time," Isabella shot back. My temper had skated a tensile thread since yesterday. It snapped.

"No, darling," my words came out a snarl. "If we waste time, you'll end up corpses. I had to clean up my Captain's yesterday, and

I don't want another. Grieving's a pretty sentiment, but not all of us have the luxury."

Isabella closed her mouth, and her chestnut eyes glistened with unshed tears. She glanced at her skirts while smoothing them down. Nobody said a word.

I let my temper simmer before I spoke again. "Obviously we need to leave port. But if we leave, we lose our chance to take care of Jensen."

"Would he stay though?" Geoff interjected. "He was a few buttons short of a blouse, but the man knows how to survive."

"Jensen? He wouldn't stay, but where would he run?" I crossed one leg over the other and tapped my foot in the air. Geoff placed his maps onto the table. His neat handwriting marked all the coordinates to important drop sites we'd visited in the past. My finger pressed onto the black inked numbers, and I dipped my hand into my pocket. "Hold on a tick." I fished out the paper I'd found the day before. "This. I found this tucked in with Jensen's stuff. Do you recognize the coordinates, Geoff?"

He took the paper from me, scanning over it for a moment. Geoff glanced back and forth between the maps he had placed on the table and the wrinkled piece of paper. "That far West, we're already in the area." His finger followed along the map until it stopped right on the large dot marking Reno.

"That fool boy," Isabella spoke, her voice gentler than

before. "He'd be going straight to the nearest city in running distance. Of course he'd be in Reno."

"If we port there though," Spade said, "we're slapped with another docking fee we can barely pay, and the Brits could easily dock. If they find us, we're wide open to attack."

"If we stay here we're boned too." I hunched over, resting my elbows on my knees. "Our ex-employer wanted the box and no strings left attached. We're screwed if we leave, screwed if we stay. I'd recommend leave, but are there any side ports besides the Reno main?" I glanced toward Geoff who already pored over the open map. His long finger travelled along the lines of the map but stopped and hovered right to the side of Reno. I leaned over, squinting for a closer peek.

"There's a smaller lesser known dock past Reno proper and in the nastier parts of town," he said. "The port wouldn't be safe, and we'd have to keep a tight watch on our girl. But we'd stay under the radar, and the fee's next to nothing."

"Geoff, you're brilliant." My heart jumped in excitement. I slung an arm around his neck and pulled him close, but the nearness reminded me of the night prior. Just as fast I moved away, though not before a slight blush tinged his cheeks. I picked up the paper with the coordinates to cause a distraction. "What about the second number? The SSN-571?"

Geoff shrugged. "No idea. Those numbers sound more like

an identification tag than any navigational lingo."

"At least it gave us a direction." I crumpled the paper into a ball and tossed it onto the ground. "We'll travel tonight. If we're not on a clear horizon we have less chance of being seen."

"After," Isabella stopped, and her voice shook. Her lips formed a thin line as she forced the words out. "After the Captain..." she trailed off.

"Yes." Familiar numbness clenched my jaw, blurring my vision. "Tonight." We left the cabin, and I gave orders for a rowboat, tinder, stone, and some soil. The Captain deserved better, but we would send him off the best way we could manage right now.

***

Sundown came faster than any of us prepared for. Some of the crew had wandered off during the wait while others holed up in their rooms, and more roamed the deck like aimless orphaned children. I hid in my chambers. A blank pad sat before me, ready for when I started writing what to say, but instead I just tapped my finger stylus against the desktop.

A pocket knife dangled from a cord, attached to the jutted wooden desk corner. I stole that knife from a Morlock the day

Isabella got shot. Captain and I looted the bodies, trying to find something to salvage from the botched operation.

I searched for words, hour after hour, but nothing surfaced in my mind. Nothing solidified the void he left, or the emptiness wrenching my insides. Out the window, the first signs of sunset cast amber rays along my desk, causing my heart to race like the aether batteries of our engine. Crimson streaks trickled through the broad horizon like loose threads on a frayed tapestry.

My limbs seized. I didn't want to go. I couldn't. The crazy events over the past two days still held a touch of unreality, and that sense of wading through a nightmare kept me going. Once tonight faded, the Captain's passing became real, and I couldn't return to the past. A deep breath hardly settled me, but the air coerced my muscles into motion. I grabbed a bottle of rum from my dresser and left. With each step towards the surface, my emotions wound tighter like a cork readied to zip from the bottle. I approached the deck where the crew rallied.

Without a word, I tapped Seth on the shoulder. I didn't have to explain his job as Morris's oldest friend. We trudged into the captain's quarters and lifted the body, carrying his inert form wrapped in the blanket. I didn't glance down, just focused on getting him up and onto the deck.

The rowboat I'd asked for shifted back and forth in the waters below. We maneuvered the corpse down the rope ladder and onto the docking bay. I focused on the bottle of rum in my holster, thudding against my hip rather than the man wrapped in the blanket. Slowly, the deck filled up around us, and our crew trickled down, but I scarcely paid attention. This task consumed the remaining sanity I clung to. Seth and I placed Captain Morris in the rowboat.

For a moment, I stopped and stared.

Despite the blood and the terrible way he died, Captain Robert Morris seemed peaceful. Though his skin had turned an ashen white, and a chill emanated from the blanket, his eyes closed in final rest. The scar on his lip glowed under the battered sunset and forced through several rough memories of that job so many years back when he saved my life. The sun descended against the horizon line with a finality reserved for this occasion.

Seth and I heaved the buckets of soil and stone overtop his still body to create the tumulus. No one offered any help because nobody wanted to. Burying the captain wasn't a task I ever thought I'd have to do. Next on the pile we placed dry wood, and several deckhands brought some over to help us. We scattered the tinder over the rowboat, and Seth stepped back. I pulled out the rum, kissing the bottle before spreading the contents over the kindling. No one in the crew uttered a word, as silent as the setting sun until I found my voice from its hiding spot and stood before the boat.

"Captain Robert Morris," my voice faltered. Seth reached from his jumpsuit and offered me his fabled flask. He never offered anyone the flask. I took a deep draft of spiced rum thicker than syrup, letting it strengthen my resolve. "He built her. From the ground up, built this girl and treasured her, more than most knew. You could tell by more than just the ship though. The Captain's care, his strength, and his pride shone through us. He pulled most of us from crap situations and took us under his wing. The Desire became our home when we had none." Tears glittered in the eyes of many of the crew, and more than a couple choked sobs echoed across the deck.

"He offered us a home, offered us companionship. Taught us, trained us. His impact will never be lessened. Ever. Captain Morris will live on through every single one of us. His ideals will resurrect when we protect ours and every time we take care of his girl, the one love of his life. Desire's not just some ship. She's a treasure of the skies, and he always knew it. So we'll keep his dream alive and protect her with our lives."

I lit the tinder and dropped it onto the kindling. Seth helped me push the boat out into the waves as the fire spread. The flames licked across the tumulus, and the glimmer of fire rivaled the golden burning sun as it crashed onto the horizon line. We watched in silence, his entire crew, as the boat drifted further and further into the ocean until the burning vessel melded with the fiery hues of the sunset in the distance.

"To Captain Robert Morris." I saluted the disappearing boat. A murmur of repetition sounded behind me, and we watched as the vessel carried our Captain away, out to meet the depths of the sea.

CHAPTER FIFTEEN

We filed back on board, and true to our plans, Spade and Geoff set sail. Lucky for us the captain already paid her fee, so we were free to go. Unlucky for us, we hadn't bought the new parts Seth needed to fix Desire. We'd have to find them in Reno and pray we didn't have any interceptions along the way.

I stalked along Desire's whorled wooden planks and wandered over toward the navigation bay. Her limbs creaked as we ascended into the night sky, and a full moon cleared our path. The stars glittered like gold in a pan rushed by a stream. I leaned against one of the beams supporting the canopy, and my shoulders slumped. Desire's steam engine kicked in as her ivory balloon inflated in full again. Moonlight glinted off the steel bands around the lookout, and the nickel plating held the navigation bay sturdy.

With her full colors on display, the ship ascended, and we cleared the dock. Spade stood by the helm with both hands guiding the wheel, and Geoff took his position at her thrusters. He pressed on them in slow spurts to drive the power necessary for full sail.

"I hope the sudden change didn't shock you boys out of your panties. I assumed you'd both be man enough to handle the position." I passed them a saucy wink. Spade smirked back, but

Geoff's expression didn't change. "Anyway," I continued, "I hate to break up this perfect romance here, but we'll be finding you a new helmsman, Spade. When we begin our search for someone else, I'd like your input since they'll be working alongside you."

I placed a hand on Geoff's shoulder. Warmth emanated through his clothes like the heat of a boiler tank, and I briefly recalled the honeyed taste of his lips. "And you get to do your favorite thing, keep me in line." He didn't say anything. Had last night had been too much for him?

Geoff shook his head, and strands of his wild brown hair swung with the motion. "Well, someone needs to. Let you run rampant with a ship and a crew and within weeks we'll resort to cannibalism."

My voice dropped low. "Good. I'm glad you're okay with it. I'm sure you never wanted the burden, but there's plenty of that going around these days. How far to Reno?" I turned to Spade.

"Morning." He grunted. Shadows coated his stubble, emphasizing the seriousness of his gaze.

"Lovely," I replied. "Why do I get the feeling I won't sleep a wink tonight?"

"Jitters?" Geoff raised a brow. "That's unlike you, doll."

"That was before I had real responsibility. Now I have to wave my fingers and make these 'decision' things. And they affect people now too, not just my own sorry hide." I ran my fingers through my tousled strands. Jitters indeed. More like tensed violin strings right before a concert. The wind picked up with our speed and ruffled my long curls to sweep against my shoulders. We were aloft again, and that alone usually inspired fisticuffs with one of the boys on deck or a game of Faro to bet the little money I had. Emptiness twisted my stomach because I wouldn't feel that carefree again for some time—if ever. I punched Geoff in the shoulder.

"And hey, moving into the first mate cabin, you'll get into my bed!" The joke slipped out, but once I said it, I knew I shouldn't have. Geoff's face darkened, and he didn't respond. Spade avoided my gaze. That time I pushed too far. I turned my head to avoid the hurt I caused, even though it tightened my chest. Loathing crawled through me like a horde of roaches, and I wandered off towards the cabin steps before awkwardness and shame halted my steps. I'd have to apologize for that later, but right now I needed to be away from all these feelings.

Great job as captain, tuck tail and run. Stupid. Why had I said that? Of course he'd be hurting, and Geoff had done nothing but comfort me throughout this whole ordeal. The scuff of my boots echoed down the stairwell. I didn't deserve a friend like him, nor did I deserve the attention he gave me. Shadows curled around the lamps lighting the hallway, making their glow more desperate.

The door to the infirmary lay at the end of the hall. I sped down the corridor and tugged at the doorknob, ready to distract myself with something else. Isabella and Edwin sat at the table. A couple of days ago Jensen sat with them, and his hulking shoulders loomed over everyone else. My blood boiled at his name, but I still struggled to disassociate any good memories of him. After such a heinous action, I could never forgive him.

"Does anyone have a stiff drink?" I asked and stepped into the room. Adelle lay on one of the beds with her wounded ankle propped up over a pillow.

Isabella's face softened, and she tried on a smile. "Now Bea, you haven't been taking Seth's advice on captainship have you?"

"If I took Seth's advice, I'd already have a flask handy." I pulled up a seat at the table. "What are you folks doing to pass the time?"

"It's hard to think of doing anything with Captain Morris gone." Edwin tapped his fingers against the table. "I spend all this time fixing up the crew and then we go and lose him."

A familiar lump rose in my throat again, and I straightened my back. "Didn't you hear, Edwin? We're playing the light conversation game," I said. My fingers dug into the cushion of the chair, imprinting divots into the vinyl.

"We'll grieve however we choose to." Isabella's words were clipped. She passed me a glare, and Edwin stifled a sob as she placed an arm around him. He pressed his shaky palms against the table, his body shaking as silent tears poured down his cheeks.

Isabella leaned against him, holding tight.

Bitterness roiled around my stomach. Neither of them witnessed Jensen's betrayal, nor did they clean up the mess. I was the one who had to tough up for the crew, so I could bury and burn my Captain. All I wanted to do right now was to shoot the hell out of something or tumble into bed with someone.

I pulled my chair over by Adelle's bed. Since we brought her in, I barely had the chance to speak with her, and besides, I needed some sort of distraction before I pissed off my entire crew. Adelle turned her head, studying me with those inquisitive almond eyes. She wore the same dirty overalls, the fabric dimpling from the size.

"How are you feeling?" I asked. "The ankle doing better?" Edwin must have wrapped her ankle because the gauze sealed up tighter than an engine piston. The man might be scatterbrained, but no one cleaned wounds like him. I ignored the hushed sniffles from Isabella and Edwin behind me.

"It's okay. Mr. Edwin gave me something to drink, so it doesn't hurt any more, but I'm not allowed to walk around on it much. He said it'll make my ankle worse." She folded her arms over her chest, and I caught the minor glare in his direction. I hid my grin. Definitely still a teenager.

"Edwin makes some pretty crazy drafts. You'll do well to listen to him. He's a skilled doctor. Are you feeling more comfortable on the ship?"

She nodded with the hint of a smile. "I like it better. The slaver caravan wasn't..." She shuddered, and I remained silent, waiting for her to continue. "Before that, I lived with a bunch of other people. My parents sent me off to a boarding school when I got too smart, but I think they just didn't know what to do with me. I haven't seen them in years." Parental neglect, something else I could relate to.

"Well, you have a place here as long as you put in your work." I winked.

She gave me a tentative grin, but it faltered. "What happened to that man who welcomed me on board? Did someone kill him?"

My tongue prepared a sharp retort, and anger surged into my stomach. But I stopped. The poor thing was a teenager, new to the ship, and had no idea what happened. I took in a deep breath and calmed myself. The simple action of pausing before I spoke gave me the prescience to stay composed.

"That man was our Captain. A crew mate, Jensen, stole our cargo and murdered him."

Her eyebrows wrinkled in confusion. "The other one who helped me?" she asked. I nodded but couldn't wrangle the words. "That's very sad." The statement struck me like a slap. So simple, so unassuming, but completely true.

"You're right," my voice lowered to a hush and cracked.

"Captain Morris was an honorable man. The best of us." Isabella and Edwin's gazes heated my back, but I didn't bother turning around.

"Are you in charge now?" She tilted her head, and long strands of her black hair shifted down her back. I nodded again, not daring to speak after showing that much weakness. My eyes stung, and my throat tightened.

"Yes," I said after a moment. "I'm leading the crew. But I'm going to take care of everyone, don't you worry. We're going to catch that traitor and make him pay for hurting our Captain."

She nodded, satisfied with my response. "I know you will. You saved me."

This girl didn't hold back the emotional punch. I bit my lip to keep it from trembling. Several deep breaths calmed me again, and I pinched the blue cameo around my neck to regain control before picking up her hands in mine.

"You know what we say around this ship?" I told her, "We protect ours. Even though the captain's gone, that won't change one bit. I will always protect mine." My voice took on a ragged edge, but I kept my breathing even. Edwin and Isabella's sniffles were not helping in the slightest. "We're heading to Reno. We should be there in the morning, and we'll hunt down that traitor then, don't worry." I reached over and ruffled her hair.

"Not quite morning," she spoke. "We'll be there in less than

a half hour since we're maintaining a steady pace of thirty knots."
My jaw dropped. Just a teenager, my ass. I tilted my head to the
side.

"How...how did you figure that out?" I glanced back to
Isabella and Edwin, but between the wide eyes and confusion, I
assumed they were just as surprised as I was. "Did either of you say
anything?"

"Like I'd know where we are." Isabella snorted. Edwin shook
his head.

Adelle spoke up again. "Well, it's easy to calculate the
airspeed based upon the drift of the ship and our position over
land. We're midway there since Reno isn't that far, and we're not
passing ocean. The winds over the Pacific bring in a different
calculation due to the water's tampering with solid airflow."

I raised both my eyebrows. "Easy for whom?" I muttered.
"Where did you say you went to school again?"

"I didn't." She shrugged. "But I attended the Vernian School
for Gifted Children. I didn't like it very much though." A distant
look overtook her eyes, the same one the captain used to get when
struggling with a bitter old memory. Apparently the slavers hadn't
captured some random girl—she must have been one of their
prized ones. Renewed hatred for those cruel men penetrated my
skin, crawling around underneath.

"How do you calculate that being here inside the cabins?" I

hunched over and rested my elbows against my knees. "You can't even see outside."

"I don't need to. Wherever I am, I've always found my way around—I just feel it." A hint of a smile quirked her lips. "You know when you're little and your mom loses you at the marketplace? She may not have known where I hid, but I was never lost. I've been like that for as far back as I can remember. It's like having a map inside your head for reference at all times."

I exhaled real slowly. "Well doll, that's an important talent you've got."

Edwin opened the book on his table and soaked the pages with his tears before he joined us by her bedside. The surprised lift of his brows wrinkled his forehead, elongating his face. "You say it's been like this since you were born? No implants? No bionics or chips used to alter modes of thinking? Maybe a GPS chip feeds information to your cerebral cortex in blips." He wiped away the remaining liquid around his eyes with his long sleeve. Leave it to Edwin; his professional intrigue trumped any grief he'd dwell over.

"Well, I'm not a robot or anything. I just grew up with the ability. My parents weren't rich enough to pay for those fancy implants you're talking about. The government gave them a hefty chunk of credits to take me into the program."

The bony man quivered with excitement. "I've never heard of a geographical sense trigger. Perhaps in the cerebrum, the lobes honed in on accelerated movement diagnostics." Edwin peered over her. She folded her arms over her chest and rolled her eyes. Brilliant navigational genius or no, the girl still acted like a teenager. I bit back a laugh, stepping away from the bed as Edwin scurried into my spot to bombard the poor girl with tons of his precise scientific questions. Meanwhile, her abilities gave my mind some jerky to gnaw at.

I turned to leave, but a hand tugged at my shoulder. Glancing back, Isabella stood behind me.

"Don't worry sweetie, no one will tell that our fierce ol' Captain choked up." My jaw tensed. Right now her teasing enflamed my temper. Isabella fixed me with her patented no-nonsense look before continuing, "Bea, stop beating yourself up and taking it out on us."

I opened my mouth, ready to retort, but couldn't. Isabella knew me too well and for too long. Hopefully Geoff would understand too.

"Will you be ready to move out once we hit Reno?" I asked her. "Are you still getting dizzy spells from the poison?"

She gave my shoulder a quick squeeze before flashing me an attempted smile. "They've all but stopped at this point. After being out yesterday back in action again, I'm convinced I'll be fine. My leg doesn't have the spring it used to." The shift of her skirt when she lifted up her left leg exposed her caramel skin. "But I can still run, and I've been strength training. Don't leave me behind. I'm going to hammer the nails into that bastard's crucifixion cross. Not even a week ago I—" she stopped but the thought finished itself.

The reason why Isabella would be taking this particularly hard dawned upon me. Only a day before the traitor killed the captain, I woke the two of them up after they spent the night together. I placed a hand on her shoulder and met her eyes with some understanding at long last.

"I'd been with him too," I reminded her. Fresh tears streamed down her face, and I brought her in for a hug. "It'll be okay. We'll throw him overboard." I managed an awkward pat on her back before Isabella pulled away. A smirk twisted her face despite the sticky tears.

"Don't strain yourself too hard." She wiped the tears away. "All this emotional crap, you might get a hernia."

I laughed as I exited, summoning my courage to return back onto the deck where Geoff waited. After the near encounter we almost had and with everyone's emotions brimming at the surface, I knew how my comment hurt him. The man deserved—well he deserved something I couldn't give, but at least my talk with Adelle smacked some sense into me.

The night sky coated the deck in a velvety blue hue, and the full moon sharpened those shadows, casting long jagged lines over the span of the ship. It illuminated the sky with a pearly luminescence, and I yearned back to the summers I spent ashore chasing fireflies before I had any cognizance of the mess of a relationship my folks had. Simple.

Life was simple back then, and I missed that black and white. Hell, I missed the clarity I had when Morris took the lead. He emblemized the good guys for me, and our crew threw their heart and soul into our tasks. Or so I'd thought. The perfect white orb in the sky lay too far out of reach from my gray deck. So many shadows crept over the moon, and I didn't think I'd ever find a way to grasp it.

Spade and Geoff conversed over by the navigational bay. Time to face my actions. Heaving a sigh, I stalked over to interrupt them.

As I walked over, my hips swung with the lazy sway of the ship. Spade and Geoff stopped talking when I approached, and the tension I had left descended once again.

"We're almost at Reno," I said. "I'd say we'll get there in less than a half hour. Ahead of schedule. Right?"

Geoff narrowed his eyes in confusion. "Did one of the crew tell you? We just figured it out ourselves, and there's no way you out-navigated us. No offense."

"None taken." I lifted my hands. "The young girl we picked up holds as many mysteries as that box. She rattled off our current course down in the infirmary. I'm not talking a decent sense of direction—she's a living, breathing map."

Spade let out a hard exhale. "Really? So young though."

"Verifiable genius. Edwin almost had an orgasm right on the floor when we found out." Geoff fought with a smile. I caught his eyes, those deep dark brown ones with the hurt shining through. 'I'm sorry' I mouthed. Spade chose that moment to ignore us and focus intently on the aether manipulator. We didn't need to talk to communicate, since Geoff knew me better than that. I slipped a hand onto his back, and his muscles relaxed. The hurt still shone in his eyes, but he nodded. He understood, for now.

"Once her ankle's healed, we'll try her out up here. We may have found ourselves a helmswoman. See how you two get along."

Spade passed me a wary glance, though his hands never left the wheel. "Don't want any babysitting."

"You're just jealous." I laughed. "This girl could school you with her navigating skills."

He cracked a smile. "We'll see."

In the distance, thousands of colored lights lit the city line, glowing with the soft luminescence of frosted lamps. My hand still rested on Geoff's back. It felt so comfortable, so natural there, and with the realization, I yanked it back faster than a quick draw. "Is that Reno?" Before either man noticed the heat that crept onto my cheeks, I wandered over towards the side of the ship.

Tall skyscrapers nudged the violet clouds, and bulbous buildings suspended by balloons littered the mid-zone. Not like we could afford to even breathe in one of those casinos. Ladies and gents inside carried copper cards, not coins, which had no spending limit. The original 'Sin City' claimed a desert oasis, but Reno's scalloped shores combined pre-sunken California's beachside fronts with that same glitz and glamour as old Vegas.

A zeppelin floated by with an advertisement for "Southwest Airships—The Cruise of Your Dreams!" Ten Desires could fit into one of those bloated monstrosities. The city of Reno lit up like a twenty four hour fireworks display. They must have taken the clearance neon paint and striped the town with it because the buildings glowed.

Reno was the city of fame, tourists, and wealth. It also housed one of the largest criminal populations in the States and more poverty than you could cram into the dozens of shelters lining the streets off the main stretch.

And we headed straight into the underbelly.

CHAPTER SIXTEEN

As the Desire progressed closer towards Reno's electric display, the main docks jutted into view as if someone took a marker and drew arrows pointing to them. Those weren't the ones we sought because I'd bet my last lucky cameo the British Merchant ship waited there. In the poorer district we just worried about our ex-employer and the Morlocks.

I squeezed the ledge before heading toward the cabins. How had our situation become this bad? A couple months back we ran through smuggling jobs under Captain Morris without a care in the world, but the day we procured that box, our troubles began. For the hardship it brought us, we couldn't just toss the cargo overboard, not after the he died over it. I pulled the box from the trunk in my room and carried it over to the captain's quarters.

None of his belongings had moved, but no one sat, smoking a cigar behind his large oaken desk. This room would be mine now. The unattended aether lamps cast their green sheen over his ships, which still lay scattered across the floor. Despite the tattered books along his shelf and folders of old job contacts, emptiness dominated the room. His presence, the loyal, bellowing man who resided in these chambers, had left.

I sat the box on the table and stared at the stupid thing, which was locked tighter than Seth's old gun collection. What could be inside this thing to cause so much chaos? The small carvings along the sides of the box glinted under any sort of light, making them impossible to distinguish. I pulled out a paper and pencil from the captain's drawer and placed the sheet against the box. The rubbing clarified the markings, but they looked like a foreign language. Definitely not the international English I learned back in school.

Tucking the folded sheet into my back pocket, I pushed open the door to the captain's bedroom. No one would search for it there, so I wedged the box inside his dresser. I'd take Isabella and Geoff with me, but someone needed to keep an eye out for the cargo. While I still retained some trust, recent events had given me pause. Leaving the captain's quarters, I descended the first flight of steps on the way to the engine room.

The steam greeted me on the final stairwell before the whirring sound of the engine.

"Oi, Seth." I entered the room. A crash was followed by a tinny thud as I opened the door. A smirk hovered over my lips. "Hope I'm not interrupting anything. Need to give her one last peck before you part? I won't judge." Seth fixed me with a flat "no-sass" look, and I sighed, swinging my arms by my sides. "We'll be docking soon, and I'm taking some crew with me. The box is in the captain's quarters tucked in his dresser drawer. You and I are the only ones who know the location. Understood?"

He nodded. I always appreciated Seth's straightforwardness. His ruddy cheeks shone redder than normal, and he offered me a sip from his flask. I gladly accepted while Seth took two sips of his own. He'd grieve in his own way—I wouldn't judge. As long as he kept our ship running, he could drink a jug of whisky a day. Anything was better than these tears.

"Also," I continued, pulling out the rubbing I'd made, "Do any of these look familiar to you? I'm trying to figure out anything more about this box. All I have to go on are these markings around the rim. Morris said he was doing it for Old Germany."

Seth gave me a sharp glance at the mention of Old Germany and took the paper from my hand. "I'll check. I fought in the war with Morris back then...so maybe it'll make sense." Seth placed a beefy oil-smudged hand on my shoulder.

"Take the box down here if you need to for examination, but just keep it out of sight." I ran a hand through my hair.

"Here," he said and handed me a folded paper, weighted down by something inside. I opened it to see a handwritten list with a card tucked inside. "Those are credits the Captain allotted me for repairs. Can you send a crewmember for the parts? I'd trust Spade."

"Of course you would. The two of you would write the shortest book in history," I said. The corner of his mouth tweaked up. "I'll pass it off and get you all the parts you need. With all of these enemies, we need her in top shape."

He grunted, and I left. As I ascended the stairs, the Desire shifted upon descent. The slow deceleration and the slight tremble of the ship as they lay off the thrusters culminated in the eventual landing, but the decline took much longer than flying through clear air. I swung by my room.

The first sleepless night of many passed, and nervous energy still thrummed through my veins. My bed lay dejected in the corner. I bypassed it and tugged on my holster, filling my bag full of rounds. None of the upscale casinos allowed weapons through their perimeters, but the down and dirty streets around this port played by different rules.

I stalked onto the deck and watched as we skated into the ocean again. The main stretch of Reno drew so much attention with flashing neon lights from electric blue to a sizzling green. Glitzy signs advertised hotels like the Time Machine and The Earth's Center. The surrounding glamour made the dim lighting of the lower district landing docks gape like a blackout. Spade and Geoff bustled around the navigation bay hard at work to give Desire a smooth drift into the docks.

The ocean breeze threaded the air when we descended, and I breathed in the salt spray. Isabella approached from below deck. Her salmon off-shoulder gypsy blouse and bobbed skirt made her caramel skin glow. A familiar glint gleamed in her dark eyes with a fierceness I associated with one of ours, which matched the arsenal of pistols strapped on and several knives lining her knee-high black boots. At least she didn't walk with as much of a limp anymore. The cincher around her waist accentuated her already evident curves but fit her like she'd never gone without it. My olive breeches and tailored leather tunic suddenly hung on me like bundled bed sheets.

"I'm all gussied up, Captain." She flashed me a smile. "Now where are you taking me?" The word still jarred me, and I half expected Morris to be standing behind me.

"We're going on a stroll once we touch down. I'm hoping some of the nearby casinos and parlors will have some information. Either about our dear old ex-employer or if anyone's seen someone of Jensen's build. He's not exactly meek and unassuming."

"Knowing him he ran his mouth at someone and threw them into a tizzy anyway. Follow the trail of angry people and we'll have him." She tensed her jaw.

"Maybe you can win at the casino tables while we're at it. We could use the money." The Desire trembled as we hit the water and glided toward the docks. In comparison to the backwater town we landed in before, their docking mechanisms were more advanced, but the rusted beams and piles of trash along the deck lent the bay a grungy subterranean appearance. The balloon clicked onto the metal frame and ground against it as we slid into place.

Geoff emerged from his cabin, having changed into clothes more suitable for walking around town. I hadn't even seen him leave the navigation bay. Geoff knew how to dress, and I ran my tongue over my top lip to keep a wolf whistle at bay. The man looked damn good. His chestnut breeches fit snugly around the waist, and over his black button down shirt he wore a burgundy waistcoat. The ragged black duster his brother gave him hid his weapons. I hadn't been out on a job with either of the two in some time, and nostalgia warmed my bones.

"Looking handsome, sweetheart," Isabella purred when Geoff walked over. "You'll have the ladies crawling over you." He offered her a grin.

"Do those ladies have information? Because if so, you get to be bait." I patted him on the back.

"Lovely. Anything for a worthy cause." He said, looming over us due to his height. I peered over the edge expecting an official to be scurrying our way any second.

"They won't be coming." Geoff glanced over at me. "Officials don't operate this port. We'll be charged, but we don't have the paperwork and forms to fill out. That's not how this section of Reno operates."

"You speak like you know from experience," I commented.

"I may be a brilliant navigator, but no computer. I spent some time slumming around these streets before the captain found me."

"Yeah? Are we in for a family reunion?" I asked. Geoff averted his gaze, and I took the hint at once. "So that makes you one of those Pacific characters? I heard they eat their young. Before hopping aboard the Desire, I never saw a city past Chicago."

He rolled his eyes. "And I heard Atlantic broads punch each other for a greeting."

"You heard right." I showed my teeth with my smile.

Spade waved to signal we'd landed. I walked over, handing him the paper and credits Seth entrusted me with.

"Seth needs these things while we're docked. She's not going to run as well without the parts to fix the cannon damage, so I'd appreciate if you'd go get them. He asked if you'd do it. Something about no one else getting the job done right."

"No problem." Spade nodded and pursed his lips as he scanned the list. Before we set off, I grabbed two of the deckhands wandering around.

"Hiram, Abbey. We're going ashore. Can you send Jack and someone else down to the bar? They'll need to ask around about someone of Jensen's build and stature. As for the rest of you, I want this ship watched. We're in a shoddy section of town, and I don't want anyone getting ideas about taking what's ours."

"Aye, aye, Captain." Hiram saluted before he and Abbey

scampered off.

"Look at you, giving orders like a pro," Isabella teased.

"I can't help if I have a naturally commanding nature."

"Domineering is more like it," Geoff muttered under his breath. I arched my brow and placed my hands over my hips.

"If it gets the job done," I cracked back. Relief trickled into my chest at our banter. "Let's get going. Jensen may not have arrived yet, but the sub-bus could've transported him here in that day's head start he had."

"I haven't ridden one of those in an age." Isabella threw the rope ladder down and took the first steps off the ship. Geoff and I followed right after. Unlike the last dock, the rusted beams leaned in an awkward slant against one another, and muddy sludge coated the boardwalk in large blobs and crusted corners. I stroked Matilda out of habit before we set forth into the city streets.

Skyscrapers jutted into the horizon overtop the multilevel buildings, but their shadow swallowed anything smaller. Three-tier row homes lined either side of the pavement with elegant scalloped edges decorating the row down, but the paint had weathered and edges chipped like jagged teeth. The shingled roofs gave the stretch an even appearance, though many had either sunk into the top floor or created a checkerboard with the missing tiles. Once in awhile a building with flat rectangular windows and octagonal angled panes buttressed the lineup, but for the most part, uniformity played a key role in this degradation. The row homes stood as masked sentinels with windows that glared like hollow shells.

"Friendly place to bide your time," I said. Geoff nodded.

Abandoned streets meant the place was either a ghost town, or we had to be morons to walk there at night. We were probably column B. The sun rose in the distance, but all the flash and glitz from Reno's main strip drowned out any of nature's real glamour. Up ahead casino lights blinked on and off.

Three signs within close proximity battled for attention. The Captain's Wife and the Golden Doubloon made a valiant effort with their flash, but the Green Eyed Lady stood the clear winner. Its square body with descending rails led to an underground entrance. A translucent emerald dome overtop refracted any light in the area and glittered like a coal besmirched gem. The faint clinking sounds of slot machines traveled over to where we stood.

"Maybe we can win back some money from these failed jobs," Isabella said. "It's about time karma paid us double in return. I tend to be efficient at games." A feline smile curved her lips, since by 'efficient' she meant she cheated. Regardless, if we got enough to keep the Desire running, Isabella could use her skills all she wanted. I dipped my hand into the leather pouch and pulled out several coins.

"Try your hand. If you get a crowd, scatter, but use your

time at the tables to dredge up some information from the dealers and such." I looped an arm through Geoff's. "You'll be coming with me. Less of the gambling, and more of the drinking. A shared drink inspires camaraderie and gets people to talk."

"To each his own vice." Geoff shrugged, following my lead as we walked down the musty steps covered in rotten leaves. From the stairwell, loud strains of cabaret fare with lusty vocals and punchy instruments filtered in, the recording occasionally crackling. I pushed open the doors, and pale gold light cascaded down from glass lamps strung by brassy chandeliers.

Isabella departed from our side, and a trail of leers followed as she walked by. Geoff steered me over towards the bar and away from the flashing slot machines. In the casinos on the main stretch of Reno, well-dressed women in petticoats stood around dealer tables wearing baubles worth more than they bid. Here, those ladies would be shark food.

Mostly men roamed this bar, either sitting and gambling their stolen pennies or spending them drinking absinthe. Mugs littered the dirt-streaked and chipped wooden counter, but the bartender just stood back and yawned. At least I fit in here. Cigar smoke filtered through the room with a choking gusto, and I took a deep inhale of it with satisfaction.

Before sitting, I tested the stool with my foot. It creaked, and the seat slanted to the side. I'd been through enough ruffian bars to know better, so I took a gentle seat on the firm end and signaled for the bartender. He folded his arms across his chest. Geoff stepped beside me as if he'd interfere, but I stretched an arm in front of him and placed a coin on the counter.

"I'll be having two pints of grog." I raised my voice. "And if you don't hurry, I'll step behind the counter and get it myself. I'm pretty parched and don't like to wait." The bartender didn't say anything or even bother glancing my way. He pulled out two mugs from the ledge, filled them with grog, and plunked them onto the countertop. Some grog spilled over the side, but he didn't say a word, and I didn't offer any thanks.

Places like these, if we didn't swagger in and establish ourselves, the other men would mark us as easy targets. I took a deep sip of my drink, scanning the other patrons. Bartenders here didn't talk because gossip ended with a bullet through your chest. They overheard so much that if they chatted up every patron, they'd become a liability, fast. I passed one amber pint over to Geoff.

"Mm, grog." His tone was dry.

"It'll do." I laughed. "I need something to continue my alcoholic trend. Watch out though—if I start talking in half sentences, I may turn into Seth." Down the line I spotted several mercenaries enjoying cognac glasses of absinthe. You could always pick them out because they spent the most, but not in the sense of some stuffed shirt peacocking around expensive jewelry or flashing too much coin. Regardless of how much coin they squandered, their weapons glinted from their belts whenever they moved, so the bar knew they were armed. Closest to us, a drunken wastrel sat with his nose an inch from touching the ale in his mug. I took another swig.

Behind us, folks with vacant eyes slumped over the slot machines, cranking the lever and gambling their savings away. Sharks ran these tables, so I hoped Isabella would lead them on a waltz of her own. They cheated just as much as she would. Whoever had the faster hand won, and I'd seen Isabella draw a gun before, so I'd place my bets on her. I scanned the casino for anyone with the hulking build of Jensen, but no one fit the bill. Slumping back over my mug, I stared into my muted reflection.

A shout carried from across the room.

I whirled around at the sound, and my heart sped. Isabella sat over at a table with a span of cards still in hand. My gaze followed the wall until I spotted the source of the noise. A man stood in the corner of the room, as broad as Jensen, but with taller stature. Three men surrounded him, brandishing their weapons. Glad that Isabella hadn't gotten herself into a scuffle, I relaxed, at least until I caught their markings. A fur pelt looped around their holsters, and one wore a dark blue monocle signifying rank. The glimpse at the tattoo on their biceps of the M with the cog around it confirmed their identity.

"Morlocks," I growled.

CHAPTER SEVENTEEN

My fingers gripped Matilda tight, but Geoff placed a hand on my shoulder. The cornered man loomed over the three Morlocks, and his shotgun glowed under the hazy bar light. Still, there were three Morlocks and only one of Mr. Tall and Strapping. The rest of the bar quieted. Some of the men by the furthest slot machines inched towards the door, one slow step at a time while the mercenaries already grabbed their pieces. No one jumped to help, but everyone in the bar tensed, waiting for a fight.

"You owe us a debt, Mordecai, and it's time to pay up. You've been in our database for some time now, and we don't like live reports in our wanted files."

The tall stranger gave the Morlock officer a half-lidded stare, making no effort to move. He wore a black trench coat that swept the ground, and matching slate pants that accentuated his green eyes. "This is unnecessary. Civilians could be harmed. Why don't we take your issue with me elsewhere?"

"You'd just run. Like we'd let you get away again." The younger Morlock sneered. The Morlock officer kept his gun aimed at this man they called Mordecai. While the dark blue monocle hid the officer's one eye, his other expressed all the coldness I needed to see. They were the eyes of a dead fish. Watching them corner this man brought back the memories of my last job with the captain.

Isabella met my gaze from across the room. A Morlock officer, like that one, had shot her in the leg and started our streak of horrible, horrible luck. The trouble that led to this unwanted cargo. The trouble that led to Jensen's betrayal. The trouble that led to my Captain's murder.

My temper strengthened to a boil. Chances were the captain, Isabella, and I held files of our own in their stupid 'wanted' database after the last encounter. Hatred burned through me. This man was probably like us, on the receiving end of some bad luck and cornered by these bullies who called themselves pirates.

"No one crosses the Morlocks and lives." The officer growled.

"Why is it always the same lines with you guys?" My voice broke through the quiet, and I aimed Matilda straight at the ranked Morlock. The seats of the bar patrons squeaked behind me as they shifted back. Geoff let out a sigh and drew his gun to back me up. "Could you just once not deliver a stock scumbag line?" I asked. "Or do they teach that in school? Good little Morlocks must find every cliché in the dictionary and memorize them by heart." At this point, the other two turned their guns on us. The officer still kept his pointed on Mordecai in the corner.

The bartender shot first.

Thankfully he aimed at the Morlock men and not at us because the moment his gun clicked, my muscles tensed to duck. The bullet missed and pinged against the wall, but the sound sent the bar into an uproar. Panicking, the three Morlocks opened fire onto Mordecai. My feet moved as I surged to help him, but I shouldn't have bothered.

He didn't pull out the shotgun by his side. Instead, something glinted from inside his trench coat. It blurred faster than my eyes followed, and lame bullets bounced onto the ground. His fluid motion stopped as he sheathed his sabre. My jaw dropped. The Morlocks needed more men if they hoped to best him because I'd never seen swordsmanship like that. The Morlocks had known they wouldn't be enough for this man too—four more of their men kicked in the door. That bartender smashed one of the mugs lining the countertop and cursed.

I aimed a shot at the nearest Morlock, but with people standing in the way, the bullet missed my target, burrowing into his leg. He let out a gasp and lifted his gun as his face purpled with rage. Geoff and I dashed towards the slot machines for cover right as the bartender aimed several shots at the Morlocks by the door. Startled, since they stormed into a gunfight, they let loose a hail of erratic bullets.

My senses reeled from the combined noises of the casino machines, the roar of gunfire, and the scratchy voice of some siren playing on the gramophone. Bullets pinged off the steel hulls of machines and drove into the wall while some clattered onto the floor. Others found marks, and several bystanders dropped. In a bar full of scumbags, criminals, and lowlifes, that was the last thing they should have done.

A bullet flew past the drunkard by the bar, startling him out of his stupor. The man screamed and scurried behind the counter with the bartender. Isabella, bless her soul, had ducked under the table for cover at the first sign of trouble, and a bubble of relief burst in my chest once I saw her safe. The mercs sitting in the corner fondled their guns in irritation at the interruption of their well-paid drink. One scowled, stood from his stool, and unloaded a clip on the Morlock team who entered.

Every man fell.

Meanwhile, Mordecai kept the original three Morlocks busy from helping their friends. He wielded his sabre again with a finesse I envied, as the nearest man rushed him. The novice Morlock still had a trick to play—the shimmer of a fireburster around the muzzle of his gun snagged the light. My voice caught in my throat as I tried to call out a warning. A glint flashed as quickly as before, and with a flick of Mordecai's wrist, the Morlock's arm fell clean off.

"Leave," his deep voice bellowed. The man whimpered, and blood sprayed from the open wound at his shoulder. Several flecks hit the stranger, but he didn't blink. The mercenaries from the back corner popped their guns back into their holsters, starting a chain reaction of rustling leather. My shoulders relaxed. Until two more Morlocks appeared through the door.

Pop. Pop. Both dropped.

I glanced back in surprise that they drew their guns so fast. The mercenaries hadn't. Their eyebrows rose with appreciation as they stared in the other direction where Isabella crouched under the table, both pistols drawn. Smart girl. Even after her hiatus, she hadn't lost her edge. Geoff's gun blared next to my ear, and I winced. The officer fell with a howl, collapsing onto the floor when the bullet burrowed into his right leg. I couldn't bring myself to fire another shot since they lay helpless on the ground. Their eyes widened in panic when they realized the whole bar stood against them.

The stranger stepped in front of the Morlocks with his arms spread. He turned his head.

"Leave now and you'll have your lives," he offered. The men groveled on the floor before scrambling away. One's arm spurted a river of blood, and the other two shambled from their leg injuries. Right as they reached the door however, the bartender dropped them with three shots.

"Not in my bar." The sullen barkeep's jaw jutted out, and he settled back against the ledge, finally picking up one of the countless mugs lining the counter to clean it.

Mordecai's lips wrinkled in distaste. He stood a foot taller than anyone else with waves of dirty blonde hair down to his shoulders. His head tilted for a second as he studied the room like a sparrow, but then he stopped, tucked his sword back into the sheath, and strode through the broken door.

"That's the type of recon man we need," Geoff whispered into my ear. I nodded and marched straight to the mercenaries. The bartender had since gone back to neglecting his bar, and men stepped over bodies to return to their slot machines.

"Who was that man?" I jerked my thumb at the door. Several leers greeted me, as if they'd never seen a female before, but the one who shot down the Morlocks spoke.

"Mordecai Blacksmith. Although, I don't know what he was doing down here. The man's brilliant at finding anyone and staying invisible himself. Morlocks tried to recruit him for years, but it looks like they've marked him as kill on sight," another mercenary interjected.

"I've heard rumors of the Shadow Ward, but I've never seen the man before now. Pretty handy with a sword."

"Where is he normally found?"

The mercenary's grin widened, and a hunger filled his eyes. "That'll cost you." He scanned me up and down, stopping at my chest. I placed a hand on my hip, ready to argue back when Isabella stepped between us to press a coin into his palm.

"Here's your payment, big guy," she breathed and passed me a quick wink before taking a step behind me.

The mercenary shrugged, placated. "I've heard he swings around Nautilus, the casino on the main stretch. As for seen, that's a whole other thing. Good luck finding him, he's better at staying out of sight than anyone. Rumor says he could stay invisible in plain sight if he's trying."

Isabella gave him an innocent glance and thrust her chest out. "Cherie, you wouldn't have happened to see some large brutish guy in here, would you? He's built like an ox with lighter eyes and armed with an arsenal of weaponry most of the time. He's incredibly American—loud, obnoxious."

"We've seen a lot of types. He sounds like most of the mercenaries I've worked with." The guy shrugged. Isabella sighed.

"You tried." I clapped a hand on her shoulder and turned on my heel. "Thanks," I called and threw a wave. The casino patrons ignored us—after all, in this part of town, a bar fight surprised no one. I tiptoed past the broken doors, careful not to worsen the damage, while Isabella and Geoff followed me out. My eyes had adjusted to the aged light inside, and I squinted when we exited into broad sunlight.

"So we'll be hitting the main stretch, aye?" Isabella's eyes sparkled under the early dawn's rays.

"It looks it." I sighed. "Geoff, you're right though, that's the exact type of recon man we need. Besides, if this man can find anyone, he'd be able to pick out Jensen." The road back to the ports stretched out before us. If we travelled back, we could get some blessed sleep, but during that time, Jensen could travel further and further away. Checking my gun, I was surprised I only fired one shot in that last fight since I normally blew through ammo. After reloading Matilda, I placed her back in the holster. "We're underdressed for Nautilus," I said. "Hopefully they don't judge. If it's a bar on the main stretch too, they'll take our guns, so we'll have to use caution while we search for Jensen."

"Are you reminding yourself?" Geoff grinned. "Because I'm pretty sure you were the one who stepped in back there."

"Three to one." I folded my arms over my chest. "Those odds are not fair."

Isabella shook her head. "I don't know. Tall, strapping, and handsome took care of himself well." A wicked smile lit her face, and I mirrored hers.

"My, what a pity if we have to deal with him."

Isabella bit her lower lip. "Mmm," she added for extra emphasis.

"I swear, you ladies are worse than any man I know." Geoff's smile twisted wryly. "You treat us like pieces of meat." We broke into laughter and walked further into town, following the S signs for the sub bus. A chill of a wind sent leaves tumbling across the dirt covered streets as we strolled past empty houses.

"By the way Isabella," I said as we walked, "How did you make out with your gambling?" She passed me a handful of coins, the initial amount I'd given her. However, her full leather pouch jangled with extra coin.

"I made myself plenty more to gamble with." She winked. "We may not have any jobs working for us right now, but we'll get the money to keep Desire going somehow. Us gypsies, we know how to survive, love. Whatever means necessary."

She was right. Even though cheating was a coward's way to make money, I couldn't argue with the results. "Good, because even if we're desperate, I'm not letting Edwin start another hydroponics garden."

"Yeah," Isabella snorted, "I think it went downhill with his hybrids. His zucchicarronip tasted like raw sewage." Up ahead, the sub-bus stretched across the landscape with a ruler's rigidity.

Geoff scratched the back of his head. "I haven't been on a sub-bus in some time, especially not the Reno one." His voice trailed off, and we lost him to his own deeper thoughts. Geoff didn't talk much about his past, but he had run away from home like me. The sub-bus ran beneath a thick arched convex walling of geosynthetic resin, which created a translucent barrier that protected the transport system from the weather's wear and tear. Several black doors stood out against the transparencies, marking themselves as the entrances and exits.

After we entered through the doors, the environment morphed into the perfect temperature with none of the clingy humidity from outside. The arched barrier kept in the warmth, but to keep the humidity from ruining the machinery, periodically stationed vents dehumidified the area. It resulted in a warm and dry climate. The transit system whirred in the background, and I tapped my palm against my thigh as we waited. A couple benches lined the way, and my legs begged for rest, but if I sat down I wouldn't get back up from sheer exhaustion. I wrinkled my nose.

"We left our mugs of grog back there," I said. "What a waste."

"It's not a waste if its grog, just if you're spilling ale or absinthe." Geoff stretched his arms behind his back.

"Spilling absinthe? That's a crime against humanity." In the distance, the lights from the sub-bus reflected off the arched ceiling and demanded our attention. "This is the direction into the city, right?" I asked.

Geoff hit his forehead with his palm. "Really? You have the worst sense of direction out of anyone I've met."

I threw my arm around his shoulders. "But that's why I have you. And Spade. And Adelle now too." Geoff stared back at me with a flat-lidded gaze, and I sighed. "All right, you can restart your navigational lessons with me after all this rigamarole." The sub-bus thundered louder, and its sleek white exterior shone like an untouched casing. It zoomed towards us so fast the monstrosity nearly rumbled by, but at the last moment, the brakes squealed, and the sub-bus shuddered to an immediate halt.

The door slid open, but no one left. Apparently this wasn't a popular spot. No idea why, those broken-down, abandoned city streets teemed with friendliness. Balling my hands into fists, I strode onto the sub-bus. Fluorescent lights lined the ceiling, bleaching the walls with a bluish tinge, and a lack of windows gave the chambers a claustrophobic feel. A map with a holographic console flickered at the head of each compartment on either side of the doors. Geoff placed his hands down, and a keypad appeared. His fingers raced over the optic keys.

"Nautilus, right?" he asked. I nodded, and he plugged in the information. An address and location popped up on the map. Geoff pressed the marker and input the number of passengers. When the fare charge came up, Geoff tapped his foot as he waited for me to dig up my card. "It accepts credits, not the rustic coinage you sling for beer."

"There isn't much on it but that should be enough." I passed it over, and he slid the card into the indicated spot. Once the console processed the money and printed us out a ticket, the sub-bus started up again. A couple other people sat in our chamber. Two rows of seats lined either side, both covered in hunter green plush cushions. The edging facing the aisle glistened with a golden sheen, but under the medical lighting the metal shone green too.

Isabella swung into the nearest open row and squished against the wall. A screen hung over the doorframes on either side, signaling the stops. Geoff sat next to her, and I took the edge. The second my back hit the comfortable cushion, I bit back a moan.

"Let's start placing bets here on who falls asleep first." I sunk into the curve of the seat, and my back performed a lovely slouch.

"Now, Captain, it's your job to stay awake and see us through this fiasco." Isabella closed her eyes with a feline smile still on her lips.

"Excuse me, I'm going to die of boredom before we ever get there." My eyes flickered from the lack of sleep. I frowned and folded my arms over my chest.

The sub-bus zoomed along, and aside from the slight buzz, it was a smoother ride than any other mode of transport I travelled. A woman with more petticoats than fingers tossed the occasional glare our way, and her sour pinched lips enhanced her haughtiness. She must have picked up the sub-bus out in the country to spend a night aboard the airship casinos in Reno. Must be nice. An older man slumped over like us with a bowler cap that fell over his forehead and touched the tip of his nose. Sleeplessness sent waves of irritation through my muscles, and I shifted in my seat again.

A destination scrolled over the header above the door while the polished voice of machinery circulated around the speakers near the ceilings. The transport thudded to a halt, and the creak of doors opening filtered throughout the chambers. I turned to look at the map on my right, squinting to see how far along we were. On the board, an illuminated circle marked the Nautilus an inch away from our current location.

Our compartment door opened, and a slim young girl walked in. What she lacked in hips, she made up for in bosom, and her short ruffled cocktail dress exposed plenty. Creamy skin and almond eyes gave her exotic appeal while the nametag clipped to her front, and the miniature nautical captain's hat suggested a uniform. A man who had drifted off woke up and gave her his full attention. He wasn't the only one.

"Claire?" Geoff's voice sounded next to me. The girl's head jerked in our direction, and her eyebrows furrowed once she caught sight of Geoff. Her small lips formed a shocked circle, and tears began pouring down her face.

CHAPTER EIGHTEEN

My eyes widened with curiosity, but I forced myself to sit back and watch. She took several steps towards us, her feet dragging as if she were under a spell. I glanced at Geoff. His jaw dropped with genuine surprise, and his fingers dug into the cushion of the seat in front of us.

"I thought you'd..." Her words came out with hesitation. She stopped in front of our row and wiped the tears from her cheeks with her forearm. I raised my brows before glancing back at Geoff.

"Claire, I had to leave. I couldn't say goodbye." Both stopped and stared at each other, neither willing to continue. The sub-bus already started back up, and according to the holographic display, we zoomed into the main stretch of Reno. Claire's tears deepened her blue eyes, offsetting her smooth skin. She was one of the rare few whose tears enhanced her looks.

"I never stopped thinking about you," she started again but bit her lip. Geoff's face darkened. I recognized that expression: guilt. This girl had meant something to him, but listening to their vague, unclear sentences grated my nerves to ribbons.

"Give me a snack and maybe I'll watch this melodrama unfold, but as it is, I'm hungry and sleepless. Both make me cranky, so, who's the lady?" I jabbed a thumb in her direction as her dainty features narrowed into a glare. I extended a hand in her direction, since a little friendliness never hurt anyone. "I'm Beatrice, nice to meet you." Claire hesitated and glanced between me and Geoff before she placed her soft hand against my blistered one.

"This is Claire," Geoff introduced. "She's an old friend from back before the Desire when I lived around here for a time." The girl's eyebrows shot up at the mention of the word friend— obviously they had something more between them. I leaned back in the seat and crossed my arms over my chest. Isabella slept next to Geoff, oblivious to the situation.

The sub-bus stopped again, and people boarded. Several passengers entered our compartment, so Claire took a seat in the row before ours. An awkward silence descended amongst us as the sub-bus set into motion again.

"Cute get-up," I commented. "What's the job?" Claire didn't say anything at first as if she still debated whether or not she wanted to speak with me.

"I work at Nautilus." She stared at Geoff rather than me when she responded. Not that I didn't love an awkward interchange, but in this triangulation of the conversation I played third fiddle.

"We're heading to the same place then," I attempted again. Her expression didn't change, and she kept staring at Geoff who refused to meet her eyes. I tapped a finger on my knee. Our stop couldn't arrive fast enough.

"So what was Geoff like back in the day? I mean before he boarded the Desire?" The lanky deckhand I'd first met had grown into a man before my eyes, now first mate to my captain, though he still wore that same duster with all the bronze buttons and stains.

I punched him in the shoulder, but he didn't respond. His eyes sank towards the floor, and a frown crowned his face. He couldn't be enjoying any of this. Claire pursed her lips, not responding to me, but three times was my limit. My temper escalated. If she had some long held grudge with him, fine, but no one treated me like I was invisible. Beyond her disregard for me, the way she upset Geoff marked her off as a floozy in my books. My fingers curled into a fist, and I clenched my jaw to keep from snapping. Geoff must have noticed, since he placed a hand on my shoulder.

"I'm sorry," he apologized to both of us. "You took me by surprise, Claire. If you want, we can catch up real fast before you have to go to work."

"I'd like that." Her words were terse.

I rolled my eyes. This broad didn't deserve five minutes with him. I stood up for Geoff to get out, and I'm sure when he did he noticed the angry flare in my eyes. They sat several rows ahead of us surrounded by empty seats. I sat back down and folded my arms over my chest.

From her small manicured hands to the tears sticky on her face, everything about her screamed hyper-feminine, and I couldn't ever imagine Geoff being with one of those girls. Trickles of their whispers filtered into my hearing but no phrases loud enough to distinguish. I tried to ignore the burning sensation in my chest, since I had no right to get irritated. Geoff could talk to whomever he wanted to, floozy or not. But, still. I huffed and kicked the side of Isabella's boot. If I had to sit here in silence, I'd burst. Isabella woke with a start, giving me a sulky glare.

"What was that for?" she grumbled.

I pointed. "Geoff stumbled into an old flame."

"So?" Isabella tilted her head and stretched her arms.

"She's rude." I settled back into my seat, fiddling with the strap on my holster.

Isabella entertained a grin, and she shook her head. "She's not you, you mean. Sorry darling, he's allowed any woman he wants. You've never given him a chance, and you've had plenty."

"Not like that. Geoff just deserves the best." Irritation stormed me like a nest of bugs.

"You're so dense." Isabella rolled her eyes before turning back on her side.

"What's that supposed to mean?" I shot back.

"I'll let you mull on it."

When I glanced over, her eyes shut in slumber again. Isabella was dead wrong. Annoyance prickled all over me but not because of his interest in someone else. No, I just didn't like her rudeness. I shifted in my seat again and simmered in a silence that dragged on like waiting for a watched pot to boil—or burn in my case.

Finally Nautilus blinked onto the overhead screen. Geoff and Claire stood. I kicked Isabella's boot again and roused her.

"Wakey, wakey, we're off here."

She blew away long strands of light brown hair that had drifted over her face and pushed herself from the seat. We exited through the doors. From the clouded shell of the sub-bus, all of Reno's lights glowed and flashed from indistinguishable places. Claire whispered something in Geoff's ear before she strode off ahead of us through the black exit doors. Nice of her to offer a goodbye. He sidled back over to us but didn't say a word, and I didn't ask. Anyway, Nautilus provided a quick distraction the moment we exited the sub-bus doors.

A giant sign blinked on and off, spelling 'Nautilus' in cerulean light. The hotel itself rose high into the sky, more stories than I dared count, and the colored walls shifted from slate green to cavernous blue with electronic ripples like the tide below.

Translucent aquamarine windows added to the effect. In front of the hotel, the giant submarine lurked like a subterranean threat. The three of us stopped, gaping at the spectacle before our eyes.

A docking walk traveled up to the entryway of a giant hulled out submarine. The numbers 571 glowed in white print against the hull, and a large sign read: USS Nautilus. Although I preferred airships myself, I couldn't help but admire the curves on that hulking monstrosity.

Steel rivets lined both sides of the slate green panels covering the submarine's exterior. The casino's shell hearkened back to a time well before modern technology, but the ancient monolith had panache the newer models lacked. Her tail arced from ridge to bow, and the globed portholes shone from the interior lighting. The entire ship from a distance took on a shark-like quality with a sleek design not unlike the Desire.

"Time to make some coin." Isabella grinned. We walked up the sullen planked boardwalk leading to the main entrance. Large bouncers dressed in matching navy uniforms stood by the doors to make sure people didn't carry side arms—none of our ruffian rabble allowed. I wrinkled my nose. No one was allowed to take Matilda from me. Plus, with how many enemies we'd made, going without spelled suicide.

"I'm going to give you my holster," I told Isabella. "I need you to sneak by the guards. Geoff and I will enter simultaneously and provide the distraction, but you're the best at subterfuge. Once inside, meet back up with us." She nodded, and I passed her my holster, leather pouch included. Geoff relinquished his gun and ammo. Isabella strapped my holster and his gun on, saluted me, and disappeared into the boarding crowd. But that's when I spotted him.

A hulking figure walked through the swinging doors of the Nautilus with a hunch I'd recognize anywhere, a man I'd stood beside on countless missions in the past. Even though I just glimpsed his back, I didn't need the confirmation of his hazel eyes to know who he was.

Jensen.

My heart leapt into my throat, and I jabbed Geoff.

"Look ahead," I whispered. "Don't make a scene. We have to get to him as quickly as possible." Geoff glanced up, and his eyes widened as Jensen disappeared into the building. We strode up to the guards who patted us down, but when they found nothing, they pushed us along. My nerves pulsed with fresh adrenaline at the sight of Jensen. We needed weapons. Isabella already disappeared into the crowd, and I hoped she'd found her way inside. Nautilus' navy blue doors swung open, and we entered.

Copper chandeliers hung from the submarine ceilings, and their flowing lights reflected a trail of sapphire crystals. The two floor casino spanned the length of the submarine while artificial light invaded every spare inch, even the corners. I scanned the crowd for any sign of Jensen. The tense sounds of a violin played over the speakers, rising with the crescendo. Loud burbles of an indoor waterfall carried throughout the entire casino even though it cascaded from the center of the second floor down to the first.

Men dressed in tuxedos, and the women wore bustled full dresses with boned bodices and petticoats on the smaller second tier. With my fitted leather tunic and loose breeches, I stuck out like an eggplant in a cabbage patch. Give me a mercenary, a drunkard, and a bar fight any day.

Someone bumped into me from behind. My hand leapt to my side for my gun, but I groped air. A woman, with the same uniform as Claire, pushed by me toting a tray full of drinks for the patrons by the slot machines and tables. I glared. My own rack wasn't meager, but these women's shelves carried their trays for them. People swarmed in clusters around the Nautilus, and everywhere we walked, snippets of conversation flowed into my ears. Jensen had blended into the crowd. I glanced around but spotted no sign of Isabella either, which caused a sweat broke out against the nape of my neck.

"Geoff, I need you to find Isabella. I'll wait for you by the bar. With any luck, Jensen didn't notice us, so I'll try to mingle and blend into the crowd. If both of us are together, he'll recognize us faster than we'd draw our nonexistent guns." He nodded and took off.

The owners of the casino put some extraordinary effort into

making the submarine a work of art. While the exterior glared sullenly slate, colors inside blossomed like a tropical garden. The walls resembled an underwater landscape with a cerulean base color shifting to different darker shades in sections while giant murals of jellyfish, octopi and schools of fish decorated the entire building. Seaweed drifted between them in such realistic detail the painting appeared three dimensional. I tapped my foot. My brain ran in search overload between looking for Jensen, Isabella, this Shadow Ward guy, and now Geoff. Bottles glistened against the bar in the distance, and I headed in that direction.

A hand tapped my shoulder.

I whirled around, fists brandished and ready for a fight. The middle-aged gentleman who stood behind me fit in with this whole crowd, wearing a bowler cap and a spotless tweed tailcoat. Like so many old aristocrats, he even had a monocle for the gods' sakes. My panic fizzled. He was no threat.

"You stood out like a lost lamb, my dear." The man's voice was thick like resin and bogged down by a vaguely familiar accent. I lowered my fists, taking in a deep breath.

"I'm sorry. I thought you were someone else."

"Someone you don't want to meet?" he asked with a twinkle in his light gray eyes. "Or maybe you do want to meet them. And they may not want to meet you."

I kept my eyes on the crowd but turned to face the man.

Mingling helped me stay under the radar, not stick out like a feisty, punch-slinging sore thumb.

"An old friend. I owe him a debt I can't wait to repay." I started edging in the direction of the bar, hoping to lose this guy. Instead, he walked alongside me.

"Is this your first time in Reno?" he asked. "It can be overwhelming for newcomers."

"Before, but briefly." I took a deep breath before continuing, not wanting to disclose too much information to this total stranger. "Here on business. Yourself?"

"Why, business as well." He gave me another charming grin that creased into dimples. "I've hit a bumpy patch with negotiations, but my plans will smooth out soon."

I nodded, half-paying attention. "Maybe you've seen my friend," I said. "He's taller than most of the people in here and has broad shoulders like a riot wrestler. He's dressed out of place, like me. The guy wears a bowler cap too, like you."

The man scanned out into the crowd with raised brows. "I can't say I've seen this friend of yours, but if I do, I'll be sure to let you know."

Geoff ran up to me, his chest heaving up and down from exertion.

"Bea, I searched for her all through this casino, even the

upper floor," he said, slouching over. "I haven't caught sight of either since we entered." I bit back a groan. We needed to find her and soon.

"Oh, Geoff, meet—" I turned to where the gentleman had stood, but he'd vanished. Geoff crooked his eyebrow at me, but I shrugged. "I was talking to someone and trying to mingle, but he took off." We both lapsed into silence, and awkwardness spread between us like an ink stain. I shifted from hip to hip, and neither of us spoke. The murmur from the chatter behind us blended with the splash of the waterfall.

"Have you spotted him at all?" Geoff asked. My heart thudded against my chest in anxiousness from the initial glimpse of Jensen. "Why hasn't Isabella caught up yet?" Geoff cut through our silence, echoing the worry on both of our minds. Slot machines next to us pinged and jangled, the sounds straining the speakers. The one closest displayed a set of cogs to match different shapes and sizes of brassy clockwork.

I patted my hips, "I don't like being without my holster and gun with Jensen wandering around here. Isabella took my coin too."

Geoff lifted his pouch. "I still have mine." He scanned the room. "Where can we stay the most inconspicuous?"

"The corners are too crowded to get a clear view of the layout. If Isabella is trying to find us, she'd aim for a main location. I pray Jensen didn't—" I stopped there, and Geoff stared me straight in the eye, worried as hell. Time to change topics. "Where'd your strumpet run off to?" I squinted at a line of women passing by but no Isabella. Geoff grunted. The noise sounded foreign from him.

"Claire's working. Look, I'm sorry she was rude to you. She, well, she's had a rough time."

My temper began to bubble, so I took a couple steps forward. "No time for her big bad sob story."

"When is the time?" Geoff grabbed my shoulder and turned me in his direction. "Any occasion there's tension between us, you dodge the conversation. I would like to know when we'll talk about any of it."

I placed my head in my hands and dragged my fingers down my face. We were weaponless, on the hunt for Isabella, the traitor roamed through the casino, and he wanted to talk about our relationship now?

My voice lowered to a serious tone. "When we get back to the ship. Once we're in air with a full crew we can talk—I promise we will. It's just, since I'm the captain now, the Desire has to come first. I swear to you though, I won't duck out after this is settled." A strange look overtook Geoff's face, and I placed my hands over my hips in defense. "What?"

"Nothing." His mouth quirked into a half smile. "I don't believe I've ever seen you so responsible. It looks good on you." I frowned, opened my mouth, and closed it again. He grabbed my hand and tugged. "Let's get over to the bar. It's the central part of this place, and I'd rather be able to see my enemies from afar. Maybe we'll even stumble into this Mordecai guy."

I scanned the crowds for a man in a trench coat or our dear gypsy queen. Jensen should have stuck out amidst these well-dressed people, but I hadn't seen his large form since he first entered the Nautilus. Even loitering around the corners or lining the walls, none of the people matched their general build. I shook off the uncomfortable feeling that Jensen watched us. He could lurk anywhere around this place while he waited to take us out. And without weapons? I shivered.

Gentlemen strolled around the room smoking cigars and sipping glasses of absinthe from nearby cocktail waitresses. They wore tailcoats, top hats, and some even had monocles, but no trench coats like the Shadow Ward. Ladies slipped into their finest as well, from corseted dresses with full skirts to the field of petticoats some donned. My fairy godmother hadn't dressed me for this ball, but I wished she'd visit. Clean chemises dwindled, and it'd been an age since I bought a new skirt.

"Why don't we wait by the bar?" I pointed. "Maybe your girlfriend can score us some free drinks."

Geoff shook his head. "Alcoholic."

I threw my hands up. "I can't help it if I'm bitter over my wasted grog. I fully prepared to enjoy that."

"Since you bought that round, I'll treat." Geoff led the way over to the center of the ship.

The bar lay in the middle of the submarine, a rewired and stripped old control center. Bar hardware covered the old navigational functions, and rounded wooden paneling replaced the button boards. Navy and copper striping overhauled the old-style seats. They were scattered around circular glass tables creating a parlor effect, and cocktail girls delivered the drinks. I spotted Claire behind the bar, mixing a whisky and lemon tonic to take elsewhere. The moment she spotted us, I waved, hopping up and down while in turn she frowned and ignored us.

"All I do is try with that girl." I clutched my chest with mock dismay. "I don't know why we're not best friends yet."

"I can't imagine," Geoff muttered.

"I don't know." I kept a serious face. "My personality charms the pants off chipmunks."

Geoff snorted. We took a seat at the first open table, and I settled back. Since we were out in the open, Isabella could spot us from anywhere in this joint. Unfortunately so could Jensen. I prayed he hadn't figured a way to smuggle his stupid revolver in.

"What about finding the Shadow Ward?" Geoff sat in his cushy high-backed seat.

"He can find us. At this point, making sure Isabella's okay is priority. I hate the thought that Jensen might have found her."

We could have sat around the main bar circle, but I preferred a more comfortable perch at this stage of sleeplessness. Claire sashayed over in our direction. Of course she provided a sweet piece of eye candy with the way her voluptuous curves spilled out of the top and bottom of her tight navy blue dress, while the little sailor hat and heavy makeup accented. She balanced a tray on her palm carrying two cognac glasses filled with the sensual green elixir. Absinthe. I cocked my head to the side and glanced at Geoff. He shrugged.

"Hey, Geoff." She didn't offer a glance in my direction, and my temper flared again. "I brought you these."

"Not that I'm complaining, but we never ordered them." I swallowed my anger before I continued and pointed out just how little her outfit covered.

She shook her head. "No, they're on the house. I brought them over for you." She stared at Geoff, avoiding my gaze. Despite my extreme dislike for the girl, my mouth practically watered for the first sip.

"Thanks Claire."

She winked at him and strode off with the tray in hand. We picked up our drinks and clinked glasses in a toast. Out of the corner of my eye, I noticed the monocle-wearing gentleman who spoke with me before sneaking glances in our direction. I wrinkled my nose—not my type. I hoped our five second chat hadn't given him the wrong idea.

"That's the man from earlier." I pointed over to the bar. "I think he's after you, boy-o." Geoff's grin caused his crooked tooth to poke out before he took a deep sip. I followed suit.

A numb haziness overtook me like the effects of a night's drinking rolled into one punch, and sweat pricked my neck. I glanced over at Geoff. He'd paled several shades and gripped the table. Over by the bar, the man with the monocle grinned so wide his teeth glinted like a shark's while several hulking men approached our table from the other direction. Their suits helped them blend into the crowd, but they strode towards us with a definite direction. They weren't Morlocks or redcoats—shit.

Our ex-employer.

CHAPTER NINETEEN

"Geoff," I croaked, "We need to get out fast. That absinthe was drugged."

His brown eyes flashed, and he followed my careful glance over to the slow moving mercenaries. Stupid. We'd been careless. At this point finding Mordecai or Isabella didn't matter; we needed a way out of the Nautilus. Jensen wandered through the crowds inside this sub, and he wouldn't hesitate to kill us. Neither would these mercenaries.

My hand leapt to my missing holster. As I groped the air, panic heated my mind in a sharp, numbing wave. I tilted my head over to the bar, hoping Geoff would understand. The mercs wouldn't break into open fire, not in a flashy, public venue like this since they'd draw too much attention, and they couldn't afford that. But whatever they put into our drinks hit with a sucker punch I couldn't shake off.

We rose from our seats, inching towards the bar. At least behind cover we'd have the chance to mask our movements, however the effects of the drugged absinthe made even walking difficult. My fingers and toes numbed, and I tripped over my clunky feet on the way over. Pins and needles raced along my arms and legs, but we managed a steady pace. Claire noticed us and walked by.

"Don't tell me that absinthe was too much for you." She placed her hands on her hips.

"Get out," I attempted, but the words slurred.

"I work here." She threw back sass. "I'm not leaving."

"No, really." Geoff shook his head. "Get out of the way," he managed, and we stumbled past her.

Her face darkened. She set her jaw, and tears welled up in her blue eyes, but hurt feelings didn't matter. If she talked with us, she drew negative attention onto herself. The mercenaries reached our table right as we slid behind the circular bar. Thank the gods too, for the spins struck me like a hammer to the skull. I clutched the polished wooden ledge as my world careened around me. The alluring blues and violets of the murals along the walls whirled around into a spiral of colors. My fingers trembled, and I let go of the ledge.

Geoff caught me before my back slammed against the floor. The pained expression on his pale face mirrored the turbulence in my stomach.

"We have to keep moving." He pointed towards the corner slot machines lining the far wall. Their muted jangles echoed in my ears as I followed his gaze towards a side exit. His finger swayed up and down mid-air, but I couldn't decide if he or my vision wavered.

"Hurry." I crouched again, and we stumbled over to the slot machines. Not too many patrons paid us attention since drunks commonly bumbled around Reno. I chanced a glance back, but the same men followed us, creeping over to the bar. We entered into some insane predator-prey dance where neither group ran. Running drew too much attention, and the motion would force the poison into our veins faster.

My hands found the chilled metal frame of a slot machine, and I steadied myself. We crept below them, out of sight. The mercs knew our general direction, but this gave us enough cover, so they'd get bogged down in their search. My stomach twisted with the hollowness of a pulped orange. Geoff split into three before me, and sweat trickled into my eye. I tried to bat the liquid away but missed, almost colliding with him when he staggered ahead of me.

The far wall zoomed before my eyes and darted away again. Feet belonging to patrons meshed into blobs and back into leather before my compromised vision. I shook my head to clear my mind, but the motion sent my world spinning.

We crawled on the floor at a sluggish pace, and each movement sent shudders up my spine. The carpeted floor was a temptation—so springy and soft like a navy blue ocean. I could rest there. A distant voice screamed at me, but my brain barely reacted. Still, the sound irritated me enough to manage another step forward. Walls jumbled before me in an array of blues, yellows, and reds like a stream of paint. The door no longer stood out, and peachy black blobs drifted in my peripheral.

A slap stung my face, and for a brief moment I submerged from the listless pool. Claire's angry face greeted mine. I needed that wake up and fast because Geoff had collapsed onto the floor. Before the poison dulled my senses again, I seized Geoff by the arms and yanked him onto my back, stumbling forward on what little adrenaline I had left. My surroundings whirled. His body pressed against my back but for some reason felt light as a scarf.

Claire's voice and shouts of surprise buzzed in the background of my hearing, but none of that mattered because the door loomed in front of us. My feet slapped the floor, and I surged ahead. I ran. Yes, the poison hit me faster, and yes it drew attention, but I didn't care. The door meant escape. Sounds around me muted to a dull fuzz, and my quickened heartbeat thumped in my ears.

The men behind us could catch up. Didn't matter. Had to make it to the door, which was blurring before my eyes. Shit. I pushed forward faster, exhausting reserves I didn't know I had. My body shook, but I tightened my grip around Geoff because I couldn't afford to lose him. His feet trailed along the ground and snagged, making him even harder to pull along. Breaths faltered, and with each inhale I sucked down sludge. Determination pounded through me with every step I managed. No option. Had to make it.

My shoulder hit the door first, but I didn't even feel the pain. I threw my body against it and Geoff with me. No result. A bar jutted into my stomach and at first nothing registered. My vision flickered in and out as I threw my hip at the bar. A dull click echoed in my ears, and we tumbled out the door onto the pavement. My senses screamed at me, begging me to run, but the pavement was comfortable. Warm.

My sight snapped away for a moment, before I returned to broad daylight. The sun sent me spinning. Black overtook my vision again, and I lost consciousness.

***

"Takes some time to filter out." A rich male voice echoed through the room. A hushed female tone accompanied him from somewhere around me. My bearings hadn't returned yet, and my eyes still crusted shut.

"Shouldn't be as bad though, right?" A shadow hovered over me, carrying along the faint smell of rose perfume. I recognized her voice. My eyes fluttered open, and I stared at Isabella's face as relief flooded through me in a balmy torrent. Strands of her light brown hair dangled over me, and her dark eyes softened with concern. When she realized my eyes had opened, she lunged over, wrapping me in a hug.

"You just can't stay out of trouble." She pulled back, and a wry grin gripped her face.

"How'd you find me?" I tested my voice out. It scraped against my throat. Panic skittered through my veins, and I sat up fast. The ex-employer. Jensen. The blood rushed into my brain, and the motion sent a streak of pain through.

"Where's Geoff?" I croaked.

Isabella gestured to her right. "Asleep on the bed. You're both okay, but you were drugged. We found you collapsed outside the Nautilus around the time you started running, and those mercenaries gave chase. It caused some noise around the casino, but everything you touch turns to chaos."

I relaxed, tilting my head. "We?" I asked. Isabella's lips curved into a smile, and she tossed her gaze back.

"I might have helped a little." The deep voice sounded behind her. I peered past. He stood by the window under an afternoon sun, and the rays filtered through, lightening his blonde waves. Green eyes flitted in my direction, and his sword poked out from underneath his black trench coat. Mordecai Blacksmith, the Shadow's Ward.

"How?" I glanced between Isabella and him.

"Please." She arched a brow. "Mordecai here's gypsy borne—I knew it the moment he used that sabre. He couldn't evade me if he tried. He's agreed to help us find Jensen, for his price of course." The memory of Jensen entering the Nautilus hit me like a strike to the head.

"Did you find him in there?" My fingers balled into fists. Isabella cocked her head to the side. "Geoff and I saw him enter the Nautilus. When—when we didn't find you, we were worried he'd caught up with you." Her jaw dropped.

Mordecai leaned into view. "I believe I may be able to help in your search for him."

I pursed my lips and glanced to Isabella. "Where are we getting this coin you promised him?"

"From my winnings of course." She flashed her teeth with a grin, perching on a dented gray stool.

"You're some kind of woman." I sat up in the bed, though my back begged to return to the grip of the thick ivory mattress. Whitewashed walls sparkled under the sunbeams from the window, shifting light causing Geoff to stir from the other bed. He stretched his arms out in front of him, blinked several times, and rolled over onto his side.

"Where are we?" he asked, his voice thick with sleep.

"Not sure myself," I said. "But Mordecai and Isabella here were kind enough to save us."

"They slipped valerian lupulus into your drinks. Though the common herb is used as a sedative, a variant of it knocks you out within minutes. I've used it myself before and not only by the way you reacted, but the lingering scent on your tongue validated their drug of choice." Mordecai leaned back against the wall, crossing his arms over his barrel of a chest.

"We should get moving." I stretched out my legs and cracked my neck. "Jensen's just going to get further and further away. What happened to those mercenaries chasing us?"

"I wasn't paying attention." Isabella shrugged. "It was enough to get you out." Mordecai frowned at her while her eyes danced away from me.

"Mordecai," I addressed him. "What happened to those mercs?"

"They took that girl, the one who chased after you. Her and a couple others. I suppose they hoped to get information of your whereabouts." His mouth formed a tight line after he stopped talking. Geoff clutched fistfuls of the blanket in front of him, and his neck tensed.

"That doesn't matter," Isabella said. "They don't know anything, so they'll be let go. We can't afford the time to chase them down, plus we don't know where they may be."

"I could find them," Mordecai said. "For a price of course."

"It's a price we can't afford, darling." Isabella shook her head. "We have enough for Jensen." I glanced over to Geoff. His jaw tensed, but the poor boy was too devoted a soldier to argue back about searching for Claire.

"Isabella's right," he agreed, although his eyes flashed with contained bitterness. "We can only go after one, and Jensen's our target. Let's get moving."

I flipped the sheets off me and stood. "May I have my holster and piece back?" I asked Isabella who passed them over. As I strapped the familiar weight around my hips, my shoulders relaxed.

"That's better, I can think now. Ready to hunt?" I turned to Mordecai, and he nodded. "Good, we're going after those mercenaries."

Isabella's eyes narrowed, and Geoff's mouth dropped.

"I'll not be having innocents captured on our account. That makes us no better than Jensen, and we need to always keep that distinction clear." My eyes flashed in irritation at those damned mercenaries for poisoning our draft and jeopardizing our chance to take Jensen down. Giving up our lead on Jensen pained me, especially for someone rude like Claire, but the choice was clear. Mordecai's green eyes studied me with that birdlike curiosity.

"I know you don't like leaving people in trouble, but this may be our one shot at Jensen," Isabella's tone softened.

"If it comes at the expense of others, I don't want it." I placed my hand on my hips since my mind was made up. Geoff snatched up his coin purse from Isabella and strapped on his pistols. "Let's make this quick folks, because we need to return to the ship. How long have we been asleep? How far could they have gotten?" My eyes focused on the white door, which would have blended into the wall without the brass doorknob.

"You've been asleep for half the day. It's afternoon." Mordecai stood, and his head brushed the ceiling. "They took them off west, towards the seedy areas of Reno."

"Good, closer to the ship." I crossed my arms over my chest. "Do you have an inkling as to where they may have gone?"

"My dear." A wolfish grin spread over his face. "For a paid customer, of course I do. They don't call me the Shadow Ward for nothing. They'll most likely be in the abandoned houses lining the strip from the dock since nobody apart from mercenaries, Morlocks, and cultists go there." No wonder those streets emptied out at night.

"To the sub-bus we go." I pointed toward the door but furrowed my brows. "Where are we?"

"No one will return here for a couple days." Mordecai glanced to the ceiling. "We're a couple blocks off the main strip of casinos," he said, taking the lead. I didn't ask, just followed. We exited the tenement and rushed along sidewalks teeming with tourists. After three turns down streets I'd never seen before, the sheen of the sub-bus entry glistened at the end of the road.

We boarded, and I settled back into my weathered seat. As the transport zoomed ahead, Isabella showed off her knives, lifting the pieces on her palm to show the balance while Mordecai nodded in appreciation. He gestured to the sword at his side, but my attention dropped after they began to discuss the sort of smithy needed to make his sabre. Geoff hunched over and stared at the ground.

I placed a hand on his back. "She'll be safe. This isn't your fault."

"I could have ignored Claire on the way in." He gripped his knees. "She already went through hell on my account. When I boarded with Captain Morris, I'd hit rock bottom. Claire and I had been together, but we were more like street rats binding under hard times than anything I considered real." The sub-bus stopped, and a destination flashed onto the screen. Geoff's dark brown eyes distanced.

"She cared a great deal for me," he continued, "but when I had the option to leave, I took it. I didn't say goodbye to anyone, including her. At the time they were part of a past I wanted to erase, but that wasn't fair to Claire. I ditched with no regard to how my disappearance affected her."

"Well you couldn't know," I reminded him. "You were young, and we all do dumb crap when we're younger."

"Dumb things to ourselves, yeah, but to others?" Geoff rifled a hand through his longer strands.

"Even to others—if you hadn't learned from it, you wouldn't care now. And I don't even know why you're worrying. We'll get them out safe," I said, giving him a confident smile.

"You're right. Thanks, Bea." He exhaled and straightened in his seat. The sub-bus zoomed ahead several stops until a familiar one splashed onto the screen. Mordecai stood first, ever vigilant, and we followed him off. When we stepped onto the streets leading back to port, I checked Matilda to make sure I'd filled her with ammo.

Late afternoon beams transformed the town with wispy golden rays and orange shadows. The green dome of the casino from earlier glistened despite the internal wreckage I'm sure they still cleaned up. Before we approached the row of homes, we stopped and surveyed the road ahead. Night or day, the road remained empty, and I half expected a tumbleweed to bumble through.

A slight breeze swept by and stirred doubts. What was I doing? Isabella kept a level head on her, and part of me thought she'd spoken true. I was a fool to waste our one chance at Jensen to save some people who may or may not be hurt. Claire hated me anyway and would be as ungrateful as a landed fish. Money we couldn't afford to spend, and I'd gone and thrown it into a rescue mission when danger hunted my own crew's every step.

The Brits tracked us, Morlocks put us in their 'kill' database, and our ex-employer wanted his cargo. With so many new friends, it was a wonder we got anywhere.

"Do you have any inkling as to which one of these lovely homes the mercenaries would shove them in?" I asked.

Mordecai shook his head. "Could be any. I may be skilled at finding people, but I just follow the signs. No psychic powers or anything, as much as that'd help my career. Look for indicators of movement or footprints. These houses are generally abandoned." The path ahead appeared, well, dirty. My eyes weren't trained to seek out footprints and details like askew doorframes. Or overturned rocking chairs. My gaze paused on the sight three houses down.

"You think there might have been a struggle?" I pointed in the direction of the felled rocking chair.

"It's worth a try." Isabella twirled two knives between her fingers. "Better than anything we have right now."

I peered at the windows lining the top floor but they were too darkened to see from, and the first floor ones had been boarded up. Great attack plan: march in through the front door. Mordecai walked up the porch steps first, but for a man of such large stature wearing heavy leather boots, he didn't make a creak. His blonde hair trailed down the middle of his back and flowed with his lithe movements. Isabella followed him with a gentle sway to her hips.

I tried placing my foot on the step lightly like them, but the wood groaned when I pressed my boot down. So much for stealth. Mordecai's eyes narrowed, and I raised my hands, biting my tongue to keep from pointing out our front entrance approach didn't help either.

No one aimed a sniper shot at our heads, so they hadn't stationed guards. Although, if they pressed their hostages for information, the mercenaries might've made a call and disposed of the bodies. A shiver ran through to my fingertips. Mordecai pressed the door open, and we filed indoors. Streams of light poked through the couple cracks in the walls, but shadows suffocated the rest of the place.

The keen smell of rust and mildew filtered through the room, mingling with the cheap air. This entire house unsettled me, even as my eyes adjusted to the pitch black. Long wooden floorboards stretched out, for the most part unbroken, and a couple of tarp-covered chairs and couches crowded the back wall. No one made a sound, and we all listened. Though in the far distance seagulls cawed and the breakers crashed, utter silence dominated the inside.

A spiral staircase cut into the middle of the room. We crept over to it, and Mordecai tested the first step with his boot. Good. The wood hadn't rotted through. I drew my gun while we scaled the stairs because readiness had saved my life several times over. We reached the top step and stopped. I crept behind Mordecai, squeezing by him to peer past the wall. A corridor branched into three rooms, but still, no noise. Either the mercenaries were adept or...I shuddered. An early evening crow cawed right outside the window, causing me to jump in surprise.

Taking the lead, I stepped forward. The visibility on this floor was much clearer, and a musky sienna light streamed in through the windows. I stepped into the first room, but it lay empty aside from a rotted mattress. No mercenaries waited in the corner for us or any tied up victims. We crept through the corridor and peered into the other two rooms but found them empty, empty, and more empty. I stamped my foot in frustration upon entering the final one. A dusty chest sat against the wall, so I took a seat.

"Where are they?" My impatience and temper rose. "Will we have to search every last one of these row homes?"

Mordecai leaned against the wall. "We may have to."

"I hope we aren't too late." Isabella voiced what each of us thought. If anything happened to Claire, Geoff would lose whatever tenuous composure he held onto.

"You saw them carried away by the mercenaries, right? Did you notice anything else? Who did they pull from the crowds?"

Mordecai's emerald eyes narrowed in concentration, and he tapped a finger against his lips. The motion of his arm brought his sleeve down around his elbow, revealing a tattoo of a black and grey iron cross surrounded by a spoked wheel on his tanned forearm. Geoff paced around the room, back and forth. Waning light cast from the window caused shadows, which swept around the room like dangerous thoughts. I pushed the muddled memory of Claire slapping me away.

Mordecai finally spoke. "One mercenary grabbed the girl who approached you and Geoff. She jumped on you and tackled you down."

"Claire's very fond of me," I commented dryly.

"She was short, tiny features, wore one of those cocktail outfits with a miniature metal hot air balloon pinned to the lapel."

I lifted my eyebrows, impressed. "You have more than an average memory. We've got a girl like you on board. She's pretty much a living map."

"Just steady recall. If I'm paying attention, I pick up every detail. It's why I'm an expert at finding people."

"Okay." I placed my palms on my knees. "So what else did you notice? Who else did they take?"

"Another man, one of the bartenders." He squinted. "He wore that modernized military suit jacket with a little navy cap. Shoddy representation if you ask me. They pulled away one of the patrons too, a well-dressed gentleman. He wore a tweed suit jacket and chestnut pants with a monocle."

I froze. It couldn't be. We weren't the true targets. The blackened thought from before surged into my stomach again, churning it with panic. A thin sweat broke out on the nape of my neck because my intuition hit marks like target practice, bullseye every time. I knew exactly where they'd be.

"Shall we go search the other houses?" Isabella tapped her foot. "It's getting late, and I'd still like some visibility to our advantage."

"No," my voice scraped out at a whisper. Mordecai delivered a sharp, surprised glare. Geoff stopped his pacing. The cogs whirled around in my mind faster than I wanted them to. "Geoff, you have your holster on, yeah?" He nodded, still giving me a confused frown. "What about your coin bag?" He groped for the pouch by his hips, but his hand came up empty. I fought to keep my voice level. "Now, what did you have in your bag besides coins?"

He scratched the back of his head. "Uh, a pocket-sized aether lamp and a map of Reno."

My jaw tightened. "Did you have that map marked with the location of our ship?" I asked. The answer I already guessed socked me in the gut. Geoff always marked the Desire's location when we journeyed on land.

"Yes." He hesitated before comprehension sunk into his features.

Isabella pursed her full lips and glanced between the two of us. "What's so important about that? So he was mugged. The two of you got drugged in there—I think that matters a bit more than a mugging."

"The important part is our ex-employer's mercenaries now know the location of the box on our ship. Which puts our crew in danger."

"They've gained half a day. Do the mercenaries know what airship you fly?" Mordecai strode to the door.

"I'm not sure," I said. "Hell, I don't even know how they found us. I thought we knocked off our pursuers at the drop site."

Geoff followed Mordecai out the door, his face a mask. "During the day there's the chance of docking officers and the other men who run those docks, but you saw how empty it was before dawn. Even with a head start, they'd wait for night. No hassle that way and more cover. Mercenaries think smart."

"Claire must have taken it when we fell trying to escape. She was grappling with me. I thought she slapped me, but my mind was too addled to tell." I brought up.

"We don't know that—anyone could have pick-pocketed me there." The firm tone of his voice closed the topic.

I glanced out the window. "So what you're saying is we have until sunset?" The sky turned lavender under the first waning rays of shadow. "Gods protect us, let's go."

We threw regard out the broken window and ran.

CHAPTER TWENTY

Our feet pounded down the steps, and we flew past the door. The docking bays were located at the end of the street, so I pushed harder, kicking up dirt along the road as all four of us sprinted. Mordecai took the lead with long loping strides that outdistanced the rest of us while Isabella and Geoff lagged a couple paces behind me. Long days of training helped me keep pace despite the drugs still filtering out of my system. My heartbeat pulsed through my hearing like a jangling alarm. The sun wavered along the horizon, but the deepened colors reminded me.

Sunset was coming.

Failure burrowed into my chest, burning like an open wound. Our one shot at finding Jensen, and I blew it to help traitors. Maybe that was my problem. I was too trusting. My heartbeat pounded in my ears as we raced along the dirty streets. Hell, if I hadn't been naïve in the first place, maybe the captain...I squeezed my eyes shut for a second and pushed myself harder. No time for that now.

The docking bay loomed into sight. We neared closer and closer, but the boardwalk lay right out of reach. My ship and crew were in danger. Urgency flooded me, warmed my legs, and forced me to move faster.

Our footsteps' cadence created a steady rhythm, but the fresh adrenaline gave my steps extra impetus, and I passed Mordecai. We had to get there in time, before the mercs tried boarding the Desire. No one would violate her, and I wouldn't allow my crew to be taken by surprise. My hands balled into fists as we ran. Magenta streaks raced across the horizon, and the sun halved into a copper ball of flames that sank into the sea. Worry beat like a tin drum in the back of my brain.

A slight wind picked up and carried the salty spray of the tides mingled with rusted metal. We reached the boardwalk where dozens of ships berthed, and I caught sight of the Desire's dark wooden hull. If we made it to the ship, we could pull out and ditch them before they even caused a problem. No one strolled along the deck, and the absence formed a menacing silence, which was only broken up by the occasional crash of tides.

I squeezed my fists tight. The crow of a seagull startled me as it careened way too close.

Isabella sidled next to me, pulling out a miniature brass telescope. "Let's find some cover and take a peek."

We crouched behind several barrels, and sandbags slouched against the port building. Isabella peered out from above with her scope, scanning our ship. I tapped my foot against the stained wooden planks. The sun glided closer to the horizon, and purple edged its way onto the skyline. We may have already been too late. That dropped a numbing beehive of panic into my brain, and I forced myself to take several deep breaths. Isabella's fingers tightened around the brass tube.

"What is it?" I almost didn't want the response. Mordecai crowded in closer.

"I see Spade wandering the ship." A sigh passed her lips. "So is Jack, Abigail too."

My chest burned with relief, and I took charge. "Let's move out then. We don't have the time to waste on subtlety."

"Please," Isabella laughed. "When have you ever wasted time on subtlety?"

Before bursting out into the open, I glanced down one side of the walkway, then the other. I raced towards the ship and prayed Spade or one of the deckhands noticed us. We needed them to drop down the rope ladder.

The smell of gunpowder and I had a familiar, sordid past. So, when the first bullet cleared the air, I ducked in time. In fact, all four of us did. Even though we stood by the Desire, no one peered over the edge or threw us a ladder. By the other end of the port house, someone stepped behind the teetering stack of crates, but we'd already exposed ourselves, so anything more couldn't hurt.

"Spade!" I placed a hand by my mouth and called up, "You

black hearted cur, leaving us stranded down here. If you don't lower the ladder I'll have your liver for breakfast!" I stepped back, hoping my voice carried. Mordecai drew his sabre and raised the blade in defense, preparing for an onslaught of bullets. Another shot ripped through the air, but he arced his blade fast, and it pinged harmlessly onto the ground. Either they tested us, or only one man hid behind the stack.

A familiar face peered over the ship ledge, and seconds later the rope ladder dropped down. I scrambled for the first rung but upon grabbing it, stopped. Climbing would leave us exposed and vulnerable for them to shoot us in the back. These were mercs. Smart. We made easy targets, so why waste ammo? I placed an arm out to keep the others back before tossing the ladder upwards.

"Don't let anyone aboard," I yelled back. "Snipe any intruders." I jerked a thumb towards our previous cover, and we made a quick retreat.

The mercenaries didn't waste any time once their opportunity vanished. A full onslaught of bullets peppered the air. Mordecai took the front, and his sword flashed a million different ways while he fended off the stray shots. The others studded the boardwalk. We raced back over to the barrels, and I dove. My shoulder crashed onto the mildewed planks, but I shook the pain off and drew Matilda. The port house doorway blocked a clear shot at the stack of crates lining the other side.

Another round of shots fired again but sparser this time

since we hid behind the barrels. They realized the disadvantage too.

"I wish I had a frag right now. I'd lob it and blow the bastards to hell." Geoff threw his head back. Isabella peered over the sandbag and took a shot. Her bullet pinged against the protruding doorway off the building, so she tried again, but the shot buried into a crate. We couldn't maneuver out in the open, yet they couldn't either. Ah, good old fashioned stand stills.

Someone poked out past the crates. Two people, in fact.

I lined up my shot, but before I fired, Mordecai clamped a hand on my shoulder.

"Those are the supposed hostages." Deep in my gut, I still had that sinking feeling, but I glanced back at Geoff. Even though he barely dared, hope shone through his eyes anyway. If I shot Claire now, he'd never forgive me. Besides, I couldn't aim at unarmed, open targets.

Claire and the bartender rushed towards us.

"Help, help!" she screamed and balled her delicate hands into fists. Tears streamed down her face, and I had to stop myself from rolling my eyes. Like the mercenaries would let hostages go for no reason. How stupid did they think we were? None of us moved an inch. Midway through, several bullets clipped the air again. Claire and the other man threw themselves to the ground. I shot a hand out to Geoff's shoulder to keep him from running out and frowned.

They scrabbled up again, surging towards us. The sun cascaded into its final swan dive before night and sprayed a trail of glittering light across the deck. Desperate beams glistened over waves and deepened the monolithic shadows of the ships. And the final rays glinted off an object in Claire's hand.

I whipped Matilda up and pulled the trigger, but Isabella beat me to it. A shot buried deep into the bartender, and his hidden shotgun flew from his hands. Claire wasted no time and rolled over by the doorframe. My shot sailed past her overhead. I fired another one, but she already ducked into the port house entrance. Shit. I placed a hand against Geoff's back, but he didn't move. In my experience, betrayal sliced deeper than a bayonet knife.

With one dead body on the boardwalk and one loose-cannon vixen inside, we were back to the standstill from before. Threads of night began to overtake the sunset and cast the dock in darker shadows. I sucked in a sharp breath before peering up to try another shot. My bullet pinged off a crate, throwing splinters into the air.

A round of bullets besieged the mercenaries from above.

Spade came through, and our crew fired rounds from the perfect vantage point of the ship. One man slumped past their cover, dead. The mercenaries moved fast when their cover fell through. They circled around the back, but Spade and our men kept firing.

I signaled forward. Since someone threw the rope ladder down, I seized the opportunity. We raced across the boardwalk while our crew maintained distracting fire. My fingers curled around the first rung, and I scaled that ladder so fast the rope rippled in my wake. As I tossed myself onto the deck, Edwin rushed over.

"We hadn't heard from you since yesterday. We were worried, Captain."

"I've been busy getting shot at, deceived, and drugged. Scouting's a tough job these days."

Edwin shook his head, and a goofy smile quirked our doctor's lips. Isabella and Geoff tumbled aboard with Mordecai right behind. Edwin hovered over them. "And who's this?"

"A big fluffy teddy bear." Isabella's eyes studied Mordecai, and she flashed him a predatory grin.

"Spade," I called out. "Halt the fire, we're on board. We need to get out of here at once." The peppered shots simmered down, and Spade jogged over. A dainty hand touched my shoulder, which caused me to whirl around. Adelle stood behind me, favoring her right side since a brace still wrapped around her ankle.

"What are you doing up and moving around?" I asked.

"I looked over the navigation bay with Mister Wesley." She tugged a long strand of hair.

I blinked. "I thought I knew everyone on this ship."

"You call him Spade."

"You mean his name's not Spade?" I arched a brow.

He cut between us. "What do you need, Captain?"

"We need to leave now. Those are our ex-employer's men, so we'd be safer in the air. Start up the engine, fill up her balloon, and we'll sail the skies again this night." I turned to Adelle. "You're not ready to start steering on that ankle, but do you want to watch the boys get her started?" Spade escorted her over, and I glanced back at Geoff. "Would you mind?" He stalked over to the navigation bay without a word. We'd need to talk later.

Edwin scuttled back to his crustacean depths, and Isabella wandered over to Jack and Abby. Mordecai leaned against the side of the ship with his arms crossed. I tapped a finger against my forehead before hurrying over to him.

"I'm so sorry—you already did what we paid you for. You're free to go." I bit my lip, frustrated at the foolish waste of coin. Mordecai didn't move.

"I talked to Isabella you know. A traitor on your ship, this Jensen? That's rough to stomach. And I didn't fulfill my bargain, since I never found you any hostages. You came to the answer on your own."

"We do need a recon man. The traitor was our old one.

Would you be interested?" Mordecai didn't answer and studied me for a moment. I grinned. "Sorry, did I move too fast for you? Next time I'll buy you dinner first."

"You exchanged help finding the traitor for those hostages. Why?"

"For Geoff and because I'm no scumbag." I didn't hesitate. "I don't get innocents involved on my account, especially unarmed ones who can't protect themselves. And that girl who betrayed us? Geoff's old flame. We protect ours around here. I just wish I could have protected him from that emotional smack down."

Mordecai's grin deepened. "That's not the first time I've heard that phrase." Before I could ask, he cut me off. "Very well, I'll join with you. I've grown tired of Reno anyway and could use the change of scenery. No gypsy stays in the same place for long."

"I can't promise you'll be bathing in jewels, but we keep things interesting."

He shook his head. "I've seen a bit of that already."

"We never suffered a formal introduction." I offered him a hand. "I'm Bea, Captain of the airship Desire."

"Mordecai Blacksmith, dear lady." He flourished his hand and bowed. "The alleged Shadow Ward at your service."

I slapped his back. "Welcome aboard."

He removed his trench and draped the thick coat over his forearm. The starched tan shirt made a failed attempt at disguising the sinewy muscles underneath. Without the cover of his coat, his sword hilt protruded from the frog attached to his belt. I'd seen the sword in flashes when he displayed his fancy moves, but the pommel glowed brassy under the last wisps of light. His scabbard ran long and black with a bronzed tip. Mine was longer, but I hadn't his level of skill.

"Since I'm a new member of this crew, and not some random mercenary for hire, I suppose it couldn't hurt to give you what little I've seen of your traitor."

I perked at his words. In the distance, Adelle stood next to Spade and Geoff at the navigation bay as she watched them flip open consoles and set the Desire up for flight.

"How would you have heard anything? I haven't even told you the man's name or description yet." Before he responded, I figured out the answer. "Isabella. How much time did you guys have together anyway?"

"Enough." He grinned and showed some teeth. She'd have to fill me in later. "When I wandered the districts of Reno, even in Nautilus, I did catch a glimpse of a man matching your description, mere hours before I ran into the three of you. He stood a head taller than most of the crowd and wore a bowler cap. Hazel eyes."

"That sounds like Jensen to me. Any idea where he headed?"

I leaned against the side of the ship, listening to the creaks as she readied to sail.

"A Morlock tattoo covered his bicep, and the obligatory pelt weighted down his holster. He was conversing with other Morlocks, those of the eastern branch."

"You must have met the wrong man." I frowned. "Jensen might be a traitor, but the Morlocks?"

"I can tell you what I've seen, but not what's true or real." Mordecai shrugged. I stepped back and rolled on my heels. Whatever his motivations had been, Jensen left behind the person I spent missions running around with. He lost the right to those memories when he killed our captain. If he joined with the Morlocks now, his new identity painted him in comfortable black and white enemy clothes.

"As for where he was headed..." Mordecai continued. "Well, it wasn't a coincidence the Morlocks cornered me in that bar. I overheard word of the eastern sect meeting over the Atlantic. Those coordinates are supposed to be secret, like news of the meeting, but I happened to sneak into one of their bases."

I raised an eyebrow. "You don't just stumble on those bases. What were you doing there?"

"First off, I don't like being in any sort of database. And secondly, I heard they were after cargo that could turn into a catastrophic nightmare in their hands—involving my birthplace of

Old Germany at that."

My heart paused in my chest, and my eyes widened. "What did they say that cargo looked like?" the words left my lips in a whisper. How did others know about this cargo? My blood froze. Worse, what were we going to do if the Morlocks found out we had it?

Mordecai squinted as he recalled. "A box, small size with a hell of a hard lock to break was stolen from a British merchant ship. Old German writing detailed the sides."

I nodded and tried to betray no emotion. The Desire's limbs groaned with the start up, and the ground trembled underneath my boots. "With the Brits after us, our ex-employer, and the Morlocks, I have to say, anywhere is better than staying still. I appreciate what you've shared with me. You'll be a valuable member of our crew," I said, clapping a hand on his shoulder before I walked off.

My mind whirled with thoughts of our cargo. What could be inside worth this trouble? By the docks, a door opened, and Claire slipped through the shadows along the side of the building, vanishing with the other mercenaries. I clenched my jaw. No one hurt Geoff like that. The next time we met that strumpet I'd be armed and ready to take her down.

The balloon inflated and puffs of steam trailed off into the night sky from our roaring engine. Night fell. A somber moon glinted off the metal frame of the balloon, casting idle beams over the deck. The steel structure squealed against the rusted beams holding her in place, and the ship skimmed against the sea. We soared into the night sky, away from Reno.

CHAPTER TWENTY-ONE

The next morning when I woke up, my head dizzied with

the intoxication of sleep. Geoff and Spade started our girl flying,

and we sailed over the land mass of the United States en route to

the Atlantic Ocean. Whatever these Morlocks congregated about, if

Jensen followed them now, he'd be ours. I blinked and scanned my

room. Today I'd have to start moving my belongings over to the

captain's chambers, even though that room still loomed in my mind

like forbidden territory.

I stretched my arms over my head and stood. My chemise

was wrinkled, so I threw on a more suitable ensemble of dark

brown breeches and an absinthe green bodice. I cast a sad glance

over the clothes scattered around my room and the baubles lining

my countertop. My cameo collection would have to be packed away

along with my prized brass knuckles.

When I stepped out into the hallway, I tilted my head to the

side and sniffed the air. The breeze carried the savory scent of sage

and butter through the cabin. I narrowed my eyes. No one cooked

real food on this ship.

The last good meal I'd eaten was the jerky we had with

boiled potatoes because Isabella managed to heat them without burning the meal. Before then, Edwin's fruitcake stood out in my memory, despite the chunks of half cooked egg inside. My feet directed me towards the source of the aroma. One flight of steps down, the scents became clearer and more delicious. I couldn't identify any of them, but perhaps if I could then I'd be able to cook.

Muffled voices came from the galley and mess hall. Once in awhile people tried to cook something down there, but more often we grabbed a meal bar from the cabinets or ate a dinner in town whenever we could. I rifled a hand through my tresses before entering the room. Generally, empty rectangular tables studded the otherwise clear mess hall, but today proved different. Most of our crew of about twenty scattered around the seats, including a couple deckhands in the back, Jack, Abby, even Hiram. Mordecai and Seth sat together, deep in discussion at one of the closer tables. Spade finished a plate of food beside them, and Seth waved once he caught sight of me. I nodded back.

A hissing sound came from our galley accompanied by the source of those delicious smells. I entered our cramped kitchen, which had two granite panels for the countertops, a stove, oven, and a sink. Adelle stood by the oven with a checkerboard towel wrapped around her hand, and Edwin peered over her shoulder. A skillet full of meat and vegetables in some sort of gravy sat on the stovetop, and several dirty dishes littered the sink.

"What's going on?"

She jumped with surprise at the sound of my voice. "I

figured I'd cook some breakfast. I mean, you had some dried meat, and we picked up vegetables at the port. I'm making Cornish pasties for the crew."

"Thank the Gods. We finally have a cook aboard our ship!" I hugged her tight. My mouth watered at the sight of the delicious pasties with golden handmade crusts, which had been crimped with a fork edge. She gave me a shy smile while Edwin peered into the oven.

"I believe they're done baking, Adelle." His lanky form hunched over like a triangle. "Did you want to pull them out?" I let her go, and she used her makeshift oven rag to pull the tray of tiny treasures from the oven.

"Where did you learn this magic?" I took a deep whiff of the savory baked treat and had to restrain myself from shoveling handfuls of it into my eager mouth.

"The school I was sent to. It was a boarding facility, so we learned to cook for ourselves early on. Some students had an aptitude for the art, and we took a round of classes. It's not that difficult."

Adelle still wore the same overalls from when we met her. My nose wrinkled on reflex. "I'm going to go through my belongings today. Let me see if I have anything too small for me, so we can get you properly outfitted. No helmsman of mine will wear rags."

Her eyes lit with excitement.

"You don't care when I do, Captain," Spade called in from the mess hall.

"That's because if you put a pug in a dress, it still looks like a pug. But if you'd like a lovely little bonnet, I'd be happy to oblige," I hollered back. A couple laughs, including Spade's, trickled in from the other room. The pasties had sat for a few minutes, so I reached down to pick one up. My hand jumped back from the burn.

"Ah, careful, they're not done cooling," Adelle warned too late. "Try picking one up with a cloth. They'll still be steaming for a bit, but once it's broken it'll cool down faster." She passed me her oven cloth, and I scooped up the pasty, dropping it onto one of our chipped gray plates. I groped around the drawers for utensils, but the rest of the crew already snatched up the few we owned. They probably played pass the fork out in the mess hall.

"Thank you doll." I mussed her hair. "You have no idea what a hot meal means to the crew. You're absolutely lovely."

Edwin nodded while stroking his bony chin. "This baking and cooking thing is such simple chemistry. I should be able to comprehend it, and yet the end result still eludes me. Perhaps it's because of the cognitive functions of our cerebral development."

"English, Edwin. Do you speak it?"

He wiped his hands across his waistcoat. "Based on the

processing of our childhood experiences involving food, perhaps we develop different ways of tasting, which leads to a proficiency in the art or an inability to intake and understand it."

I blinked at him several more times.

He threw his hands in the air. "My mother was a terrible cook."

"Ah." A grin lit my face. I whirled away from the kitchen with my plate in hand and carried it over to the first table where Seth and Mordecai sat. Spade had left; I assumed back to man the helm. He and Geoff always traded off with ease, both willing to compromise when the other needed a break. I placed my plate down, and Seth pushed a mug over to me.

"So you don't steal mine." He nodded towards it. I lifted the cup to my face, taking a deep swig of grog.

"Thank you kindly, sir. So what are you men discussing over here?"

"His time during the military," Mordecai said. "Seth here had a pretty phenomenal campaign even though he's being modest. I'd heard tales of Eagle Eye from all the way back home."

I sat up in my seat and glanced at Seth. "Hidden depths, eh?" My pasty still steamed, so I poked a hole in top. Heat bit my fingertip, and I drew back fast. "How come you've never told us these stories, Seth? I've known you for years now."

"Never asked." He shrugged, and a blush covered his ruddy face all the way to his ears. He didn't like boasting and wouldn't bring his own accolades up.

Mordecai chewed on the final bite of his food and swallowed. "You never told me you had such a wonderful cook aboard."

"I'm discovering many things today. The taste of a savory meal is about to be one of them." I shifted on my seat, waiting for the pasty to cool.

"You all started eating without me?" Isabella's smooth voice sounded from the doorframe. I turned around to spot her standing next to Geoff.

"I can't help it if you sleep more than a cat." I jerked my thumb to the kitchen. "Grub's in there."

"What's this breakfast novelty?" Geoff muttered and shook his head. "I don't think I can ever remember a time we had this."

"Once." Seth had a faraway look in his eyes. "Before you all came aboard. After a lucrative job, Morris hired a wench to make us a meal the next morning."

"Why didn't Morris hire wenches for us?" I asked, still glaring at my scorching breakfast.

"He did," Geoff called from the galley, "He brought you aboard, didn't he?"

I held back my smile in lieu of mock indignation. "Hey, that's Captain Wench to you, boy-o," I yelled back.

Geoff reemerged with a plate, followed by Isabella. He sat next to me and dug a fork into the pasty.

"How did you get a fork?" I frowned.

A wicked tooth poked out with Geoff's grin. "Spade likes me more than you."

Relief settled in my chest seeing Geoff joke around. After last night and his old flame's betrayal, I had worried he'd delve into a dark place. Steam stopped rising from the hole I poked, so I lifted the pasty. Since the crust no longer burned my fingers, I could finally eat it. The warm first bite filled my mouth with gravy from the pocket: salty, savory and beyond delicious. I chewed vegetables and the softened meat along with the buttery pastry crust. Adelle was a phenomenal cook.

"Inhale it a little more why don't you." Isabella sat beside Geoff. "Seth, what did you do to that thing?" We glanced over to see he had cut his pasty into precise square segments and worked away at it with his fork.

"I like order." He shrugged, jabbing one of his little squares.

"You like playing with your food. I'm not opposed, but I prefer a different setting." She winked and stroked his arm. Seth rolled his eyes, keeping focus on his meal. He was the only man I'd ever met who didn't get flustered by her charms, which fueled her to try harder. Edwin strolled in from the kitchen.

"I believe I've figured out how she's making these." He jabbed a finger at my pasty. I moved my plate away with a protective arm and devoured another delicious bite. "I watched her proportions and the length of time she leaves the tiny pies in the oven. A jelly of sorts, like gooseberry, would improve the filling."

"Edwin, if you ruin her good cooking, I will end you." Geoff spoke while chewing another bite of food. "Don't put your jellies or weird potions into our meals."

"I think it would taste decent." Edwin sniffed the air, and his mouth turned in a slight pout. "The chemical composition should complement the rest of the pastry." He sat at the end of the other table, facing us. "Does anyone need a wound dressed?" he asked. I shook my head and ignored the graze on my arm.

His eyes glinted as he glanced at my sloppy bandage job. "I have a new formula for a healing ointment that involves a flour paste and the elderberry extract I found in my back cupboard stores. I also placed some mild sedative in it to calm the nerves. The experience should be rather relaxing." A crazed look overtook Edwin's eyes. "Would anyone like to test it out?"

"No stabbing for science." I leaned back in my seat and took another bite. Edwin's shoulders sunk into a sulk.

"Fine, I'll have to wait for the next person to get wounded in battle. Shouldn't be difficult as none of you can seem to stay out of trouble."

I shook my head. "You have a point there, sir."

"I wouldn't say none of us can." Isabella frowned. "I don't get into too much trouble."

Edwin raised his scraggly eyebrows, and he glared at her over his beak of a nose. "You've been in my infirmary, why?" he asked. "And that traitor, Jensen, he had just been there too. Poor darling Adelle, she's been there. Bea, you should have come down to see me for that graze because it'll fester in days. Geoff, Seth, and since I've never met you, Mordecai, I'd say you three are exempt." He fixed us with a supercilious teacher's stare. "The rest of you are walking talking ant farms of trouble."

He shrugged. "Although, if no one got hurt, I'd be rather bored." The way he said the phrase didn't comfort me. I finished the last bit of my breakfast, and my stomach settled happily. I couldn't remember the last time a warm meal filled my stomach. We needed to do this more often.

Adelle came in from the kitchen with strands of her hair curling and rosy cheeks from the heat of the oven. She carried over a plate with a pasty on top.

"Come sit with us, enjoy your meal," I called out.

She walked over and took a seat across from Edwin.

"Thank you for the wonderful breakfast," Geoff said, passing her his fork. "What did you think of the navigation bay?"

"Such a tiny slip of a thing, how are you going to reach those consoles?" Mordecai chuckled.

Adelle poked a hole into the pasty with the fork. "She has a reliable system, but her bearings are off. Just minor degrees, but they can be adjusted. You and Spade too, that romance needs to go. It's totally distracting." We paused in silence for a moment before she broke into a grin.

"There we go, you're one of mine." A wide grin stole my face as I tossed an arm around Geoff's shoulders. "Hear that? I'm not the only one who thinks you and Spade are too close. Sharing forks. I'm afraid to even know what comes next."

Seth burst into a loud laugh, and we all turned to gawk at him. "The girl's got lip on her. Welcome to the crew."

A bright smile lit her face, one I hadn't seen on her before, but seconds later tears watered around her eyes.

Edwin's brows furrowed in confusion. "Are you okay?" he asked.

I chased a crumb around my plate and tried to ignore her tears.

"I'm fine." Adelle wiped her forearm over her eyes. "It's just—I haven't had a meal like this in awhile with so many wonderful people. The school, well, not much interaction was tolerated. They separated us after awhile. And those slavers." She shuddered.

Isabella stroked her back. "Shh, you're here now. You're safe."

"Aye, we're a lucky bunch to have a crew like this." I stood and surveyed the room. "Many would die for such a team."

"Many have." Seth nodded. Our table grew somber for a moment, and I could guess what most were thinking. The other tables of crew members hadn't overheard our conversation though and carried on with their own.

"The ship careened and tossed us around." Jack stood with one leg rested on the bench as he threw his hands in that motion. "But from the crow's nest you can see the entire ship, and the whole crew was scrabbling over the deck like ants. Byron, you hid below during that maelstrom, but you should have seen it. Our ship handled that storm like a pro with Captain Morris, Geoff, and Spade at the helm while Bea singlehandedly pulled the sails to steady her. The cracks of lightning that ripped through the sky? I've never seen anything like it in my life."

I grinned, remembering our last storm not so long ago. Whole years passed with less commotion than the previous couple months.

"That was quite the gale." Isabella turned to Adelle. "From

below deck, the bucking almost drove us all sick. I was sitting there trying to rest while the beds started moving back and forth. The least they could do was to try and steady her so us patients would be a bit more comfortable. And Edwin ran about the infirmary with his hands over his head, screaming about the end of days."

"I did not." He sniffed. "I merely held some concern for our immediate safety." Adelle wiped away the remaining tears and let out a watery laugh. I brought my dirty plate over to the galley, pausing at the doorframe.

In the back, Jack still told his story to some of the new deckhands, and the old ones leaned against the wall with their arms crossed. Isabella kept her hand on Adelle's hunched shoulders while the two of them chuckled at Edwin's indignance. Seth hunched over the table, watching the whole thing with an amused smirk riding his face, and Mordecai interjected with an occasional comment as smooth as his silken voice. I clutched the frame and bit my lip. We hadn't eaten as a crew in some time, and I missed that togetherness. No matter what happened, I'd protect them.

Before I left, Seth caught my eye and approached. I cocked my head to the side.

"Bea, I need to speak with you. In private." He glanced back over towards Mordecai and signaled for him to join us. Both men were discreet, so no one paid much attention when we exited the room.

"Where are we going?" I asked.

"Down to the engine room." Seth lowered his voice, "It's about the box."

CHAPTER TWENTY-TWO

As we descended the steps to the engine room, my heart sped up in my chest. Did Seth crack the code to open the thing? The mystery of what the box held ticked inside my mind like the sound of the rusted clock on my dresser. Tufts of steam drifted from the entrance in hazy clouds, threading the air with a thick humidity.

"Did you ever find out what the inscription meant?" I tried to not specify what we were talking about since Mordecai joined us. Seth nodded and jerked a thumb at the Shadow Ward.

"He'll recognize it. Anyone from Old Germany would. The inscription is the ancient military mantra, "no German boots on foreign soil"." Pulsing aether tubes greeted us the moment we walked into the engine room as the green liquid flowed up and down with a rhythmic chug.

"They changed that around the time of the Great European War," Mordecai spoke up. "A warrior death over a cowardly life." Our engine dominated the right side of the room, cased in a large steel cylinder to keep the internal parts from damage, and I knew every last detail from the camshaft to the piston. Seth directed us to a circular table away from the heavy machinery. A light bulb dangled from overhead, lighting the oil-stained tabletop.

"This was the old mantra, from before the war. Someone's had this box for a long time." Seth pulled the cargo from the locker he'd kept it in and then moved his wrenches and hacksaw onto the shelving against the wall. He brushed metal clippings and dust onto the floor, placing the box square in the middle of the table. "Here it is Captain, safe like you asked. I've been trying numbers, but no luck yet."

"Well, we already knew it had to do with old Germany." The box mocked us, as impenetrable as before. My shoulders sunk as I sighed, and Mordecai clapped a hand on my back.

"Don't look defeated. You have a veteran from the Great European War, a lockpicking gypsy who spent a long time in old Germany, and a lovely mind like your own. Between the three of us, we can figure out how to open this thing." We pulled folding chairs around, and for five minutes, the three of us sat, staring at it in silence. Tension crawled around the room like a living beast, and drops of sweat pricked the back of my neck, causing impatience to flush through me like spicy cinnamon.

"Let's heave the damned thing overboard."

"Focus on the numbers," Mordecai said. "I can pick that lock with no problem. The mechanism has to be disabled first though, so all we need are three numbers."

"Oh, three numbers, that's not hard," I muttered. "Let's go

over every past event in German history and pick the most important ones."

Mordecai raised his eyebrows. "That's not a terrible idea. This is the ancient mantra, so it spanned from the Second World War to the Great European War around 2030. Someone clinging onto an old motto like that is similar to someone clinging onto the past." We lapsed into silence again and pondered it over. Well, Mordecai and Seth did. I hadn't a clue about old German history.

"So it obviously wouldn't be Surrender day since it ended the Great European War," I started off the conversation.

"What about the Berlin Wall falling back in the 1990s? Maybe that was a big step for them at the time?" Mordecai proposed. Heat crawled through the engine room, coloring our cheeks.

"Oh yeah, wasn't Germany split up for a time?" I brought up. "Granted, that was over half a century ago."

Seth shook his head 'no.' "Has nothing to do with a war, and that's why the motto came around." We all lapsed into a resigned silence again.

"V-E Day, way back when," Seth broke our quiet. "May 8, 1945, was the first marked German surrender to the Brits." He rapped his fist against the table. "But those are too many numbers, and we're looking for three."

"I may not be a gypsy level pickpocket, but I've been on enough jobs where we crack codes," I said. "Year's not important. We've got the first two numbers, five and eight." I spread my palms against the table and stared hard at the inscriptions on the box. People used a million different devices to pick those last numbers. The final one was where someone would try to get tricky by using their age or the number of letters in their name. My eyes darted to the inscription on the box, and a smile breached my face. I fought to keep the corners of my grin down. "The ancient mantra was six words, and the second one was seven."

"So which one is it?" Mordecai glanced at me. Close scrutiny and analyzing always failed me on a job, but my gut instinct never let me down. I stared at the box, and a drop of sweat tickled as it inched down the side of my face. I clenched my jaw and trusted myself.

"Seven. The geared mechanism's newer and would have been installed around the time the new mantra was around. Try five, eight then seven."

Mordecai crouched before the box with the pins laced between his fingers on standby. He cycled through the three numbers, and all of us waited around the table, holding our breath. We watched as the gears whirred and clicked on the mechanism, and the little cogs turned until the side lock released with a tinny click.

Jitters of anticipation trembled through my veins. Some sort of treasure had to be inside this thing—a cursed ruby or an ancient weapon.

Mordecai paused and cast a longing glance at the box.

"Old Germany, eh?" He inserted his pins, jimmying with the lock. "She was stunning back in her day. My camp lived right by the river as we had for a good number of years. I was young then, and we all helped out wherever we could, as one big extended family." I bit my lip as I watched him work. His eyes stayed on task, but he continued. "Even though I grew up without a father, my mother made up for that, the sort of woman who worked just as hard as the men. Her baking inspired legends along the Ruhr, and people from villages away travelled down for a single loaf of her cinnamon bread."

"Madeline?" Seth spoke up. Mordecai glanced up from his work right as the lock clicked.

"How'd you know her name?"

"I'm from the Ruhr. I'd heard of her famous bread." Seth let a small smile loose in remembrance of his home. I took a deep breath as Mordecai pushed the top of the box, but it didn't budge, so he went back to work.

"That all changed on Surrender Day," he continued. Seth nodded and clapped a hand on his shoulder. "The British soldiers swarmed our lands. They stormed the villages and forced people from their homes on the death march to the Stuttgart line."

I glanced over at Seth whose eyes bored into the box with the distinct look of someone trying to repress a memory. Bubbles in the aether tubules pulsed up and down with a rhythmic regularity as Mordecai let out a deep exhale. "My mother fell during that march." His jaw tensed, and the lock clicked again. "I'd give anything to return to old Germany by an open fire with a glass of fresh milk and a slice of my mother's cinnamon bread."

We all sat in pregnant silence except for the hiss of the engine as it released more steam. My hand clenched and unclenched, but it didn't quell the buzzing in my brain. Mordecai stood from the box with his hand on the lid, and my chest squeezed out shallow breaths. I had to stop myself from reaching past him and smacking the top open. He lifted the lid, revealing the contents inside.

A pile of papers.

My nose wrinkled in distaste, and I kicked the leg of the chair.

"Really? After all this chaos, all this hell, we've been carting around a couple of papers that someone forgot to shred? No jewels, no coin, and no fortune—this thing is worthless."

Seth still hadn't said a word, and Mordecai's jaw dropped as they both hovered over the box. Neither man spoke.

"What are you gawking at? Waiting for them to talk back?" My temper flared. "My captain was murdered by one of my best friends over some stupid papers? What is it? Tax evasion documents on some millionaire? Everyone knows paper documents don't hold up any more." I gritted my teeth and stepped next to them to view the useless cargo that hordes of enemies pursued us for.

"Oh look, it has a golden seal. Maybe we can pawn that for money," I muttered, reading from the first paper. "Provision for the Surrender of Germany to the British Repu—" I paused and caught a better glimpse of the papers. I gingerly picked up the ancient documents and scanned over the illegible text. Not tearing my eyes away, I took a seat.

Amidst the political mumbo jumbo were the agreements of the papers that signed away most of Old Germany. All the treaty had granted them was a country the size of Slovakia, but this document was off. I passed the first couple of sheets over for Mordecai and Seth to read. The Stuttgart line drew the border for the remaining land of Germany, a small Southern sliver near the Danube River.

However, that's not what this document stated. This document gave them from Dresden to Cologne, at least three times the current amount of land. I passed the remaining papers over to the boys.

"I knew it," Seth spat on the floor. "Our leader would have never signed off on that much land, unless manipulated and coerced into the situation. We all knew it, and this proves it."

"Proves what?" I asked, still unsure of what this meant.

"This is our official seal." Seth jabbed a finger at the paper. "These were the documents our leader signed before the British took him into custody. He signed on more land. They must have forged that treaty after they took him away. Our homes destroyed by their military and our lands stolen while we had to stand by and watch, all because the dividing line was down South."

"I grew up in Frankfurt." Mordecai's jaw tightened. "We could have stayed. My mother—she might have..." He stopped, unable to process the rest.

Seth faced me, and his dark eyes glinted. "We have to deliver this to the authorities in Germany. They have a right to know what's theirs."

I glanced at the papers again—this was serious. If this buried political secret surfaced, the situation would get ugly.

"Seth. If your people knew what had happened, what would they do? Would they fight?"

"Yes." His eyes burned. "Down to the last child we would."

"They'd all be slaughtered. Germany's army is pitiful, regulated, and still recovering. You throw them against a superpower like Britain, and they'll all die." I placed a hand on his shoulder, meeting his gaze. "Captain was a nationalist, and you are too, I know that, but he wouldn't throw away hundreds of lives.

Think about the situation, smart-like. We have to deliver this to the United Front since they're the ones who handle debates between countries now."

Seth let out a deep sigh. His finger pressed hard against the wrench in his pocket, but he didn't argue with me. Mordecai slumped against the table with his head resting on his hands. I placed the papers back into the box before snapping the lock shut. "One thing is for sure. None of our enemies can get their hands on this thing. We'll talk about our plans tomorrow morning." I left Seth and Mordecai sitting at the table and took the cargo with me.

The captain's room hadn't been touched since I last cleaned it up, and my stomach churned from the faint smell of blood still lingering throughout the chambers. I plucked the old candle from my room and lit it in this one—after all, I couldn't sleep here while that scent resurrected all those horrible memories. My candle flickered, dispensing loose wafts of tobacco and vanilla. I darted out again, returning to the first mate cabin to collect my belongings.

The handles of my leather trunk creaked from disuse, but I stuffed my loose clothing inside and clamped the top shut. My trunk rumbled along the wooden floor as I dragged it down the hall, kicking it into the bedchambers. With each consecutive trip, the tinny scent of blood dissipated. Plus, once I placed my clothes, gun collection, and lucky cameos inside the captain's quarters, the less I'd stomp in on sanctified ground.

I switched on the captain's aether lamps, which caused the

emerald liquid to flow up and down the tubes, illuminating my cameos scattered over his desk and my guns cluttering the shelving. The heat from mid-afternoon filtered into the room, since I'd been hard at work for the last several hours.

At this point, the first mate cabin was nearly empty, and the dresser lay barren aside from the choking dust I'd unsettled. Though my bed still had the same sheets, I held no attachments there. I scanned the floor and the corners of the room, but even with so many little knick knacks, I'd managed to corral them all. I stubbed my toe on a flat little box, forcing me to squat down and pick it up, dusting off the piece. The brass latch came undone, and the top swung open.

My first compass lay nestled inside. The brass contraption was a sundial compass combination that Captain Morris gave me when I became his first mate. He said if I was going to stand at his side, I'd have to know a thing or two about navigating. A snort flew from my lips, and I sat down on the bed with the box. The metal glistened against its black velvet, and the arrow on the compass steadied towards North with a delicate circle of a sundial surrounding the top. I swung my legs back and forth at the edge of the bed.

The day Morris gave the compass to me, I'd run straight to Geoff for help. I hadn't a clue how to use one despite being on the ship for five years, but I sure as hell wouldn't ask Captain Morris. It was a pride thing. I stifled a watery laugh and gripped the worn sheets on my bed. Geoff had tried many times to explain his magical juju to me and go over navigational techniques like the use of an astrolabe, but I only grasped North, South, East, and West. I always trusted that he'd always be there to take care of the ship. Like I believed the captain would always be by my side. I ran my thumb down the smooth sides of the wooden box, taking in a deep breath.

A knock came from my open door. Geoff stood by the doorframe.

"I got confused when I saw your empty room." He tilted his head back, and several messy strands of hair draped over his eyes, but I held back the urge to reach out and brush them away. He entered, and I placed the box into his open hands. "Is that the old compass Morris gave you? Man, it's been some time since I last saw this beauty. How long ago was that, three years ago you became first mate?"

I lay on the bed, stretching my arms out above me. "Yep. Three years ago, I acquired some crazy responsibility. I just thought I gained a fancy new room."

"Wasn't what you signed up for?" Geoff slouched at the side of my empty bed.

"Never. I thought I'd be following our captain's orders around the globe, getting into trouble, and exploring the world. Never planned on responsibility." I cracked a half smile. "Come on now, Geoff, you know me." A silence spread between us with the unspoken words we wanted to say. He leaned forward and pressed his palms to his temples before running his fingers back through his hair.

"She was a traitor, Bea. Another one." His voice broke over the words. "The first time I kept it together, but this? Again?" He turned his head away from me to hide his expression. The sheets crumpled under his white-knuckled grip. "I felt guilty for leaving her behind all those years back, and while I know she betrayed us, part of me has to wonder if it would have been that way, backstabbing and working with mercenaries, if I'd stayed. Or if we could have struggled together and risen out of the muck. But Reno back then...even still. It was bad."

"Would you have been happy though?" I asked. He didn't respond and didn't turn to look at me, but he needed the logic. "If you'd stayed in Reno, maybe working a job or having a family? Claire would have given you those things, I mean, her childbearing hips alone could've."

The candle on my dresser flickered with a hazy light, and wax dripped down the sides. Dimmed beams cast shadows over Geoff's face as he stared at his knees. I placed my fingertips under his chin and gently lifted his face towards mine until he looked me straight in the eyes.

"Gods, you're right. There was a reason I marked the time Morris picked me up as the beginning of my life. It was the day I finally started living it." Inches away from my face, his hot breath tickled my lips, which sent a silent thrill rearing inside me. We both moved in closer. With my motion, the compass clattered onto the floor, startling us out of the moment. I scooped it up from the ground and scratched the back of my head to regain some composure.

"See? You'll be okay as long as you're with me." I lightly punched his arm. "Besides, I can't have some wench stealing away my first mate. You're an important member of this crew, and I can't afford to lose any more."

"So what about your promise to talk?" Geoff put down the compass and faced me. I frowned. After that intense moment a couple seconds ago, I couldn't avoid the discussion, and I'd given him my word. Taking another deep breath, I steadied myself and followed with another for courage.

"All right. Why don't you join me in the captain's quarters? You're going to have to move your stuff in here soon anyway now that I'm cleared out." I picked up the compass box and exited the room.

Geoff followed me, like I knew he would. Sweat pricked my palms—give me a gun fight any day over dealing with feelings. We walked into the captain's room, now mine, and I placed the compass on a shelf before sitting back in the leather chair behind the desk and taking a deep breath. I glanced up to him, hoping he'd let the discussion go, but one look confirmed he wouldn't. So after heaving a reluctant sigh, I started talking before my brain caught up.

"You're asking something of me that I don't know how to give." I flipped one of my loose cameos between my fingertips, focusing on that rather than the intensity I knew I'd find the moment I looked at him. "You want answers and believe me, I'm not blind. I'm aware of what's between us, but I'm not capable of those kinds of feelings."

Geoff took the seat facing me. "You care about your crew and deeply at that. How is this so different?"

My heart sped up at the passion in his dark eyes and the way they shone when he spoke to me. Every bit of me wanted him, heart and soul, but I just couldn't give him what he longed for.

"It's..." I sucked in a deep breath and choked the word out. "It's the emotions of it Geoff. I'm proud of my crew, and I'm proud of you. Those are comfortable, they're okay. But baring your soul to someone else? Being naked under their personal microscope? You've known me long enough—why would I ever subject myself to that?" My lower lip trembled, just for a second, but he caught it. His gaze steadied as he reached across the desk and brushed several strands of hair behind my ear. That touch sent a thrill through me, so confusing I couldn't think straight.

"Bea, there's such a thing as being too tough. I don't know where you obtained this skewed impression, but caring for someone else always requires some level of vulnerability. That's why Jensen's betrayal hurt us all so deeply. If you didn't give a damn, it wouldn't have upset you. It may be easier to shut people out and not care about them, but a life like that isn't worth living. It's no different than if I'd stayed to try a farce of a relationship with Claire."

I sank back into my seat and closed my eyes, inhaling the musk of good leather. One more second of staring at his gorgeous face, and I would get myself into trouble. He didn't understand. I couldn't tear down the walls I built regarding intimacy overnight. Hell, I hadn't even let myself cry when Captain Morris died, and he was a better father than my own. I took a shaky breath before opening my eyes again.

"You make a hell of a lot of sense, but I don't know. Let me think on it?"

He nodded. I yanked open one of the desk drawers where the captain's ships were still crammed inside with little flecks of blood marring the hulls. The sight sent a wave of nausea through me, and I tasted bile. I remembered that night, even though I yearned to black it out. The Spanish galleon I'd lifted up shook between my unstable fingers.

"Is that?" Geoff peered at the flecks decorating the hull and stopped when he came to his own realizations.

"I saw it all." My breaths came sharper. "And cleaned up the mess too. Is that what being the first mate means? You have to be prepared to bury your captain?"

Geoff shook his head. "You have to be prepared for anyone. Betrayal never hurts any less when it happens, but you move forward and do what we are now, hunting the traitor who committed the crime."

"Jensen's going down." I sat up in the seat and leaned over the oak desk. "Mordecai told me the one bit of anything I've heard about him. He saw a man in Nautilus matching his description down to the hazel eyes and bowler cap, but the only difference was the Morlock tattoo. Do you think he joined up with those scumbags?"

"It's just as hard to believe he killed the captain. We lived with him and shared meals for years." Geoff's jaw clenched, and he hooked his thumbs into his pockets. "If he's capable of that type of betrayal, then the Morlocks would be the perfect place for him. Their ranks are full of turncoats, traitors, and scum."

I shrugged. "That's why we're sailing for the Atlantic. From the rumors we've heard, the Morlocks are congregating there en masse for some reason. Maybe they have their annual convention of evil. Either way, our highest chance of finding Jensen is there. He's close. I can feel it in my bones, and my intuition's never failed me."

"Are you ready to face him?" Geoff asked.

"More than. I'll place a bullet through his blackened heart

and leave him for the birds to peck away. That traitor killed my captain, and it's my job to avenge him." I sat back in my seat, letting the familiar anger burn inside my chest.

"Whatever happened to the box?" Geoff asked. I paused before I spoke. After so many betrayals over the stupid thing, even a mention made me suspicious. When I didn't say anything, he frowned. "Bea, really? When did you get this paranoid?"

"We've gotten double crossed by so many people I couldn't spit on the lot of them. I don't ever think you would, but the box ...unnerves me." I jerked a thumb back to the captain's, I mean, my bedchambers. "It's tucked away in there, bottom dresser drawer. I trust you Geoff." He didn't make any moves to get it, and I relaxed.

"Why not throw it overboard? The stupid thing's caused trouble since we picked it up. Our ex-employer wants the cargo, the Brit's want theirs back, and even Jensen wants it. If we didn't have it, wouldn't we lose most of our pursuit?" His words lobbed my stomach with a hard punch because I knew he was right.

"We opened the box and it's some government secret from Old Germany. If it lands into the wrong hands, either Germany stays wronged, or we could be looking at a widespread war."

He caught my eyes. "But before you opened it, what made you hold onto it?"

We sailed straight down into emotional territory. I gripped the arms of the chair so tight my knuckles bleached.

"Captain Morris, for him to not go out in battle and over this box? Nothing was worth our Captain getting killed. I can't lob the thing overboard now because this box could start wars, but, his life meant too much to go down like that, killed by one of his own, unarmed in his room. You didn't see it." My voice broke, "He never even stood a chance."

Silence filled the room and crept into the cobwebbed corners. Neither of us took his death well, but we were supposed to lock our feelings tighter than that accursed box. No tears. I cracked a half-hearted smile and switched the subject. "See, look at that. You wanted vulnerability? I'll deliver it on a platter. You've got a broken captain clinging onto the past who's too afraid to break down so I can move on. I'm a wreck, Geoff, but I can't be. I have to stay tough for the crew."

"And you think that Captain Morris wasn't? He felt every injury his crew suffered. Caring doesn't make you weak. It makes you a better captain."

I took a deep breath. My fingers still clutched the tiny spattered sailboat, and my mind churned like a violent bowl of jelly. Geoff was dead right—he knew me better than I did sometimes.

"What would I do without you?"

"Probably crash the ship. Even if we have Adelle, our new female supercomputer, no one steers her better than me." He stood from his seat and leaned in close. "You'll get us through this. I believe in you."

The rising murmur in my head quelled at his statement. If my crew believed in me, I'd become a captain they could be proud of. Someone to protect kept me swinging even if life threw me the wickedest storms. The smell of cinnamon and musty parchment drifted over, Geoff's scent, and I took in a deep inhale. His support reminded me of Desire and of what was really important: a map and the open air.

"We'll find that bastard and kill him." I slammed my fist on the table.

Geoff hid a smile. "There's the feisty woman I know." He bent over and placed a light peck on my cheek, but this time, I was the one who blushed. "Sleep tight, Bea, we'll be chasing Morlocks from their dens in no time," he called back as he strolled out of the room. I stood from the desk, and my legs strained with me. The candle I'd lit long ago still burned with a diffused vanilla scent, but wax dripped down the sides onto the flat iron holder. I opened the bedchamber door and carried the light in with me.

Unlike most of the mess, Captain Morris's bedroom lay untouched. Aside from slightly rumpled bed sheets, his clean desk and clear dresser shone with the gloss of a fresh polish. I placed the candle on the ledge. The flickering light cast shadows over the walls with long jagged edges, setting the darkness clearly apart. I sat atop the bed and gazed at my new room. My brown leather trunk sat in the corner all buckles with a bronze rim, the largest piece of furniture I owned. It made the place more mine, but I still couldn't shake the feeling that I'd scattered ashes over someone else's sanctified shrine.

Out of the corner of my eye, I noticed a familiar scrap lying on the ground. I'd left it when I went to clean the Captain's body. I hopped off the bed and plucked it off the floor.

The Captain's aviator cap.

He had rarely left his room without his cap. In fact, I could count the days on one hand when his full head of hair saw the light. Reason being, Morris always said every great captain of a ship wore a fancy hat, so he bought his aviator cap the same day Desire rose for her first flight. He sure as hell had been one of the great ones. The leather, so worn and weathered, crinkled under my fingertips. Several flecks of red stained the cap, but they were scarcely noticeable against the dark brown fabric.

I clenched my jaw and tossed my blonde waves back. If every great captain wore a fancy hat, I wasn't about to be left behind because I didn't dress for the party. I pulled the aviator cap onto my head and stood before the porthole mirror, which was accented by brass rivets that glowed under the soft light. Although Morris had a larger head, I had thicker hair, so it didn't fall over my eyes like I thought it would. The woman who stared back in the mirror at me had transformed into a different person than even a month ago. Not just the bags under my eyes or the seriousness in my gaze.

My whole life changed when I became captain. Not that I'd been completely irresponsible and careless before, but I never planned movements like I did now or thought my actions through. I lay on my bed with the cap on my head and stared at the ceiling. Under the dim candlelight, my eyes fluttered until sleep stole me away.

CHAPTER TWENTY-THREE

I woke to cold steel pressed against my temple.

The slithering feeling of metal hit me the second I became conscious, so when I opened my eyes, I did so slowly and carefully. My sleep-crusted vision blurred before me, but upon inhale the odor of diesel oil coated the room like slime.

"Stand up, Bea. Don't make any sudden moves. You know we'll shoot." The voice was familiar. Too familiar, one I'd heard countless times on so many different jobs. It rang with the same commanding tone as always.

Jensen.

For a moment, my world whirled around me in panic, and I lost gauge of my surroundings. I blinked several times, waiting for the blurriness to dissipate and my mind to settle. My surroundings were familiar—I still lay on the bed in the captain's quarters where I'd fallen asleep last night.

Jensen stood beside me with his trusty old revolver pressed against my temple. His appearance proved Mordecai's observations true. Just as I'd changed during the time after Morris' death, he had too.

The hulk of a man appeared menacing like always with tree trunk arms and thick muscular legs, but his eyes changed. Once a soft hazel, they had lent him an air of gentleness despite his brusque demeanor. No longer, they were sunken and red veins crawled into the whites. His ripped sleeves made the Morlock tattoo on his right bicep visible, and his skin glowed tender from the fresh ink. He still dressed in the same ensemble of a bandolier with a bowler cap and suspenders, but a different man than the Jensen I had known wore them. Behind him, another Morlock stood with his semi-automatic pointed in my direction, wearing the navy blue sniper glasses that marked him as a ranked officer.

I took a shaky breath and kept my cool. My feet touched the ground, and with excruciating slowness, I leveled them onto the chilled floor. Jensen kept his revolver pressed against my head the entire time. Once I planted my feet, I stood and lifted my hands.

"I'm unarmed." Just like the captain, the thought roiled through my turbulent mind, as fast and sudden as a storm. I fought to keep my tone even. "What brings you in for this visit, Jensen? I was telling Isabella, you never stop by any more. If I'd known you were coming, I might have put on a pot of tea, maybe polished up Matilda." I took another deep breath to stay steady. "Didn't your mother ever teach you manners? It's polite to give some warning."

Jensen bared his teeth at me, the way he always had when we bantered. Now though, his expression twisted into an ugly smirk.

"Always a talker. I can't say I've missed it. Working with the Morlocks, I finally have some peace and quiet." He pressed the muzzle deeper into my skull. "Now, where's the box?"

I shrugged. "You've put me off the mood to talk with all that weapon brandishing and threatening you're doing. Maybe if you say pretty please."

The Morlock behind him inched closer, but Jensen placed a hand out to keep him back.

"Don't. We don't know where it is, but they know the location." He eyed me. "You wouldn't throw it overboard. Not after Morris died over the thing."

I gritted my teeth but didn't say a word.

Jensen swung the pistol, aiming straight for my jaw. The metal smacked my face sudden and fast, causing searing, blinding pain to rip through my skull. My vision blanked to white for a moment under siege of the throbbing ache. Even still, Jensen had controlled his force, because the man wasn't stupid. If he broke my jaw, I wouldn't be able to tell him the location. He wouldn't kill me outright until they found the box.

"Morlocks, Jensen?" I spat blood onto the floor. The distressed nerves wired knifing torment and panic to my brain, but I forced myself to stay calm, catching a quick glimpse of Matilda lying on the dresser, just out of reach. "I thought you had more class than that." The men next to him growled, and Jensen's lip curled with an ugly sneer. I stretched my hand out towards the dresser, hoping they wouldn't notice. "I mean mercenary I could see, you've always had the aptitude for cold hearted killing, but 'one of the cog'? Really? If they were any more pathetic, I'd laugh them off the ship." My fingers inched near the pistol.

Jensen shifted in front of my hand and blocked me. "Having a force of men at your back isn't that bad. Getting steady gigs doesn't hurt either, especially with the new retrieval job we received from a certain employer. He's willing to pay double the original price tag now. Something about a crew that wouldn't keel over and die, so he could get his cargo. What a stubborn lot."

My eyes widened. The Morlocks and our ex-employer had teamed up. No wonder the ex-employer's men tracked us without a hitch. With Jensen on their side, two of our three enemies were armed with the insider knowledge that he could provide. Only the Brits remained on the outskirts.

I sneered. "Price tag or no, selling out to become a pet is pathetic."

Jensen slung his pistol again. Lighter this time, but that didn't matter. My jaw strained, close to breaking. The nerves along my face radiated with pain, sending shards of agony sp strong I almost crumpled. My legs held steady through willpower alone.

"Let's bring her on deck with the others. There are easier ways of dealing with this than talking it out. Besides," he said with a leer, "I can't wait to see Beatrice without her swagger. Is it Captain now?" He flicked the cap on my head. "No matter. Deep down, you're a scared little girl. You'll be begging me to hand over the box."

"That sounds right up your alley. Scared and unable to fight. They'll hail you slayer of cripples and vulnerable women. Has an honorable ring to it, right?" I braced my jaw for impact, but instead he shoved me forward, keeping the gun pointed at my head. As I trudged down the corridor, my mind spun. Jensen and his men must have boarded us during the night while most of the crew slept. But how did they locate us so easily? My heart sank heavy in my chest. Claire and those mercs probably gave away our direction. After all, we hadn't hunted them down and killed them, just sailed off fast.

Our footsteps echoed through the corridor, like the toll of a grandfather clock at midnight. We walked by my old first mate cabin, empty now, past Isabella's cameo, and Geoff's maps on the wall. My eyes stopped on the porthole hung near my old room, the one Jensen, the Captain, and I found. At the time, I hadn't the heart to tear it down, but I should have. The relic scarred her walls now as a reminder of a naïve time when men were like Captain Morris, with honor, and if they weren't, they were the bad guys we shot.

Jensen shoved me again to make sure I kept an even pace, and we started up the stairs towards the deck. A wave of shame swept over me, and my legs struggled to work. Under Captain

Morris, no intruders boarded the Desire. He'd been smart and always stayed three steps ahead of his enemies. My fly by the seat of my pants approach may have worked under high stress jobs and gun fights where instinct was key, but running a ship took a different mindset. Some captain I made.

Jensen knew what steps he took, thrusting me to face my captive crew and writhe in disgrace. I hardened my gaze. What a pity he'd never get the satisfaction of seeing me crumble. The early rays of dawn peered through the horizon, and the bloodied sky stood out like an omen. 'Red sky at morning, sailors take warning' was the old adage from eons ago. Couldn't be more true. I took a deep breath as we emerged from below, breaking onto the surface.

Not until I reached the top of the steps and witnessed my crew held at gunpoint by the dozens of Morlocks did terror shatter me like a broken vase. The horror in their eyes tore my heart apart and shredded my pride to pieces.

All across the deck, my crew filed out. Spade steadily steered the Desire with a gun pointed straight at his skull. His calm gaze faltered for a moment when he glanced at me. A bruise purpled on his cheek, and his left leg slumped with his weight supported by his right. They'd done a number on him when they snuck in during the night. While I might have thrown jabs at Jensen for joining up, the Morlocks were no laughing matter.

Men grabbed Isabella from either side. A scowl twisted her pretty mouth, and her tan curls formed a tangled mess along her shoulders. Her torn chemise exposed her shoulder while the short skirt she wore barely covered her thighs. One of the Morlock men leered at her, thrusting his face inches from hers. These people held no regard for lives. They'd rape the women and plunder the ship because when they made an exit, they left corpses aboard. Morlocks didn't gain a feared reputation as a pirate band of mercenaries through honorable practices and flower picking.

Another Morlock pointed a gun at Edwin's head. He trembled, absolutely terrified. Their muddied boots tracked trails all over our clean deck and blemished the Desire's surface, but that's the least we had to worry about with a Morlock takeover. Those bastards gutted ships like game and left the floating, decimated wrecks unmanned to crash and burn onto land.

Two of their men corralled the group of deckhands since many of them were too young and frightened to offer much resistance. Another Morlock stood behind Geoff brandishing a knife to his throat. He met my eyes for a brief moment, and I had to look away as the fear burned a brand inside me.

Fury swelled in my chest at the thought of my crew facing such a fate. I'd never allow it. But even if we gave them the box, our outcome remained the same. If anything, the box kept us alive longer because it made us worth something. The second that value left, we'd be tossed overboard like an empty clip.

Jensen shoved me forward in display of our full crew, all twenty of us. Dawn descended, and I choked on each heavy mouthful of the early morning mist. I'd rather he stripped me down than force me to stand under the gazes of my captive crew. Facing their helpless stares wrenched my pride like nothing I'd ever experienced. They expected me to do something and pull some scheme like Captain Morris would have done. Everyone relied on me, but I hadn't a clue how to get us out of this one.

An airship a quarter the size of Desire hovered beside ours, above the ledge by the navigation bay. Her propellers rattled, and in the distance, one lone figure manned the helm. The rest of the crew already found a new ship. Ours. Their small vessel held minimal crew with no artillery or cannons. In an airship fight, she'd be blown from the skies with one hit of our lone cannon, but they built her for stealth, not battle.

Jensen knew what he was doing, since he'd been trained by the best. We'd spent countless days up on the deck sparring with Morris. The better we grew, the more frequently he'd pull out an old military maneuver to win, but he kept us sharp. And Jensen knew every detail about us too—our disadvantages, the size of the crew, and the lay of the ship. He'd brought just enough men to handle our numbers. That sort of efficiency was deadly.

His proximity made me ill as he took his place beside me, and together we faced the crew.

"Now that we have a change of scenery, let's see if you'll be more receptive to my questions. You talk a lot of useless jabber." He gestured to Edwin. "Where's the box?"

Edwin's hands shook, and he refused to peer up at Jensen. "I've never seen the thing that's responsible for this trouble around here. I've no idea where it could be." The Morlock fired the deck beside him, and Edwin leapt almost a foot off the ground.

Jensen frowned and waved a hand to dismiss him. "He's too weak to lie to us. He wouldn't know where it was being kept."

Edwin drew himself up, and his eyebrows slanted with disapproval even though his voice trembled. "Even if I did know, I'd never tell you. A traitor, Jensen. You betrayed us all." My heart swelled for the lanky, neurotic scientist. The Morlock's punch cracked like thunder through the silence as his fist connected. Edwin crumpled.

"How dare you!" Isabella surged from the Morlock's grip at that point with a cry of defiance. She crouched down and kneed the man to her right in the groin. He buckled over. The one gripping her other arm yanked her back by the hair, pressing his cheek to hers.

"We'll be having a fun time later." He spanked her with his other hand, and tears of humiliation burned in her eyes. That prideful, radiant woman should've never been reduced to this. Pain ached inside my chest, but the cold steel at my temple forbade me from any sudden movements. The other Morlock rose to his feet although shakily, and both resumed pinning Isabella back.

A shout and the wet crack of a connected punch came from

below.

Two Morlocks ascended the steps onto the deck, struggling to keep Seth hostage. One sported a fresh black eye. The sight broke my heart, like watching a wild horse tamed under bit and whip.

"Your crew may not be aware of the whereabouts, Bea." Jensen turned his focus onto me. "But you know where it's hidden. Why don't you be a good girl and cooperate? Your death will be much cleaner that way, and I might even kill you straight out rather than pass you around. Morlock men don't see ladies too often, and they're not known for being gentle." I forced down a shudder at the leers coming from the Morlocks on board. "If you don't work with me, each bit of resistance will be taken out on your crew."

"How could you, Jensen?" Isabella's eyes glinted as she ground her teeth. His glance over her way lingered since their communication ran river deep.

"It's called being practical, darling. I watch my own back over anyone else's. Now, the box, Beatrice." Geoff balled his hands into fists and lifted his chin. Seth shook his head to signal a vehement 'no,' because he knew how important those documents were. If they landed in the hands of someone like Jensen, we'd end up with a devastating war.

My heart pounded against my chest. Drops of sweat crawled along my arms and dripped around the cold steel muzzle at my temple. Of course the bastard would use my crew against me. He hadn't held any regard for the Captain's life. I took a shaky deep breath.

"Fine," I said. Isabella's eyes narrowed, and Seth's shoulders sunk with disappointment. "I'll reveal the location of the box but not to you. I can't stomach your traitorous stench. Instead I'll tell Mr. Jump the Trigger over there." I pointed to the Morlock officer who'd escorted me onto the deck with Jensen.

Jensen narrowed his eyes, but he withdrew his revolver from its resting spot on my temple.

"All right. You tell him fast now. But my gun's loaded, doll, and you're unarmed. Try anything stupid, and I'll make sure you suffer. There are plenty of men here who'd like to make you uncomfortable." Each pace over to the Morlock officer echoed in my ears, and my feet dragged across the worn planks of the ship. I leaned forward. He moved in a step closer, so I could whisper the location into his ear. Jensen crossed his arms over his chest and waited.

My teeth clamped on his ear, and I jerked.

The piece of the officer's flesh flopped onto the ground, and his blood pooled into my mouth, spraying from his torn ear. The Morlock's fist collided with my stomach. Hard. I keeled over, and fierce defiance flashed through my eyes. The deck swirled under me, and I fought to keep the contents of my stomach inside. My effort threw me onto my knees.

"What did I say about anything stupid?" Jensen glowered at me with his arms still crossed over his chest. I glared at him, and a crazed grin spread on my face.

"Did you really believe I'd tell scum like you?" I spat at him. The lob of saliva mixed with Morlock's blood hit his arm before it slid onto the deck. His expression didn't change, and his face remained a perfect mask of calm. He pointed over to Geoff and the Morlock standing beside him.

"Overboard, now."

I surged to my feet, but before I could rise, the Morlock shoved Geoff over.

CHAPTER TWENTY-FOUR

My heart stopped in my chest, and I collapsed on the ground when my legs ceased to support me. The deck swirled around as I gagged, reeling in sickened horror.

Geoff. Not Geoff.

Five million memories rushed through me in an instant. Geoff's broad smirk, the one that slipped when he'd made a witty comment. The way he smelled like ozone after a fresh rain, and how the scent of those cinnamon sticks lingered when he left a room.

Even though I interrupted him every time he tried to teach me navigation and spent the other half of the time poking fun, he was always patient, and he always cared. He brought me a tiger lily after one trip because he knew it was my birthday, and I'd kept that flower until it had rotted away and bugs began collecting around the vase. I just didn't want to let it go.

During every one of our talks, he'd held his temper, no matter how much I raged and roared. Even last night when I'd tried to comfort him, he ended up bringing me back from my own self doubt. I couldn't imagine not having the tension that had been there from the start between us, or the shy glances we exchanged when we thought the other wasn't watching. Every peck on the cheek and caress. The electric feeling of his touch on my skin. The sweet taste of his lips.

Five million memories gone.

The rest of the crew quieted. Isabella's jaw dropped open, and Edwin's eyes widened as he slumped over on the ground. Seth—well Seth's gaze sank to the floor with defeat. I had failed. The Captain always said, 'we protect ours,' and I failed to protect the two most important men in my life. Misery swept through me in an aching torrent, and I placed my hands on the ground before I collapsed. Pain from his loss shoved its dizzying draft down my throat, rending the world around me a darker, grimmer color. The Morlock standing by the ledge had a smile on his face.

That bastard pushed Geoff over with a smile on his face.

Several of the Morlocks jeered, and Jensen's mouth quirked to the side with that smirk he'd always had. The Jensen who spent countless nights aboard this ship, bantering with Geoff and sharing meals, had the nerve to grin. In my life, and I'd had a rough tumble, I'd never seen more black-hearted, foul men. And they'd have my crew. They'd do to every last one of them what they did to Geoff and savor it. Except with Isabella, Abby and little Adelle, they'd find different entertainment, until they tossed them over the ledge as well. I'd kill myself before I'd let Morlock scum touch me.

I thought I'd known anger before. The self-righteous kind

like the slavers kidnapping Adelle sparked within me. Anger had rampaged through my chest and drove me into trouble.

The bitter anger of loss like after the Captain died. It ached through me, tore me apart, and mutated me into a different person. Despair drove me with such vindication for revenge, and nothing so intense ever seized control of my mind like that before.

None of those compared to this hungry anger born out of sheer desperation. Flames rose within me, hot, piping and furious. They danced through my body and tossed every bit into their consuming bonfire. Heat singed my fingertips down to my toes. Anger shaped me, molded me. It replaced my heart with molten lava and rushed me in such a freeing wave.

Geoff believed in me. No matter what. He'd always supported me, from my first year onward and was my impetus to keep moving forward. All that hatred roiled within me, honing in on the man who ordered him overboard. The man who killed my two best friends. I lifted my head and glared venom at the traitor.

Jensen stepped in front of me, and his wide frame shut out most of the deck from my view. I tried surging to my knees, but my legs refused to cooperate. My arms twitched, ready for action. At least I'd go out swinging.

"You have yourself to blame. All I asked for was your cooperation." He stretched his hands out and cracked his knuckles. "Now, let's try again." Isabella's body shook with dry sobs, which she tried to stifle, but the Morlock struck her in the back. She staggered forward.

"Not the pretty one." His friend jabbed her in the side. "We have to keep her intact as long as possible." Her eyes widened, and a stray tear coursed down her cheek. Even though she fought to hide her fear, the tremble of her legs made me squeeze my fists tighter. They couldn't be allowed to get to my crew, not like that. The Desire wouldn't go down like that. I gritted my teeth, even though my bruised jaw ached. At least as the captain, I'd go with her.

Over by the navigation bay, I spotted Mordecai peering from behind the frame and trying to catch my gaze. My heart skipped a beat. I kept my face a mask, not daring to let Jensen notice. If he did, they'd be discovered, and our one chance shot with a blank. Adelle popped her head out underneath. That's right—Jensen didn't know about Adelle's little secret or my latest recruit, and Mordecai hailed as the Shadow Ward. If anyone could keep from discovery, he could. Fighting the Morlocks was a farfetched and crazy prospect, but what else did I have to lose? If we didn't break free soon, we never would.

Captain Morris didn't hire any slouches, but neither did I.

"Couldn't do the dirty work yourself, right?" I raised my voice loud and tried to keep Jensen's focus on me. "Sounds like the type of man you are. You couldn't even face the Captain armed. He was too honorable for the likes of you." Jensen swung his fist, and I saw stars.

Half mad and half stricken by grief, I laughed. I spat at him again, and for the first time, irritation wrinkled his brows. Standing in front of him, I'd reached the perfect vantage point for the rest of the ship in time to spot Mordecai emerging from behind the navigation bay. His sword glinted under the early light, and the Morlock guarding Spade slumped onto the ground without a sound. A triumphant spike of pride rolled through me like sunset's final embers.

Time for action.

I threw a fast punch at Jensen. He placed his arms up to block it, but before the blow connected, I switched my aim. The Morlock officer, sans-ear, whipped his muzzle up to shoot me. I tackled him to the ground. My body slammed against his as we rolled around along the splintered timbers of the deck. A shot pinged nearby, but the immediate threat of the officer compromised my vision. His elbow jutted into my side, and a sharp pain lanced into my stomach. My knuckles hit something soft like skin, but the deck and sky careened so much they rolled into one kaleidoscopic mass.

Once I gripped onto something steel, I clutched the weapon for dear life. Shouts rang out behind us, but tangled up with the Morlock, I couldn't see. Using the steel as leverage, I shoved it forward, rewarded by a snapping noise. A vicious grin stole my face.

My arms kept the officer at length, even as his weight pressed overtop me. I struggled to inhale short, shallow breaths from my compromised chest. His fist flew an inch over my face, but I pivoted to the right, so we crashed onto our sides. Since the punch hardly grazed me, I lashed out with my free elbow. A boot crunched down hard on my calf.

I howled in pain, and the fibers of my leg cried with it. The anger buffeted me like a maelstrom, so strong and furious that it claimed my body over the pain. Rage clouded my vision. Nothing would stop me from sinking my teeth into the Morlock bastard who threw Geoff, my Geoff, overboard. I would gut him like a snake.

A fist pummeled my stomach, and I choked out blood but brought my knee up to greet his. I hit something further down, and the officer crumbled from the pain, curling into a ball. I shoved him off me and found my feet. The metal I grasped in my hand turned out to be the muzzle of a gun, and I thanked the Gods it hadn't fired off during our scuffle. Flipping it over the right way, I held the pistol ready in my hands. The officer surged onto his knees and pushed himself up before shambling towards me.

I emptied the clip into his chest.

The man keeled over. I scrambled to pick up the sword by his side and drew it from the scabbard. Amateurs running around with live steel ended with a poked-out eye or personal injury, but I knew a thing or two about a sword fight. Not on Mordecai's level, hell I didn't know anyone else that skilled, but I could stay afloat in a fight with one. While reloading the pistol, I surveyed the deck before choosing a direction.

Isabella adopted the stance she used whenever she fought with knives, but the men around her remained oblivious. Her arm rose over her head like a poisonous adder ready to strike while she her other hand remained poised below. Lifting her knee, she balanced on the one leg. Her fluid movements became more of a dance than a brawl, but Isabella always had that flair for elegance. She swerved to the left, avoiding the Morlock's blows, and with a high kick, she knocked the pistol from his hands. The knives glinted between her fingers as she twirled behind him and aimed. I didn't even need to see the rest to know where he'd end up.

Edwin used his talents as best he could. He'd strapped a stray barrel to one of our sail ropes dangling from a higher mast and crouched on top of the navigation bay's roof with Adelle. Leaning forward, he consulted direction with her and then shoved the tied barrel over the edge to crash down onto the Morlocks. Like a pendulum, the barrel soared back in their direction, and they scanned the folks below for their next target.

One man crept toward the navigation bay, aiming for a clear shot at them. The warning caught in my throat as Edwin turned around too late. The Morlock already closed in with his muzzle aimed. Until the pistol clattered to the ground in two pieces under Mordecai's blade.

Two Morlocks wrangling with Seth had their hands full. The

short, ruddy man slung a solid right hook and knew more military maneuvers from his long campaign than most men learned in a lifetime. Over by the navigation bay a Morlock, the same bastard who shoved Geoff overboard, shot Byron in the shoulder. Jack ran over to help. My feet took off before my mind caught up as I raced in their direction.

The air thickened around me with a telling tension, and I gasped for breath. Rage flooded me with a renewed fervor over Geoff. For the time we shared together, the lazy nights aboard ship sharing a pint of rum under the starlit sky. For the potential of what we might have been. I'd been damned stupid to let my fear keep me from him. And now—now he was gone. My head spun, and I shut out the thought before it devastated me, instead surrendering to the sickly brew of hatred churning inside.

I stopped my tread right before I careened into the Morlock. My sword and pistol clattered to the ground. I didn't need a damned thing because I'd tear that man apart with my own hands. Preoccupied with aiming a shot at Jack, he missed the first hit coming. I slugged him, right under the jaw and shook my hand out as pins and needles jolted through. He recoiled, fumbling with his pistol, but before he could get his bearings, I grappled the piece from him and slid it to our lookout, Jack. I whirled around with an up-kick, and my leg slammed against his other side.

The Morlock staggered but surged forward with another punch. His fist clipped my shoulder, and with that same addled perception, he swung again. I caught his arm between both of mine and jerked it at the elbow, a move the Captain once taught me. The limb snapped at the joint with a hearty crack, and he stopped mid-swing to buckle over in pain. I took advantage of the second to aim a sharp rap behind his knees. He toppled to the ground. Right as my leg descended with another kick, an arm wrapped around my throat.

My hands clamped onto the beefy arm closed over my neck. The man squeezed tighter, and my windpipe strained, ready to break. I bucked and tried to thrash out of the hold, but with the force at my throat and lack of air, my arms dangled by my sides. My mouth watered with my failed attempts to breathe, and my vision shuddered into black. The Morlock I'd beaten surged before me, swaying and casting a crooked shadow onto the deck. His face swelled, and he limped along. Full of rage at being taken down, and by a woman at that, he lobbed a fist into my stomach. I lost breath I couldn't afford to lose, but my captor's position shifted.

I didn't miss the chance, kicking behind my strangler's knee, and the pointed toe of my boot dug into the soft spot, hard. My vision lapsed into black again, but his arm loosened for a second, and the nectar of fresh air entered my throat. As I bit down on his arm, a yell rang out behind me. His surprise gave me enough slack, and I pushed forward to collapse onto the deck. I glanced back. Of course, my assailant had been Jensen. He loomed over me, ready to strike again, until Isabella stepped up behind him, and he whirled around to face her instead.

"You have no idea how long I've waited to sink my teeth into you." Her grim smile matched her dark glittering eyes. She was a woman to be feared.

The Morlock launched himself at me, but I curled up with my boots poised upward right before he landed. When his weight slammed against me, I rammed my feet against his torso like a loaded trap, my legs snapping forward. I rolled along my spine using the impetus to spring back to standing.

He stumbled back but caught his balance. I planted my feet on our solid deck, and we circled, both waiting for the other to make their first move. The Morlock appeared about as bruised as I felt, maybe worse with several split wounds on his chin and a broken arm. My jaw ached, and my neck burned from the near suffocation. Each shallow breath I took circulated my throat like spiked razors, but the air entered my lungs with the surprising strength of a zephyr and flooded my body with renewed vigor.

My right arm bled through my shoddy bandaging, sending a stinging dosage of pain through me. I must have reopened the wound when I launched myself at the Morlock officer. If I hadn't been stubborn, Edwin's antiseptic and curative balms would have healed it by now. A fierce wind picked up and rolled across the deck. The fresh scent held the sharpness of gunpowder ready to ignite, like the fighting aboard the ship. Desire was a loyal girl. She didn't deserve these brutes stomping all over her like a bucket of splinters to burn.

The Morlock broke our cautious circling and rushed in for a jab at me. My shoulders tensed as I followed his movements, waiting for the swing I saw coming. Too late, I caught the glint of a knife in his hand. He raised his weapon overhead, ready to slice it down deep.

A shot rang out.

The Morlock staggered forward and dropped his weapon, reeling from the shock of being shot. The bullet clattered onto the ground after passing clear through his upper torso. He took two more steps before he tumbled down. Blood pooled around him where he fell and stained the deck a deep crimson. Behind him, Jack stood with the pistol I'd passed him earlier, clutching it with shaking hands.

He gave me a slow quavering salute.

"Good shot," I called over to him. "Maybe we'll make a recon man out of you yet." He tried on a fierce grin, but his attempt wilted into more of a puppy dog smile. His eyes careened up and down as the poor boy almost passed out.

Isabella whirled around Jensen several feet away, but he moved as fast. When one of her knives snaked out to slice into him, he'd dodge out of the way to the inch. Her knives slivered razor thin surface wounds across his biceps and forearms. Isabella's tactics leaned to fast movement since against him she wasn't matching strength. She might not have realized yet, but soon she'd

335

reach a disadvantage. Those cuts wouldn't slow a pro like Jensen who just toyed with her, trying to wear her out, and the two of them could do this dance for hours. Both knew every inch of the other's body

I scooped up my stolen weapons from the ground where I'd tossed them earlier and tucked the semi-automatic into my belt loop. While my hand was wrapped around the sword hilt, anyone who tried to charge me would meet a pointed, bloody end. Mordecai stood on guard in front of Edwin and Adelle's perch, fending off any who dared to come close—many didn't, since that man could best most with a blade. Their barrel system made strides with disrupting Morlocks as they aimed it yet again to crash onto one of the men slinging a fist down on Seth. Seizing the moment, he fired a shot, and the Morlock crumpled to the ground seconds later.

With weapons, most of my crew could best these men. Now that the fighting exploded amongst the rabble and my crew wielded weaponry, hopelessness no longer marched a parade across my deck. My heart surged at seeing my crew scrap against the Morlocks as they threw every ounce of spitfire and vinegar they had into the fight. We might yet take our girl back.

Spade kept a steady hand on the helm by the navigation bay. Though the Morlocks were ruthless and used cowardly tactics, they had a sense of self-preservation since they let the helmsman steer without interaction. If no one manned the ship, we might hit an air pocket or any of the other numerous disasters up in the skies, and we'd crash and burn. Until I stared in Spade's direction, I hadn't noticed the dark clouds collecting in the distance. By themselves, those roiling tufts weren't an issue, but with the chaos on board amidst all the battling, they'd provided the perfect cover.

Breaking through the barrier of clouds, a gigantic airship sailed straight towards us. She was a sturdy thing with top of the line materials, well built, but with little thought to her aesthetic construction. Along the ropes leading to the balloon, a too familiar Union Jack flag rippled through the breeze.

The British merchant ship.

CHAPTER TWENTY-FIVE

My chest twisted. Even from here their dozens of cannons glinted from the side of the ship. We'd be sunk if they started firing the heavy artillery. Our only chance was to hoist the white flag and take our vessel back from the Morlocks. At least peace talks might buy us some time. Humidity settled over us with a clammy embrace, and the tumult around me slowed in lieu of one clear thought: rally the crew. I raced over to Spade and clapped a hand on his back. He offered me a grim nod.

"Over to me," I bellowed. "Jack," I continued, pointing towards the ropes. "Hoist the white flag!" I brought my hands to my mouth so my voice carried. "Crew! Rally to me, Captain's orders. Cease fighting. Enemy ship on the horizon!"

In the distance, the monolithic ship pressed closer.

Condensation hung heavy in the air and spiked my nerves. What I wouldn't give right now for a pint of grog, but even absinthe at this point wouldn't pull me back from the brink. At the sound of my cry, many of the crew dropped their weapons and raced over to gather around me. Bodies of the Morlock invaders scattered across the deck of our ship, but enough of the live ones still battled to give pause. Jack hung from the cables by our flags. He threw his back into the pull and hoisted the rungs of the white one into the air. The slate balloon of the British merchant ship hung overhead and carried the oaken beast towards us.

Isabella joined my side, clutching several knives in either hand. Jensen had vanished out of sight, but though she'd stained her blades, she hadn't finished him off. As much as I wanted to hunt him down, we couldn't waste time when that massive ship prepared to ram us clear out of the skies. Many of the Morlocks stared openmouthed at the approaching airship and began to cluster in one solid mass at the forward end of the Desire while we rallied.

They'd never bargained for the British military when they signed onto this mission. Throw in a wee bit of danger, and the Morlocks already tucked their tails between their legs. Unfortunately for them, their tiny airship hovered on our side of the deck, and the helmsman didn't have the smarts to loop around and carry them away.

My crew huddled around me with somber looks painted on every single face. Some days the sunshine was a long time coming, but we hadn't sentenced ourselves to dark days forever.

"Captain," Isabella spoke for everyone. "What do we do now?"

"Attempt a parley with the redcoats. No cargo is worth the price of my crew."

Seth gave me a long stare. He knew, like I did, what that box contained. If I gave it to the Brits, old Germany wouldn't see the justice she deserved. I jerked my head no, and he glowered. Under most circumstances I'd do anything to keep it out of their hands, but not if it meant any more of my crew would fall. "Make sure Jensen doesn't leave this ship alive," I continued. "That traitor is mine." The words escaped me with a growl. Our white flag fluttered in a reckless breeze that swept the deck in gusts.

"What about the Morlocks?" Edwin called down from his perch atop the navigation bay.

"Throw them overboard, I don't care. Just get those men off my ship." I walked over to the back end of the Desire sectioned off by a steeper ledge and rails. The British ship sailed forward at a steady pace approaching for collision. I stepped to the edge and placed my hands along the smooth railing where beyond me, the sky stretched out, aged and tumultuous. The wind whipped around, carrying with it the sharp scent of ozone. My aviator cap clung tight to my head, but the stray curls underneath blew past my shoulders, and I clutched the rounded pommel of the Morlock blade. The British monolith pressed onward, quickly closing the gap between us.

I held my breath and prayed our white flag flew high and clear enough that they'd notice. If not, this would be the final horizon any of us would see.

On the brink of being unable to halt, the British ship

swerved to a grinding stop. Everyone aboard the Desire remained while we watched. Aboard the British merchant ship, members filed by rank. The entire airship, from the polished oak exterior to the pin straight masts, screamed organization, nothing like the rugged bumps and uneven floorboards of the Desire. They marched onto a side boat with at least five officers and their accompanying guards before sailing straight towards us.

Their boat aimed like a rifle shot due to the small propeller whirring in the back and the small sail overtop billowing in the wind. We didn't bother trying to ready any weaponry because within minutes, they'd already lined up with us. I placed a hand over my heart in relief. If they were willing to parley, perhaps we could hand over the box, dump the Morlocks overboard, and sail off in different directions. As if it would be that simple.

"You're giving them the box?" Isabella kept her voice a low whisper as those dark eyes glittered with disbelief. Her words pained me more knowing what the cursed cargo held inside. Seth and Mordecai wouldn't forgive me, but I had to protect my crew over this treaty. Sentimentality gave trouble we couldn't afford.

"If it comes down to it, yes. I'll not lose another member of this crew."

Isabella stepped back amongst the deckhands and saluted. "We're with you until the end Captain."

"On your order, ma'am." Seth's lip split, and a wicked smirk crowned his face. He didn't enter the battlefield as much as he used to, but when he did, his fight from those military days showed. The understanding in his eyes gave me the courage I needed, and I took a deep breath.

"We've lost too many." I glanced over the deck before addressing our crew. "But no more. Whatever we do from here, we have to watch out for each other. That includes the Desire. She's been our home for so long, and no Morlock filth or pompous redcoat will take her and run us overboard. I'd go down fighting for every last one of you. I consider you all the only family I've known, and around here, we protect ours."

"Apparently I signed onto the right ship." Mordecai slipped me a wry grin.

"We're behind you Captain, say the word." Edwin's fluted voice came from the perch above the navigation bay. Little Adelle saluted me, and then waved with a small grin on her face.

"As are we all, Cherie." Isabella passed me a fierce feline smile of her own and placed her hands on her hips. "I was wondering when I'd get a good scuffle. Looks like my birthday came early this year."

The British boat pulled next to the stern side of the ship where we stood. A charged slate sky spanned behind them, and darkened clouds suspended overhead. Without any acknowledgement, not even a glance our way, those high and mighty officers and guards filed out of the boat and onto our deck. One of the redcoats stepped up from the lineup of the others. All were armed with one-handed cavalry swords and muskets strapped onto their backs, their weapons glowing from polish. The guards standing behind them didn't wear such official pieces and bogged down their holsters with a mismatch of semi-automatic pistols and sinful looking knives.

"May I speak to the captain of this ship?" The redcoat refused to deign us with a look and instead stared off into the distance with a bored expression on his face.

"Aye, that's me." I swaggered up to him past the rest of my crew. His eyebrow elevated with reserved judgments, but he didn't utter a word.

One of the guards jabbed a finger at me. "Her and the tall man, I remember them. They're the ones that nabbed the box in the first place."

The officer ignored him. "We've come for our stolen cargo. Either you hand it over, or we'll commandeer your ship." He cast an eye over to the Morlocks. "And if your deck is any representation, a takeover shouldn't be difficult." Irritation scraped my skin like rough rusted metal at hearing him talk about the Desire that way, but I swallowed my conceit.

"We'll hand the box over," I started. A smug smile rolled across the officer's face until I continued. "On one condition." His brows shot up in shock that we'd even think of bargaining. "We give it to you and then you clear off. Allow us to sail away. My crew and my ship are important to me, and I won't have either harmed."

"You do realize you'll have to turn yourselves in. You stole property belonging to the British crown. Such a crime is punishable by death, but I suppose with cooperation we could be willing to reduce such a sentence to imprisonment."

My tongue dried, and I found myself unable to reply. We'd get our lives, which was a better fate than we faced at the moment, and as it stood, I couldn't afford to sacrifice any more over my fool decisions. We'd already lost the Captain and Geoff. I glanced back to my crew.

Seth's shoulders heaved up and down from the fight, but already, he bandaged his bloody knuckles and smacked them against his palm. He'd keep swinging until the end. Isabella twirled one of her knives between her fingers while keeping her gaze sharp on the Brits. I didn't envy being on the receiving end—her look promised death. Mordecai's hand strayed on the pommel of his sword, since the professional was ready at a moment's notice. Edwin and Adelle stood on top of the navigation bay with their arms shaking and knees quivering but by the Gods, ready to hurl that barrel at the nearest foe. A caged life wasn't worth anything.

"A wise man told me the day he joined up here was the day he finally started living," my words rang loud and clear. "If refusal of imprisonment makes us pirates, fine. Airship pirates we'll be."

The officer's face twisted with an ugly frown. "Poor decision. You'll face execution here then." He signaled the guards on us. "Get them."

"Crew," I screamed, and my voice scraped against my throat. "Time to protect what's ours. Show them what the Desire's worth!" I threw my hand forward and led the charge with my sword.

The moment the parley dissolved, the Morlocks made a run for their ship as the deck exploded into chaos. However, they wouldn't get far—Edwin and Adelle stood atop the bay with their barrel poised.

The leading redcoat drew his cavalry sword and met my raised one with a clash. My steel held steady, although my own cutlass would've served me better. By his straight stance and the confidence emanating from it, I could tell the British officer would best me in swordsmanship. He surged forward, feinting a thrust. I almost fell for the trick but at the last second pulled my sword back to guard. With a fast and fluid swing, he brought his blade down, needling towards my right arm. My response time faltered, since I'd already taken a beating, but I lifted my sword in defense before he lopped off my limb.

Not hesitating, he tapped down with his edge twice before circling the sword around to the other angle. His taps threw my cutlass off balance, but I heaved my sword around to greet his next attack. The moment the tip of his blade ripped through my pants and cut into my thigh, I shoved the sword away before it bit further and became a more serious wound. Ignoring the sting from the gash, I focused on keeping up with the redcoat. He'd taken a strict offensive, and given my injuries, the man danced circles around me.

I parried another strike from him, and my arm ached with the effort. The flat edge of my cutlass stopped the point of his blade when he jabbed a sharp thrust towards my stomach. Our motions turned mechanical while the officer waited for me to do something stupid. I wasn't about to give him the opportunity. We circled one another, and the tense air settled around us.

Until Jensen reemerged onto the deck.

With the box in his hand.

CHAPTER TWENTY-SIX

$\mathbf{M}$y jaw tightened and pain from my injuries sparked up into my cheeks. He would not escape. Not after all the betrayals he'd committed and the blood staining his hands a traitorous red. This fight no longer mattered. Jensen hurtled through the chaos around deck like a juggernaut, shoving aside anyone who stood in his way. I met the British man's eyes. He might have perfect form and better swordsmanship, but I had one thing on my side that stacked the deck in my favor—I was absolutely crazy.

Tossing aside our stupid dance, I charged in with a yell so loud he almost jumped out of his little red coat. My cutlass moved with me, but he didn't matter. He stood in the way of my real goal. Even though his cavalry sword whipped against my arm and stung, I drove my blade straight through the ribs and kept running. Hot drops of blood spattered onto my face, but I didn't care.

Jensen charged for the Morlock ship hovering by the ledge. Any poor soul who got in his way would be trampled. The second he reached the vessel, he tucked the box under one arm and grabbed the rope with his other. I had less distance to cover, but he could outrun me any day. My decision wavered in my mind for a second before I tossed the sensible option to the breeze. A Morlock stood in my way, but I didn't give a damn. I shoved the man over and hurtled towards the rope. Like hell he'd escape my ship alive. The wind picked up, and the first warning drop hit my face.

Rain.

Dark clouds rushed at us containing a furious storm. As if shifted by the strong breezes, the horizon transitioned over to charcoal shadows. I gripped onto the rope and hoisted myself up. Jensen scaled it fast but climbing wasn't easy while defending precious cargo. I knew. My right arm burned with the fresh slice I'd received, and my stabbed leg throbbed with a renewed ache. A steady trickle of blood trailed down my calf. I ignored the pain and made my way up the rope even faster.

Jensen climbed an arms reach away, and if I stretched out, I could grab him. He glanced down and tried to kick me off. His boot crunched onto my knuckles, causing them to throb in pain. I clung on with dogged determination. He continued scaling the rope until he reached the ledge of the ship and tossed himself over. I followed right behind him and landed on my rear.

We collided with the flat deck of the Morlock ship, and for a moment we both caught our breath. Our eyes met. I stared into his hazel ones and knew exactly what he'd do next.

Which is why I lunged for his boot before he darted away.

I yanked to pull him in closer, but three times my weight, he didn't budge. Instead, he slammed onto his side and tried to kick me off him. I rolled across the deck but latched my nails into his skin, refusing to let go. The kick dragged me closer to his torso, so I tucked forward and threw my whole weight against his midsection. So close to him, the stench of diesel and rosemary almost choked me, even after tolerating that scent for the many, many missions I'd been. With one of his gargantuan arms, he batted me from his side like a stray cat. I sucked in my stomach and tucked into a ball to minimize the blow.

Before he stood, I whirled back around, slamming an elbow into his ribs. The soft give of flesh and bone crunched underneath my blow. His hot breath cut through the rain and threaded the air with tension. I rolled away, elbows colliding with the floor before he could shove me off again. Using the motion to my advantage, I kicked his ribs, hard. A groan followed.

His leg snaked from behind and caught me in the knee. I buckled at once, thudding against the deck as the air hissed from my throat. Jensen loomed over top me, struggling to stand. He glowered down, those hazel eyes foreign. The man who killed my Captain without remorse. The man who ordered Geoff overboard. Anger flooded my veins again and clouded my vision a musty red. I surged towards him and lobbed a blow, straight for his chest.

He threw his beefy forearm up in defense and shoved back. The force sent me tumbling. My back scraped against the deck, and the chafed skin underneath burned. This time he didn't stay to tango and darted away from me toward the ship ledge. He crept towards the helmsman, whose back faced us.

"Move out," he shouted to the man. "We'll deal with the girl, but we need to get the cargo out of this mess now." Jensen took a couple more backwards steps closer to the helm.

"Oh you'll deal with me, will you?" Pure fury sang through me. My cheeks burned from exertion, and my chest rose as I gasped out every breath. "Like you killed the captain, defenseless in his room? Why would you betray us when we'd been nothing but good to you? The crew was like family and you broke it apart." I pulled my revolver and aimed it at his head. "For Captain Morris and for Geoff, I'll never forgive you."

"It'd be nice right?" Jensen sneered and whipped out his own pistol just as fast. "All the reasons tied up in a pretty package for you? Sorry. That's not the way life works. I have my cargo. Do yourself a favor and jump overboard."

I kept my gun level and aimed for his head.

"If we both shoot, we'll both die. You know I don't miss my marks, and if it means taking you down, I'd sacrifice my life. You took away the two men who meant the most to me." Droplets of rain soaked into my hair, and the chill sent shivers rolling down my spine. "Get ready to meet your end," I growled.

"I've no plan on dying, doll." He turned to the helmsman. "Shoot her down." The hammer of a pistol clicked, sending a pit into my stomach. Two against one. A gulp traveled down my dry throat, but I stayed firm—didn't try to run. Jensen would not get away.

"Jensen, she's right. You won't be leaving this ship alive." A familiar voice spoke, but I barely believed the sound. My head whipped away from Jensen right as the helmsman turned around. Chestnut hair plastered against his forehead, and those safe, steady brown eyes stared back at me knowingly.

Geoff stood by the wheel with his gun pointed at Jensen's head.

My heart leapt, and my lip trembled under the insane tide of joy that swept over me. Water welled up in my eyes. Damned rain.

"How?" Jensen's eyes narrowed.

My finger trembled on the trigger, and I stared him down. This was Jensen, my crewmate, who I'd called a friend, a brother. But that had all changed. I aimed the gun and pulled the trigger.

Jensen staggered back, but he already stood at the ledge, so the force of the shot bucked him overboard. His eyes widened, and his jaw dropped in horror. I started running in his direction to get the box. If that fell over, we'd lose any chance of proving Britain's duplicity against old Germany. He clutched it tight against his chest with a grim determination on his face that surprised me.

For a second I glimpsed the man who watched my back on so many missions in the past. The one whose redneck stubbornness gave Americans a bad name. A brief flashing moment and I thought I saw my old friend, from the memory so long ago when we fastened that porthole onto the Desire's walls. But looming overhead would always be the scene from the night that played out in my nightmares, of him standing over the captain with blood-stained hands. Before I could reach out, Jensen and the box both dropped out of sight.

White knuckled, I gripped the ledge of the ship, but he already vanished out of view. They were in for one long descent.

I took a deep, shaky breath as my eyes stung. Captain Morris, rest in peace.

Footsteps pounded beside me, and Geoff approached. I didn't believe my heart could soar so high after the plummet it'd taken earlier. Neither of us said a word, we just stared for a moment and drank in the other's presence. All my caution dashed away with the rising winds as drops of rain hit my face. I ran over to him.

He pressed his hands against my back and pulled me into a kiss before I had the chance to say a word. But talk didn't matter. I thrust myself against him and kissed Geoff with the fervor we'd restrained for so long. Every shy glance when we thought the other wasn't looking, every fumbling drunk encounter we had, and each and every peck on the cheek culminated in this. Geoff sparked within me a passion I thought I'd lost and one I'd buried away for so long. His hot breath commingled with mine and fought against the chilled drops of rain. I met his lips over and over again, tasting the spicy cinnamon.

His arm circled my waist, and he drew me closer. My hands ran over his tight biceps and across his muscled back as I reveled in his realness. Every second he didn't vanish in my arms made me all the more grateful. I'd been so sure I lost him. He caressed my waist, his warm hands filling me with the safe assurance they always had. With Geoff at my side I couldn't lose. I would never stop fighting. I hungrily sought out his lips for more and drank in the wicked scent of ozone. My chest ached with conflicting reassurance, loss, and gratefulness, however none trumped the passion that dominated me as strong as the winds.

A crack of thunder rolled through the air, and we pulled apart.

"We have to get back to the ship." I tugged him by the hand toward the rope leading down.

"Not just the storm but the merchant ship seems to be arming up."

"Ready to pull a second miracle?" I flashed him a grin. "Let's get the Desire out of here."

CHAPTER TWENTY-SEVEN

I dropped down the rope, careful to mind my injured arm.

Below, swords clanged, and the occasional bark of a gunshot interfered with the growing patter of rain against the deck. With their numbers halved, many of the Morlocks backed towards their ship, quickly losing their steam. Weapons lowered, and wary eyes surveyed the area rather than the men charging in for a fight. My boots hit the deck as I landed with a watery thud, and Geoff followed behind me.

As long as they got the hell off my ship, I didn't care if they departed dead or alive. The rain swarmed the deck, and drops mingled with the pools of blood, beating down upon the corpses. Isabella and Mordecai toyed with a redcoat, both utilizing a mere fraction of their sword skills. Blades clanged to a sweet sort of dissonance. Two of the Brits slumped dead on the deck, one of them the officer I'd killed. Three of the guards remained, but they'd resorted to a fistfight brawl against Seth and a couple of the deckhands.

I heard the sound of cannon fire too late.

The Desire quaked. With all the chaos aboard, I hadn't noticed the British Merchant ship gearing up to fire. The cannon exploded against her side, and the deck careened to the right, sending everything to the ledge. Mottled sky and jagged planks whirled around me as the buck of the ship threw me onto my back. My aching body cried out in pain, and I began sliding along the slicked deck towards the edge. The crew. I had to help my crew.

Wood grain scraped against my arm and stung as I flipped over onto my stomach. I scrabbled for a hold along the deck, but my numbed fingers found no purchase. A hand grabbed mine, and I looked up. Geoff yanked me to his side as he wrapped his other arm around a nearby mast.

"We've got to get out of here fast." His grave expression mirrored my own.

"Quick, get to the navigation bay. We need the engine jump-started for a fast escape. I'll handle the crew." His eyes gleamed with pride, and he gave me another quick kiss on the lips before he jogged off in the direction of the helm. When Geoff approached, Spade's eyes glistened with the first real tears I'd ever seen from the man. They set to work on the aether regulators, preparing the engine. I shook off the delirious adrenaline spurred by Geoff's touch and focused on the task before us.

As I approached the crew, the red against blue flag glared on the enemy ship.

"Jensen's dead," I called over the squall, "and the box fell with him." The remaining Morlocks took that news as the final push to escape, and even those still fighting made a headlong dash towards the dangling rope leading to their boat. We didn't bother chasing them down—we had bigger concerns.

"But right now, I need everyone on alert because this ship's trying to blow us out of the skies." The remaining redcoats dropped their weapons, realizing their ship marked them off as dead. Mordecai and Isabella made fast work of binding the officers with rope. Once their superiors were captured, the others didn't even try to fight and just raised their empty hands. Defeat weighted the air as they hung their heads and sank to their knees. The raindrops thickened and compromised my vision, but in the distance, the Brits loaded one of the dozens of cannons lining their sides. We had to get out of here and fast. I took in a deep breath of ozone before continuing.

"Jack and Hiram," I called out. "I need you to get the storm sails readied. The skies are going to pour."

Jack stepped up to me with a look darker than the looming thunderheads on his face. "Hiram's dead, Captain." His words hit me like the butt end of a chainsaw, and I exhaled a sharp breath. No time to grieve—not now.

"Fine, take Abigail. We need our girl readied to get out of here." Jack and Abigail rushed off towards the sails.

"Where do you want them, Captain?" Seth jerked a thumb at the willing captives.

"Take them to the brig," I commanded, knowing very well we didn't have anywhere to hole them up. He arched his brow. "Fine, stuff them in the infirmary. More for Edwin to deal with." I sighed, waving them off.

Seth shrugged and hulked off in the direction of the lower decks, corralling the men as he went. The rain hummed in my ears like the strain of a tin whistle picking up momentum. Our ship's timbers shuddered, and we began sailing in the opposite direction of the British Merchant ship. Not fast enough. The cannon boomed again.

"Incoming!" My scream scraped against my raw throat and barely carried amidst the deafening sound.

This time I latched onto the mast for a handhold as the Desire bucked from the blast. Cannon fire smelled like a burnt wet rag as it wafted up from the keel of the ship. The force of the blow tossed crewmates feet into the air, only to send them crashing back onto the deck. If the Desire took any more hits, we'd fall from the skies. My stomach dropped as my gaze slipped to the edge. Water careened into my eyes and weighed me down from chemise to boots. Thunder crackled in the distance, and stinging drops of rain pattered with a rising fury. Even if we had a location, blasting away wouldn't give us the impetus necessary since those first two hits had slowed our girl.

Our last escape had been sheer luck. What were the chances of finding a jet stream or pocket again? Isabella approached with

Mordecai fast on her heels.

"We need to distract them somehow." Isabella shouted through the bellowing winds. The rain cascaded over us in torrents, and the winds slapped errant drops with spite.

"One cannon versus dozens." I jabbed the air in the direction of ours. "In that shot, they'll have fired the final one to clear us from the skies."

"Fire at a weak spot? Maybe if we hit their balloon?" she yelled over the rain.

I shook my head. "They've got top of the line plasma shielding. One hit won't take it down." With the British ship adjacent for firing, their lines of cannons stretched on and on like the open skies.

"It looks like the Morlocks get out of this free and clear." Mordecai pointed. Several guys scampered up the rope to the Morlock ship, moving so fast the tail whipped around underneath them. The vessel pulled away from us, but being smaller and slower, it trailed behind. An idea raced through me faster than a fish downstream.

"Isabella, come with me. We're loading the cannon."

"I thought you said—" she started. I sliced my hand through the air to cut her off. She followed without another word, and we raced across the slickened deck towards our one weapon. This was a long shot. A definite long shot. But Lady Luck hadn't left me yet, and I would test her one more time today.

The Desire shuddered, and her limbs creaked from the force of those blasts. We sailed faster away from the Brits, but the wheezing timber didn't promise a fast escape. If they sent off that next round, we'd find ourselves with a fast ticket groundside and no hope of survival. Redcoats hovered around the next cannon, readying to fire another shot from the rows of artillery lining the starboard side of their ship. They had plenty of ammo, so they could keep blasting rounds until they were green in the face. The slickened sole of my boot gave, and I slid the rest of the way towards the cannon.

My back slammed against the ledge, and a sharp lance of pain zigzagged up my back. I pulled myself up using the sides for support and waved a hand at the cannon.

"Help me load her," I commanded, and we set to work prepping the bore. If we didn't load up first, our entire struggle would be dashed like smoke in the wind. The group of redcoats pulled back from the cannon, and my bet was they weren't picking daisies. From the looks of it, they prepared tinder. We had to move faster. We had to. Isabella shoved the cartridge inside and loaded the cannon ball in after. From where we stood, the British Merchant ship made a gargantuan target.

But we weren't aiming for them. I veered the cannon's view towards the Morlock ship sailing right between us and the Brits. As

I held my hands over the fuse to shield from the rain, Isabella grabbed the tinder and lit it. Our future banked on this shot—everything from the fate of the Desire and her crew to the intact bottle of absinthe stored away in the Captain's old dresser drawer that I sure as hell would open if we survived. If we failed, the British Merchant ship would load their cannons and blow us clear out of the skies.

"Fire!" I screamed, and we skidded back from the cannon.

A burnt smell sparked the air, and it exploded. We stood back as the projectile sailed towards the Morlock ship. We just needed one hit. Isabella's hand pressed against my back. I didn't reciprocate—my palms were clammy with sweat. A wind kicked up and whipped fresh droplets of rain into my face. My heart seized, because gusts like that would knock our cannon off course. I took in one more deep breath and closed my eyes. Forget watching. Forget worrying. My shot was true.

Isabella's fingernails dug into my shoulder. A deafening boom exploded in the distance, and I opened my eyes.

Our cannon hit.

Triumph sailed through me like the fireworks displays in Reno, and I slapped Isabella on the back. A laugh slipped from my throat. The cannonball caught the center of the Morlock aircraft, right in the gut of the ship. Chunks of wood flew into the air along with tufts of blackened smoke, which yellowed around the edges as the stern of the Morlock vessel caught fire. The boat plummeted straight into the cannon-lined starboard side of the British Merchant ship. Golden flames tore them up like a flash of lightning, right as the crash echoed through the skies. The static of the rain amplified the pregnant tension filling the air right before both ships tipped to plummet.

"There's your distraction, boys!" I yelled through the caterwaul of the storm and raced across the deck toward the navigation bay. My blood pulsed through my veins, shooting me with a fresh start of adrenaline. We couldn't spare another second to watch the imminent explosion.

Under the canopy of the navigation bay, my scalp received a respite from the pounding rain. My chest heaved, fighting the weight of my sodden clothing as I struggled to catch my breath. Geoff hunched over the aether regulator, and Spade had his hands on the gyrocompass, which whirled wildly around with the breeze.

"We need her moving now," I announced through the pounding of the rain.

Spade shook his head. "The gyrocompass isn't working. We've got no bearings."

Geoff spat. "And a regular compass takes time. We'd have to calculate everything by hand then, and we still don't have a direction."

As Isabella raced towards us, a couple strands of hair stuck to the side of her cheek. "Captain, the Morlock ship's heading straight for the Brits. We need to go. Our diversion will only buy us so much time."

"The gyrocompass—" Geoff interrupted and stood from the aether manipulators which pumped the green fluid up and down so wildly bubbles formed.

I slammed my fist onto the console, nearly hitting the regulator buttons. Behind us, the blazing Morlock ship flew five seconds away from crashing headfirst into the Brits. I threw a hand back and gestured. "That's our distraction. Any more hits and we're sunk."

"Excuse me?" Adelle piped up from behind me.

"Not now. We've got to figure out a way to get our girl in motion." I glanced at Geoff. "Are you sure you couldn't calculate the bearings with a regular compass?"

He slammed a fist against the back of the overhang. "Not with this lack of time."

"Captain?" Adelle's gentle voice barely broke through the loud spattering rain. "I have our bearings."

"That's right—we've got a human GPS!" I grabbed her hands in mine and squeezed them tight. "Our gyrocompass is broken though. Do you think you can still manage to find a way out?"

She nodded and stepped up to the navigation bay. "We need

to sail Northwest at once, and we'll be able to pick up the nearest air pocket to get out of this storm."

I tossed an arm around her shoulder. "Let's get going then. The Brits may have a monstrous ship on their hands, but they'll have to tango with the flaming ball of fun lobbed their way. Our Desire can race against these odds." I stepped up and wrapped my hands around the thrusters, taking control. The brittle air of the storm seeped into my lungs, and the rain hit my face with glorious, tingling drops. An excited laugh ripped from my throat. I met Geoff's eyes, those dark, warm ones, before he flipped the switches on the aether manipulators. He understood. He always did. We were going to make it out alive.

"All right boys, let's sail away! Show those bastards how airship pirates fly!"

The Desire's engine throttled into overdrive, and we zoomed straight into the maelstrom, away from the merchant ship.

EPILOGUE

I stood from the granite headstone before me. 'Captain Robert Morris' it read, 'Your fearful trip is done.' We buried Byron, Jasper, Hiram, and Cole, the deckhands who we lost in that battle alongside him with similar markers. The Baltic tides swelled in the distance, and for a moment, I thought I could smell the cigar smoke staining my Captain's khaki duster. I placed a hand on the chilled tombstone, and tears pricked my eyes with the true realization he was gone. But standing by the beaches of my Captain's old Germany, his presence lingered right alongside me.

"O Captain, my Captain..." I trailed off. A warm hand clamped on my shoulder.

Geoff stood behind me with one hell of a sad smile on his lips. "All over a box."

"So much tragedy and for nothing. Old Germany will never get the retribution it deserved." I ran a hand over Matilda in my holster. The girl had been sorely missed when the Morlocks overtook our ship. With Edwin's neat bandaging job and his new elixir with the vague scent of elderberries, my wounds were closing up fast too.

"Maybe that's okay," Geoff spoke up. "The world's been

without it for two decades, it could've just sparked a powder keg. If what happened to us was any indication, that box was bad news from the start." The tides crashed in the distance, and the salty brine of the ocean laced through the air. I took in a deep breath.

"I get that, but I don't like all the unknowns. Whatever happened to our former employer?"

Geoff shrugged. "Let's just hope we never hear or see from him again."

"Like we'd be that lucky." I kicked the dirt, knocking a couple pebbles astray. "He's not the only one full of mysteries. How did you survive after being thrown overboard anyway?"

"Skill," he said with a wink. "I managed to grab a hold onto the side of our girl. They knocked me over right near the climbing rope they used to board our ship, so I latched onto that. The deck already broke out in skirmishes at that point, so no one noticed as I climbed up to the Morlock ship. I took out the helmsman, and that's how I ended up there."

"You're a genius, boy-o." I passed him a rueful grin.

"Where to next?" Geoff asked. "We have an open sky ahead of us."

"Beijing maybe?" I shrugged. "I heard they're more straightforward there. What I wouldn't give for a little old smuggling job. We need whatever coin we can scrape together."

"You may as well just let Isabella loose in the casinos," Geoff said. "When are you going to let the Brits off?"

"When my ship's clean." I grinned and bared my teeth. The sun glinted off the lacquer on Morris' grave, and I glanced back one last time before we returned to the ship. Geoff's rough fingers intertwined with mine, and I squeezed them tight. Desire emerged into view the moment we neared port, and her dark worn wooden hull stood out against the sparkling ocean. But she held her own beauty, a sleek and strong sort unparalleled by anything else in the skies. The word 'Desire' emblazoned the pearl white balloon, and by the Gods, she was ours.

Sneak Peek into Tale of Two Airships

There's a sacred rite all Captains go through, whether of sea or sky, that turns any fledgling into the thick-blooded, heartless bastard they need to be. Every Captain, at some point in their career will reach that same precipice.

The day when you want to murder every last member aboard your ship. For me? I'd reached the precipice and was ready to dive to the depths.

Voices rose from the end of the hallway. The splintered floorboards creaked under my heavy boots as I made my way down. Most of the crew had congregated in the mess hall, because instead of eating their damn breakfast, they'd rather run their mouths. The door was wide open, and the scents of Adele's biscuits and gravy caused my stomach to rumble. I cracked my knuckles upon approach, trying to rein in my temper. To be fair, the week long stretch in the air, combined with low paying shitty jobs were partially culprit.

However, the main reason everyone took to shouting like the end of days was coming had to do with a certain letter delivered by sparrow and addressed to our favorite ex-gypsy, Isabella.

One thing you don't do is threaten one of ours. I learned that from a wise old wardog, once upon a time.

ABOUT THE AUTHOR

A modern day Renaissance-woman, Katherine McIntyre has learned soapmaking, beer brewing, tea blending, and most recently roasting coffee. Most of which make sure she's hydrated and bathed while she spends the rest of her time writing. With a desire to travel and more imagination than she knows what to do with, all the stories jumping around in her head led to the logical route of jotting them down on paper. Not only can her poetry and prose be found in different magazines, but she's had an array of novels and novellas published through Decadent Publishing, Boroughs Publishing, Hazardous Press, and Jupiter Gardens Press. For more casual content, she's a regular contributor on CaffeineCrew.com, a geek news website.

Stolen Petals (Take to the Skies #1.5)

By

Katherine McIntyre

One man has swiped bounties from Viola, the Brass Violet, for years. Longstanding rivals, they've only had brief encounters, and if she had a choice, she'd avoid him entirely. When he saunters into her bar with an offer to work together on a job, the proper response would be to shoot him down and send him back to Shantytown. However, curiosity's a wicked beast, and Viola needs to know why, after so many years of stealing her marks, he'd approach her now.

The man is insufferable, annoyingly cavalier, and tends to stir up memories she'd rather forget--but she needs assistance on this job and he's offering aid and blueprints which could cut their work in half.

Given the intense way he looks at her though, working together isn't all he has in mind. Van Clef is known for his persistence and, with his charm, he wins women over effortlessly. Viola's not so easy though--she's wise to his tricks. But if he wants to play the game, she will gladly rise to the challenge. By the end of this bounty, she'll be the one leaving him in the dust.

Shootout at Roulement Ridge

By

Einar Mercier

Vikings! Cowboys! Airships! Welcome to the Gears & Gunfighters universe, where Gearsmen can defy death and Steamhorses gallop across the frontier! When a gunfight brings the border town of Roulement Ridge to the brink of chaos, it is up to a few well-meaning citizens to restore the peace before the Mayor and the Viking chieftain seize the opportunity to plunge the region into war. The arrival of a legendary outlaw and his beautiful companion steepen the stakes and set the town on rails for a confrontation that could destroy the fragile peace between the Union of the Americas and the Sworn Territories- can order be restored before the clock runs out?

The Winter Triangle

By

Nikki Woolfolk

In the town of Stubborn, West Virginia, 1880, happily single
Cassandra Holloway has decided to come out to her father, Walter, on the
eve of Valentine's Day. Before she can reveal being a woman of "two-
spirits" her well-intentioned, but offspring obsessed father has set her up
on another blind date with someone named Morgan. When Cassandra
attempts to cancel the date she is faced with a first. She must choose
between a beautiful, deaf Astronomy Professor at the local University or
the Professors' handsome sign-language interpreter— both named
Morgan.

With a comedy filled evening that Cassandra's cupid playing father could
not have planned, she must make a choice as the sun rises on Valentine's
Day.

Which Morgan will be her Valentine?

Empress Irukandji: The Case of Charlotte Sloane

By

Heather Hutsell

Doctor Charlotte Sloane has much to worry about: Starting with her memory...

With nothing to go on but the routines of the last twelve months and the word of her best friend Professor Matthew Sterling, Charlotte soon discovers--one secret at a time--that the great mystery of her life holds more complexity than the simple, medical one she thought it was. When she finds herself poisoned and nearly killed under the oddest of circumstances, Doctor Sloane also begins to learn of her invisible enemies, the questionable reputation of The Legion, her shady, former occupation, and her highly problematic interactions with Queen Victoria...

Set in Steampunk-altered 1889 London ~for a start~ Charlotte quickly understands that there is more to her--and everyone around her than she could possibly have imagined.

Coyote: The Outlander

By

Chantal Noordeloos

No one knows where or when the mysterious rips will appear, but from
them, Outlanders walk the earth, leaving chaos in their wake.

Coyote, a charismatic bounty hunter, travels the land with her enigmatic
partner, Caesar. Together –with the help of magic and technology—the
unlikely duo tracks down these dangerous criminals from different worlds.

Along the way, Coyote discovers a secret that threatens to shatter
everything she believes about herself, her father, and her sworn enemy,
James Westwood.

Whether Outlander or inner demons, some things can't be solved with a
six shooter.

Author Note:

Hey all! Hope you enjoyed Bea and the crew's escapades as much as I enjoyed writing them. She's a character who's near and dear to my heart, since I channeled a lot of my Aries impulsiveness into her decisions. I've been obsessed with pirates since I was a kid, so to no surprise, I adored writing this story. This is the first book in the Take to the Skies Chronicles, and the next one slated to release is A Tale of Two Airships.

If you enjoyed the book, leave a review! A couple wonderful people gave me kind words at the right time, which gave me the gumption to re-release An Airship Named Desire and continue the story into a series.

Come chat with me at any of these places—I'd love to discuss anything from airships to unicorns!

Facebook: www.facebook.com/kmcintyreauthor

Twitter: www.twitter.com/pixierants

Website: www.katherine-mcintyre.com

Tumblr: www.booksteacoffee.tumblr.com

Pinterest: www.pinterest.com/kmcintyremt